Mad Love

Four tasty tales of lust, sex...and wedded bliss

by
Darrious D. Hilmon and Javaki Hilmon

Edited by
Loren M. Brown

authorHOUSE™

1663 LIBERTY DRIVE, SUITE 200
BLOOMINGTON, INDIANA 47403
(800) 839-8640
WWW.AUTHORHOUSE.COM

First published by AuthorHouse 08/08/05

ISBN: 1-4208-7480-2 (sc)

Library of Congress Control Number: 2005906873

Printed in the United States of America
Bloomington, Indiana

This book is printed on acid-free paper.

ACKNOWLEDGEMENTS

Darrious Thank You's:

On bended knee, I bow before my Lord and Savior Jesus Christ, humbled by, and eternally thankful for, His unmerited favor, and merciful grace. He is the Alpha and Omega. To every single person who by purchase, or prayer (or both :-) helped make my last novel DIVALICIOUS an Essence ® Best-Seller, thank you. It was a Christmas gift I'll always treasure!!

Gloria (Mom), Tony, Terrance, Tiny, and Pee-wee Hilmon, you crazy, beautiful, insane, hilarious people mean more to me than words could come close to expressing. Mad love for all of ya'll! My family of friends, I thank you for always supporting and witnessing me. Randi (Julia/Tess) Myles, thank you for the editorial assistance. Loren Brown, you are a wonderful editor, GG, FH, and SF. We (more Java than me!) didn't always make it easy, but you always made it work. You got next!

Javaki (Hi Java...hi!) working with you on this project has been an amazing experience. I'm sooo freakin' proud of you! Let's rock this out, Baby!!

And to the man whose demonstration of love saved this project, thank you...again.

D2

Javaki Thank You's:

To you who have nurtured my growth, and seasoned my spirit …I thank you.

Mom: You are the pillar. I don't have enough ink in my pen to recognize you. Remember the story I wrote about you in grade school? Nothing has changed. I love you.

Tony: I respect you because you're my big sister. I love you because you're you. Always be you even when I'm being…me. Luv ya.

Leonard: You've stood strong through many storms, fighting like a soldier through each battle. I'll always have your back.

Darrious: You've pushed me, and pissed me off, and caused me to call you dirty, dirty names. But you've also shown me how much you really believe in me by lending me your gift for just a little while -- a debt I can never repay. Thank you.

Jennifer: With you I've been truly blessed (if only you knew). Thank you for everything.

My closest friends: Your presence was felt and included in these pages. Luv ya'll.

Tiny and Pee-Wee: Although you two get more attention than any of us, I love you bad little pups.

To those who believe in love…I thank you.

Contents

DREAM COME TRUE

Darrious D. Hilmon

Prologue

I fought against the urge to hyperventilate as I stood there in the crème-colored, Vera Wang gown. Blocking out the eyes burning a hole into my back, I stared straight ahead. Of the 300-plus people sitting in the pews of the mega-church, few were family or close friends. The place overflowed with Detroit's social and political elite, invited to my wedding more for the sake of appearance, than a genuine desire to have them take part in the most important day of my life.

The thick air tightening around me, I eased my tongue across my Berushka Red painted lips as my ivory-hued fingernails inched up toward my constricting neckline. I kept reminding myself to breathe, but if the dizziness was any indication, I wasn't doing nearly enough of it. With blurred vision, I twisted my head tentatively to the right, struggling to focus my gaze upon the man who, in less than twenty minutes, would be my husband. He offered a reassuring, albeit nervous, smile. Standing to my left, my maid of honor handed me a silk handkerchief, discreetly nodding toward the bead of perspiration forming on my forehead. Today, even two applications of MAC Bronzed Powder couldn't keep me from sweating like a roasting pig.

While I may have felt like dog crap warmed over on the inside, I looked good enough to eat on the outside. My hair was in an upsweep with a few curls cascading down to frame my face. The diamond clustered earrings dressing my ears caused the light to bounce in all directions when it hit them. I had decided to forgo a veil because it was too traditional, even for my taste. Besides, I'd worked too damned hard beating this face to have it covered by anything. Moist brow not withstanding, my make-up was utterly flawless. To the naked eye my skin was a blemish-free, even-toned mahogany. Now that may not sound terribly impressive at first blush, but when you took into account that just two days ago, I had been in the throes of one hellava acne breakout, it was indeed something to crow about. The make-up artist from the television station where I worked could create magic with a Bobbi Brown brush, God bless her. Even close up you couldn't spot the bags under my eyes, the result of less than six hours of sleep in the last four days. Thank heaven for that, since in addition to the small army of wedding guests, there was a shitload of photographers, not to mention the four television cameras recording my every movement.

Speaking of movement, this *too-damned expensive* dress was pinching into my waist something awful. It was no wonder I couldn't breathe. I was starving too, though right now I was certain I couldn't have held down food if I wanted to. In preparation for the wedding, I'd crashed dieted myself to a shaky size six, down from my normal size eight. In the past two days however, I'd gained much of it back. The preceding forty-eight hours had been a roller-coaster ride for me. Comfort food, in the form of Doritos Cool Ranch had been my way of coping with the stress. Considering how freakin' tight this gown felt, I should have sought comfort in a Diet Coke instead.

In retrospect, it probably wasn't such a great idea to have a ten-foot train. It looks great, but it's a bitch to maneuver. I almost tripped twice coming down the aisle. Remaining upright in a pair of rhinestone-incrusted Manolo's was hard enough without the added challenge of a dress that got to wherever I was headed ten minutes after I got there. That my father had the gait of a drunk attempting to appear sober did little to help matters. I warned my old man that if he embarrassed me today, it would be another ten years before I spoke to his habitually under-employed self again. The only reason I'd invited him in the first place was for the sake of appearances. In the circles my fiancé and I ran in, there was an expectation that things not be *negrofied*, which meant the man actually responsible for your birth – and not your sixty year old mother's thirty-seven year old boyfriend – should be the one giving your ass away at your wedding.

If I could just stop my heart from beating so damned fast I might have a shot of getting through this without incident. I'd been waiting for this day since I was fifteen years old. In my head anyway, my wedding would be perfect, the kind of affair that would have people talking for years after it occurred. Teary-eyed family and friends would sit in stupefied awe as they took in the brilliant spectacle of it all. Staring lovingly into my eyes, my husband-to-be – in my dreams it was always Denzel Washington – would mouth the words *I love you* from his juicy lips as Aretha Franklin sang a soul-infused version of Ava Maria, with Stevie Wonder accompanying her on the piano.

But this was reality and my wedding was twenty minutes late starting – my father got lost...don't ask – my head was spinning and

I wasn't sure I could keep my quaking legs from buckling beneath me. I was hot and hungry. Were it not for these three-inched heels, I might have hiked up this gown and raced toward the nearest exit. Instead I think I'll just...just...

"Danielle, are you okay?" I could hear Eliyse ask as my eye lids grew too heavy to keep open.

If I could only get a little fresh air everything would be okay. My lips were so very dry. I needed to just...

"Danielle," my fiancé called out, moving in to shore me up as I weaved from side to side, fighting not to fall face forward. "Baby what's wrong?"

Before I could give him an answer, everything went black.

Chapter One

*A*madeus smiled as I stepped out of the bathroom, fumbling to make myself presentable.

"What?" I asked slightly embarrassed.

"You are...*amazing,*" he said, flashing that sexy grin he'd been breaking hearts with since high school.

If he was referring to the weave-loosening, toe-curling round of sex we'd just had, *amazing* was the correct word indeed. A man hadn't put it on me that good since...well, since Amadeus had knocked my boots and rocked my world on my prom night fifteen years ago.

"You're not so bad yourself," I said, blushing.

"Come to me," he said, spreading his legs apart as he sat on the edge of the bed.

Still under his spell, I slipped into the space between his powerful thighs. Besides being too fine for words, Amadeus had a body that was so delicious it had to be fattening. Dark-skinned with shoulder-length dreads, he looked every inch the alluringly dangerous Rastafarian. In his arms the rest of the world slipped from mental view. All I could think of was how good, how very, very good this man made me feel.

"How long are you staying in town," I said, swallowing my desire as his hand inched up the small of my back.

"As long as it takes to get what I came for," he said, rising from the bed.

The sight of him in all his bare naked glory just about made me orgasm for the third time in as many hours. Brushing against the fabric of my red St. John skirt, the head of Amadeus' manhood peeked out from behind the wrinkled skin shielding it. Many of my girlfriends simply hated the sight of an uncut penis, but something about it worked for me.

"*Oooh*, no...no," I moaned, trying to pull away from him as his full lips connected with my earlobe. "I gotta get back...to real life."

Amadeus squeezed my newly aroused nipples poking through the fabric of my off-white silk blouse. "This feels pretty real to me," he said in a moisture-inducing growl.

Oh sweet Jesus help me! This man was one lick away from making me lose my religion, and what little good sense I still had left. As wonderful as this felt, I needed to get going. Truth be told, I should have never come in the first place. When Amadeus called me at the television station this morning inviting me to have coffee with him, I should have graciously declined. I'd barely gotten through lunch with him the week prior with my panties still above my knees. That night I could barely sleep, unable to quash the fire merely being in that man's presence had sparked in me.

An award-winning photojournalist, Amadeus never stayed in one place too long. For a man like him, anything approaching the traditional bored him on a grand scale. He was far too creative and passionate to be burdened with a mundane, connect the dots existence. And though he denied it vigorously, Amadeus loved living his life on the edge. Most sane people would avoid Iraq like the plague, but Amadeus had jumped at the opportunity to spend six weeks in the war-ravished country, capturing the on-going turmoil on film for *Time* Magazine. Before Iraq it was Haiti, before Haiti it was Zimbabwe and Nairobi before that.

My life on the other hand was – prior to today anyway – a casebook study in neat and tidy. An honors' graduate with a degree in Broadcasting from Wayne State University here in Detroit, I was the co-anchor of Channel 5's top-rated morning news show. I went to church every Sunday. Because of my early work schedule, most nights I was in bed by nine-thirty. Prior to Amadeus' blowing back into town two weeks ago, everything about my life was picture-perfect…and thoroughly dull.

The muffled sound of my cell phone ringing inside my purse jolted me out of my day dream.

"Somebody wants to talk to you bad," Amadeus said, reaching under the bed for his boxers. "It rang three times while you were in the bathroom."

And with those words, playtime ended, replaced by the reality sweeping across me like a bitter winter breeze. What the hell had I just allowed to happen here? Never mind. It was too late for *couldawouldashouldas* now. The dye had been cast, the ship sailed, the horse let out of the barn.

Glancing down at my watch I cringed. "Shit," I said, snatching up my purse from the counter. "I gotta get a move on."

"When can I see you again?"

Ignoring the question, I placed a quick peck on his cheek. "This can't happen again. You know that right?"

Amadeus flashed me a sly grin. "If that's what you want," he said smoothly.

"It's not...it's...it's what has to be," I said, stammering like a fool as he continued undressing me with his eyes.

"You've got my number," Amadeus said, reeking with confidence.

"Yea," I said, racing out the door.

"See you."

No you won't I thought as I rushed down the hall. Reaching the parking lot, I jumped inside my midnight blue Jaguar, fumbling to retrieve my cell.

Taking a deep breath, I hit the speed dial.

This too shall pass.

"Hey, where are you?" Powers asked instantly. "I've been here at the restaurant for fifteen minutes waiting for you."

"Sorry, baby," I said, trying to play it cool. "Got held up at work."

"Work?" Powers asked curiously. "I thought you said you were taking the rest of the day off to do some last minute shopping."

"Eliyse, needed me to come in to voiceover some promotional spots," I lied, making a mental note to ask my best friend, and Channel 5's executive producer to cover for me. Powers wasn't the non-trusting type, but before today I'd never done anything untrustworthy.

"Well, they better get everything they need from you now," Powers said, buying my excuse, "because there will be no working whatsoever on our honeymoon."

"Don't make promises you can't keep, Mr. Washburn," I said, trying not to sound like a woman who'd just fucked her high school sweetheart. Oh, I am such a hoe. A stank, funky low-down hoe!

"Can you believe it, baby," Powers said with what for him was high excitement. "In four days we're going to be husband and wife."

Closing my eyes, I gripped the steering wheel, shame sticking to me like Amadeus' musky scent. What in the hell was I thinking?

"Danielle?" Powers asked. "You there?"

"Umm hmm," I said, reopening my eyes. "I'm right here."

"Promise me you'll never go away?"

The tenderness in his voice made my heart ache. "Baby...umm... I think my cell's about to go," I said, my voice cracking. "I'll just see you at the restaurant."

"Okay, baby," Powers said. "I love—"

I disconnected the call before he could get out the words. His love was the last thing I could handle right now. It was the last thing I deserved.

Chapter Two

*T*he valet tapped on the window. "Miss Morton is everything okay?"

"I'm fine," I said, wishing I could crawl under the dash board. "Just a little frazzled, is all."

"Well you look great," the little flirt said with a sly grin. "Councilman Washburn sure is a lucky man."

Flashing him my best anchor-diva smile, I stepped out of the car as he held the door open for me. "No, I'm the lucky one," I said, flinching as the gust of wind swirling up my bare legs reminded me that my panties were still somewhere on the floor of the hotel room, and not on my ass where they belonged.

Carefully balancing myself on the stiletto-heeled, red Jimmy Choo's, I made my way inside Seldom Blue. Instantly, every well-to-do eye in the place stared in my direction. Everyone who was anyone in Detroit patronized the very upscale eatery located inside the biggie-sized world headquarters of General Motors. I frequented the restaurant despite the fact that it was owned by the husband of an anchor at a competing station. So long as the Mrs. didn't hold it against me for beating her show in the ratings, I wouldn't hold it against her for beating me out for the best anchor Emmy this year. Hell, I'd come to Seldom Blue even if I hated her because the food here was divine. Unfortunately, my appetite was nowhere to be found, much like my self-respect.

"Danni," Powers said, rising from the table.

"So sorry I'm late," I said as I approached.

"That's okay."

Not a fan of public displays of affection, Powers gave me a perfunctory peck on the cheek before pulling out the chair for me. Oh how I wished just once my very straight-laced fiancé would draw me into his arms and lay a big, fat, wet one on my lips, unconcerned with what others thought. But alas, gregarious acts of demonstrability weren't in Powers' character make-up. Too bad for me.

The son of long-time Michigan Congressman Mitchell Washburn, Powers was every bit the uptight, intellectual the blue and white bowtie he was wearing suggested. How could he not be? He came from a long line of clenched-cheek, boogie, black-lite folk who took great pains to keep up appearances. His mom, Lilly Washburn was classic old money snootiness. A member of Jack & Jill, she was also a Delta, and a LINK. Unburdened by something as cumbersome as a job, Lilly sat on the Detroit Institute of Arts Founders' Society, and at least three other boards. What she did on any of them -- besides yearn for her next double-martini -- was anyone's guess. Old girl played along with the program – when her son was around – but Lilly had made it clear in no uncertain terms that she was no fan of my dark-skinned nappy-haired self. She'd much rather her son had fallen in love with a lighter-skinned sister whose high yellowness could better ensure that her future grandchildren would pass the brown paper bag test.

"Danni?"

"What...huh?" I asked, snapping out of my fog. Losing my mind was exactly what I deserved for what I'd done today. "I'm sorry, Honey. What did you say?"

"I asked if you wanted a glass of wine," Powers said, nodding toward the waiter standing at our table.

"Yes, please," I said, dabbing at the wetness above my quivering lip. Sitting across the table from the man I had agreed to marry, I felt every inch the hussy my little romp in the hay with Amadeus made me. How could I have done something so stupid, so close to my wedding day? Maybe I needed to go into therapy.

"I'll be right back with your drinks," the server said, then disappeared.

I tried to block Amadeus out of my thoughts, but I couldn't. He still had my body on fire. It was a good thing Powers never kissed me on the mouth outside of the bedroom, or he might have tasted a little of my early afternoon delight for himself.

"You okay, Danni?" Powers asked, his questioning hazel eyes peeking out over the top of his wire-rimmed Kenneth Cole glasses.

Averting from his gaze, I reached for my napkin, removing it from the gold holder. "I'm fine," I said, my heart racing like a crack-head's.

Powers studied me intently. "You look a little flushed."

Clutching the side of the chair, I forced down the panic building inside me. Oh shit! I must have had that high-pro glow my best friend Eliyse always talked about. It was her belief that good sex made a woman light up like a Christmas tree. "A protein facial that puts the shine back in mama's coat," was how Eliyse described it.

"I'm fine sweetie," I said, forcing a smile. "Thank you for worrying about me though."

Powers tensed a bit when I reached across the table, taking his hand. Every head in the restaurant snapped in our direction. Being Detroit's "it" couple was a lot of damn work, I tell you. For a moment I actually wondered if popularity was worth it.

"Ignore them," I said, defiantly. "We let them into our world enough."

From the time I was in junior high school, all I ever wanted was to be someone who got noticed. While all the guys were sniffing after the girls who'd managed to get their breasts, hips, and asses by the seventh grade, I stood on the sidelines, the short, fat one who never got so much as a passing glance, unless of course, I was blocking some jocks view of a hot chick. Once I got to college, I set out to recreate myself. Every morning I went to the student gym busting my very prominent ass, determined to shed the excess baggage. In time, I had crafted myself into a woman who got the second glances and whistles. It was then that I decided to switch my major from English to Communication Arts. My new body deserved to be in front of somebody's camera.

"There are certain requirements that come with being who we are," Powers said, discreetly pulling his hand back. "We're public people."

Exhaling my frustration, I reached for my glass of merlot, downing almost the whole glass in one gulp. "How lucky for us," I said drolly.

If this were New York or Los Angeles, we'd be just two black folks with great jobs. In blue-collar Detroit however, an anchor woman and the city council president were top-shelf celebrities with all the scrutiny and gossip that came with it. For the most part, I loved the attention that my job – and fabulous shoes – afforded me. I craved it, courted it even. I had my very own personal publicist to ensure that I was invited to all the right parties, and my photo splashed about the society pages on the regular. Increasing my public profile had helped hasten my ascent from health reporter to the main anchor chair at Channel 5.

"Are you sure you're okay?" Powers asked, sensing my restless energy.

"I just…" I said, hesitating. "Do you ever wish you could live your life under the radar?"

Powers pulled off his glasses. "Where'd that question come from?" he asked, looking at me like I had just cursed the Lord.

Sighing, I took a sip of my wine. "Sometimes this all gets a little suffocating," I said, glancing around at the other patrons.

The look on Powers' face made it clear he wasn't feeling me.

"Don't you ever wish you were less...prominent?" I asked pensively. "Someone with a regular nine to five job—"

"No, I don't," Powers said, not bothering to let me finish. "Are you telling me that you'd rather be a secretary than an anchor at a major market television station?"

"I'm not saying that," I said, now feeling like an ingrate. "It's just that sometimes this being in the public spotlight thing does a Tango on my last good nerve."

"Well, I for one appreciate the fact that people respect us enough to care about what we do," Powers said, haughtily. "Like my father always says...when the public stops caring about what you're doing, you're in trouble."

Of course Mitchell *never met a camera he didn't love* Washburn would say such a dumb assed thing. That man was a media whore if ever there was one. Powers had spent his entire life in the spotlight, which was exactly why he was so damned polished and reserved, nary a curly hair out of place. I, on the other hand, had grown up on the eastside of Detroit with a nurse's aid mother who liked to have a good time. Momma couldn't give a rat's ass about the neighbors' points and stares when she did things like throw daddy's crap onto the curb. When her ass itched, she scratched it without fear that she'd become a news story. These days Powers and I couldn't so much as breathe without somebody snapping a picture of us doing it.

"We are very fortunate to have the lives we do," Powers said. "For many people you and I are role models, and that means we have to take great care to project the *right* image."

"Do you love me?"

"Of course I do," Powers said, stunned by the question. "How could you even ask me such a --?"

"May I take your orders?" the waiter said, returning to our table.

Powers looked over at me. "Ladies first."

Too bad I wasn't first in his life. Don't get me wrong, Powers was a good man, and I did love him. I just wished he would show the same passion for me that he did for his career. If only he were less careful when it came to loving me. Our lives had become so predictable and pre-packaged. Like clockwork, we had sex – if that's what you could call it – three times a week with exactly five minutes of foreplay preceding it. After the second squeeze of my nipple and a dry kiss, he'd slap on the condom, climb on top of me and ride me missionary style for seven to twelve minutes. Five minutes later he was asleep and I was in search of the orgasm that never came.

"I'll have the Caesar salad," I said, handing the menu to the waiter. "And another glass of merlot."

The waiter turned to Powers. "Your usual, Councilman?"

Amadeus, on the other hand, knew how to mix things up in and out of the bedroom. It had been ages since I'd felt as alive and sensual as he'd made me feel today. Amadeus was a take charge sorta brotha who knew exactly how to draw a sexually retarded sista out of her shell.

"Yes, please," Powers said, not bothering to glance at the menu.

What I wouldn't give for my fiancé to kick open my apartment door, march up to me, lift me into his arms, throw me down on the bed…or kitchen table, or counter, or floor, and just fuck my brains out; I mean really lay it on me. Lift my legs into the air, wrap them behind my back, I didn't give a damn so long as he made me feel something, anything resembling fire and passion. But, that was too much to ask for from a man like Powers. Hitting it from the back, or heaven forbid, going down on me were far too unseemly for him. I mean really, what would other people think if they knew he and the woman he was marrying were fucking like banshees?

"Powers! Danielle!" E' called out as she strutted toward our table.

My heart leapt into my throat as she approached. Fuck a duck! How in the world was I going to give that girl a heads-up about me using her as my cover with Powers *before* she inadvertently blew my ass out of the water?

"I'll be back shortly with your orders," the waiter said, almost tripping over himself as he spied the big-tittied Amazon, also known as Eliyse Fenton.

"How are my two favorite people in the whole wide world?" Eliyse asked, giving Powers a kiss on the cheek as he stood to greet her.

"We're fine," he said, brightening like he always did when she rolled in. For as much of a prude as the man could be, he was strangely drawn to Eliyse's outgoing, in your face personality. He'd piss his pants if I wore a skirt that high, or blouse that tight, but on Eliyse – the woman he wasn't about to marry – it was all good.

"I've got a bone to pick with you young lady," Powers said, feigning irritation with her.

"Have I been a bad girl?" E' cooed, stroking his forearm. "Maybe I should get a spanking."

Turning beat red, Powers glanced around the dining room. "Will you cut it out," he said with a nervous chuckle.

"You know you like it," E' said, enjoying getting him so flustered. "Don't be afraid to let your freak flag fly."

"Eliyse!" Powers said, cheesing like the high school debate team captain being hit on by the homecoming queen. "Why must you be so naughty?"

"Hands off my man," I said, intervening before Powers sprang a leak.

"Fine," Eliyse said, taking a step back. "So, tell me what have I done now?"

Still blushing from ear to ear, Powers said, "You made my fiancée late for lunch by holding her hostage at that station."

"When? Today?" Eliyse asked, clueless.

"Yes, today," Powers said.

"Boy *puhlease!*" Eliyse guffawed. "Miss Danni was out of that studio the instant—"

"The instant you let me leave twenty minutes ago," I said, giving my best friend a tellingly raised brow.

"Umm…yea, right," Eliyse said, playing along. "The production meeting for the wedding special—"

Powers turned to me. "I thought you said you had to do voiceovers?" With him the devil was in the detail. With a memory like a steel trap, he really was the wrong brotha to be cheating on. But, I wasn't cheating. What happened between Amadeus and me, as delicious as it may have been, was a one-time slip. It was never going to happen again.

"That's right," Eliyse said, chiming in quickly. "First, we had the production meeting, then I asked Danni to finish up the vocal tracking." She eased up to Powers. "Sorry big daddy."

Giggling like a horny teen, Powers bought the lie hook, line, and sinker. Men may be smart, but thank God they were still just men.

"Say you forgive me," Eliyse said, her eyelids fluttering.

"All right," Powers said.

"What's this?" the ocean deep voice demanded.

Eliyse beamed when she saw Leroy standing there in all his six-foot-seven inched, dark-chocolaty glory. I could barely look him in the eye since she'd told me that bruh-man was hung like a derby horse.

"Come on now Congressman," Leroy said. "You already got one beautiful lady to agree to marry you. Why you pushing up on mine?"

Powers became flustered. "No....umm...nothing like that," he stammered as he stared up at the Detroit Piston's star center.

Leroy smacked Powers on the back, almost sending him flying over the table. "I'm just fuckin' with you man," he said with an easy laugh. "It's all good."

While the two men continued exchanging small talk, Eliyse cut her eyes at me. "What time is the final fitting?" she asked smoothly.

"Four o'clock," I answered. "Thank you," I mouthed.

"I'll see you then," Eliyse said.

"Your table is ready Mr. Jones," the hostess said, gushing as she slithered up to Leroy.

"Thanks," Leroy said.

Eliyse inserted herself into the shrinking space between *her* man and the young wanna-be gold digger. The sista rolled her eyes, but backed off just the same. Eliyse was drop-dead gorgeous and could pull off being a lady when needed. But, don't let the smooth taste fool you. That girl had no problems kicking off her pumps, pulling back her honey blonde locks, and tapping somebody's ass like they stole something.

"Let E' know what night you guys want to come," Leroy said, extending his large hand to Powers.

"Good deal," Powers said, failing miserably in his attempt to do the homeboy handshake with the blinged-out basketball player.

Leroy turned to Eliyse. "You ready, Golden Lady?"

"Always," she said, then smiled at me. "I'll see you at four." Leaning in to give me a kiss on the cheek, Eliyse whispered in my ear, "You can fill in the blanks then."

"Will do," I said, turning to Leroy. "Good to see you again," I said, grinning as the visual of me climbing atop his fine self popped into my head.

As if reading my dirty thoughts, Leroy ran his tongue across his thick sexy lips. "You be good Ma," he said, giving me a playful wink.

Powers turned to me baffled as Eliyse and Leroy walked away from our table. I'd explain to him later that Leroy wasn't confusing me for the woman who'd given him birth, but was being endearing in a rough-neck, street-soldier kinda way. But, right now I needed to focus on getting through lunch with my fiancé without telling on myself.

Chapter Three

I held my breath as Hilda prodded my midsection. "How does that feel darling?" she asked.

"It's a little snug," I said, trying not to lose my balance as I stood atop the circular riser. Glancing over at Eliyse, I asked "What do you think E'?"

Interrupting her self-admiration session in the other mirror, Eliyse twisted her head in my direction. "You look hot," she said, giving me a visual once-over. "I still think you should show more cleave' though."

"Of course you do," I said sardonically.

"Why have fabulous breasts if you're not going to share them with the world?" Eliyse asked. "It's selfish...and wasteful."

"You are such a skank," I said, chuckling as I turned back to Hilda. "It's fine." The form-hugging, corset-tight bodice provided more than enough va-va-va-voom for me. Even if I wanted to show more cleavage, Powers' mother would have a conniption. Old girl was still stewing over the fact that I'd elected not to wear white. My number of sexual partners didn't come close to rivaling Miss Eliyse's, but I was no virgin either. I only had to think back upon some of the things Amadeus and I did in the hotel room today for proof of that.

"Speaking of breasts," Eliyse said, fondling her own, "you think I should get more?"

Both Hilda and I shot her *you gotta be kidding* looks. "You need bigger boobs like I need a hole in the head," I said.

"Don't hate the playa," Eliyse said over the Hungarian seamstress' and my laughter. Turning her attention to my backside, she rolled her eyes. "And, I don't care what that uptight old broad told you," E' said, referring to Powers' mother. "She's trying to kill you with that long ass train."

Hilda took a step back, pleased with her handiwork. "Fit is perfect now," she said her eyes lingering on my still sucked in stomach. "But careful not to eat too much. No time to take out before wedding on Saturday."

"Understood," I said, afraid to exhale. It was my goal to be a size six on my wedding day, and come hell or high water -- or collapse from starvation -- I was going to be. What was three more days without food if it meant looking fucking fantastic in this gown? Considering the back flips my stomach had been doing most of the day, I probably couldn't hold food down anyway.

Gazing at myself in the mirror, I sighed wearily. What was I going to do about my situation? Did I dare tell Powers what happened today? Do I see Amadeus again? Should I just forget the whole thing – wonderful though it was – ever happened?

"Maybe I should get my hair corn rolled for your wedding."

"Ouch!" I squealed as the Hilda stuck me in the ass with the pin.

"Sorry," she said, cutting her eyes at Eliyse.

My thoughts drifting to the incident – yes, that's what I'd taken to calling it, *the incident* -- I wasn't paying attention to my friend going on a mile a minute. But, if the strained look on Hilda's face was any indication, Eliyse had just uttered something tasteless or plain crazy.

"What do you think?"

Rubbing my sore behind, I tried to push the visual of a buck-naked Amadeus strutting across the hotel room out of my head. "About what?" I asked distracted.

Eliyse ran her fingers through her shoulder-length hair. "About me getting cornrolls."

"Oye vey," Hilda said under her breath.

"In your hair?" I asked disbelievingly.

"No, my coochie," Eliyse said, smirking. "Of course my hair."

I guffawed. "Oh, but I don't think so."

"Why not?" Eliyse asked, genuinely surprised I didn't see the brilliance of it all. "I could rock me some braids."

Hilda did her best not to react as she continued making final alterations to my dress.

"E' I don't know how many times I have to remind you of this," I said, trying to keep a straight face. "You are not some around-the-way home girl, from the hood, but a blue-eyed, blond-haired, upper-middle class white one from Connecticut."

"Only on the surface," Eliyse said smoothly. "On the inside... where it counts I am chalk full of delicious flava'."

I laughed. "You're flavorful alright."

"Need more pins," Hilda said, heading out of the room. "Be right back."

"Of course," I said, rolling my eyes as my stomach growled. "The instant Hilda tells me to stop eating, I get hungry."

"Damn you just had lunch not three hours ago," Eliyse said, giving me a devious grin as she remembered. "And why exactly were you late for lunch with boy boring?"

"Will you stop calling him that," I said, snappishly. "Powers is not boring."

"No, he's lightening in a can," Eliyse said, mockingly.

"Okay, maybe he's not like the ass-slapping freaks you date," I said, noting the skeptical look on her face. "But he's a good man."

"But can he make you holla?"

With a dismissive wave I said, "There are more important things than—"

"Blah, blah...*blaaah*," Eliyse said, cutting me off. Moving closer she studied me intently. "Something's up with you." Her brow rose in suspicion.

"Nothing's up with me," I said, busying myself with the sleeve of the gown.

"Bullshit," Eliyse said, circling around me like a lioness readying to devour prey. "I noticed it at the restaurant--"

Saved by the bell! The sound of my ringing cell phone stopped her short. I exhaled a relieved sigh. "Will you get that please?"

"Fine," Eliyse said, strutting over to retrieve my purse off the chair. She gave me a cool grin. "But I'm not done with you Cinderella."

"Just answer the phone," I said, feigning impatience.

"Danielle Morton's cell phone," E' sang out. "Her beautiful best friend Eliyse speaking."

"You so silly," I said, repositioning my breasts in the gown. Maybe I should go a bit lower, if only to give the *girls* a little more breathing room.

"Well, you have a lovely voice too," Eliyse cooed into the phone. "And who shall I say is calling...*Amadeus?*" Her eyes widened. "Is this the same Amadeus who took my Danni to the—?"

"I'll take that!" I said, almost ripping the gown as I leaned over, snatching the phone out of Eliyse's hand.

"All right," she said, taken aback by my aggressiveness. "No reason to be attacking anybody."

"Sorry," I said, lifting the cell to my ear. "Hi there."

Thankfully, Eliyse, once again focused on her own image in the mirror, didn't seem to notice me blushing as Amadeus told me how good it felt to be inside me that morning.

"I had a good time too," I said, trying not to giggle like some silly schoolgirl. "Will you stop it? "

When Amadeus proposed our getting together for another round, my body quivered with desire. "I don't know if that would be...yes...Amadeus it was..." I said, stopping short when I felt Eliyse's eyes on me. Wiping the warm smile off my face, I turned my back to her. "Let me think about it okay?" I asked in a whisper. "Umm hmm...me too...I gotta go bye."

Closing the cell, I placed it into E's outstretched hand. "What?" I asked defensively.

"Nothing," she said, not taking her eyes off me. "Nothing at all."

"I need to hurry up," I said, attempting to break free of her stealth-like stare. Glancing down at my watch, I sighed. "I need to be at Powers' parents' house by six for dinner."

Eliyse snapped her fingers. "That's what's different about you," she said excitedly. "You're glowing."

"I'm not glowing," I said with a nervous chuckle. "I'm sweaty."

"I didn't think Powers had the skills to make you..." Eliyse said, then hesitated. Her eyes bugging, she staggered back. "No you didn't!"

"Will you stop shouting," I said, shushing her. "What is your--?"

"Powers didn't give you the high-pro glow!" Eliyse said, now damned near hysterical.

Cringing, I bit down on my bottom lip.

"You had sex with Amade—!"

"Tanya!" I said, almost pissing myself as Amadeus' sister walked into the private fitting room.

Eliyse spun around. Her surprised look quickly morphed into one of annoyance.

"Hey Danni," Tanya said, frowning when she noticed Eliyse. "Oh, you're here."

"Hello *Taaanya*," Eliyse growled through a tight smile. "Always great to see you."

"I'm sure it is," Tanya growled back.

"Love the shoes," Eliyse said with feigned sincerity. "Payless is really kicking up the quality, huh?"

"I see you're still buying your blouses from Fredrick's of Hollywood's bargain catalogue," Tanya said, staring at E's breasts bursting out of the top of the purple silk sheath she was wearing. "Do you ever wear a shirt in your size?"

"Oh, bitter, chunky, Tanya—"

"Eliyse!" I gasped.

"Oh, culturally confused, slutty, Eliyse—"

E' took a step toward Tanya. "I got your—"

"Eliyse," I said quickly. "Let's not go there."

"Didn't start it," she said, cutting her eyes at Tanya.

This sort of bitchy verbal sparring was par for the course with those two. Tanya couldn't stand Eliyse, taking personal offense to the fact that she dated black men, specifically black athletes. The fact that I'd asked E' to be my maid of honor and not Tanya -- my friend since junior high school -- only made things worse.

"Tanya what are you doing here?" I asked, swiftly changing subjects.

Giving Eliyse a hard roll of the eyes, Tanya turned to me. "I missed my fitting yesterday," she said, placing her purse on the chair. "Paul got in trouble at school."

"What happened?" I asked.

Tanya smacked her lips in disgust. "He punched some boy in the mouth."

"Ouch," I said, grimacing. "Is he suspended?"

"Thankfully no," she said, relieved. "But he does have to go back into counseling."

Not interested in hearing about the latest act of bad behavior by Tanya's eleven-year-old, Eliyse retrieved her compact and lipstick from her clutch, making her way back to the mirror.

"If his father was any kind of *real* man," Tanya said venomously," he'd sit the boy down and talk some sense into him."

Eliyse gave me a look through the mirror, but thankfully kept her thoughts on the matter to herself.

"Tanya," Hilda said, smiling as she stepped back into the fitting room. "Hello, Darling."

"Hi Hilda," Tanya said with a guilty grin. "Sorry about yesterday."

"Not to worry," Hilda said, pointing toward the champagne colored dress hanging in the corner. "Why don't you get changed? I make little correction to Danielle's sleeve, then I'm ready for you."

"Okay," Tanya said, distracted as she stared at me standing there in my wedding gown.

Had you asked me ten years ago who would be the maid of honor at my wedding, I would have said Tanya's name without a second's hesitation. Over the last decade however, our once close friendship had grown increasingly more distant. Back in high school the two of us were as thick as thieves. It had always amazed me that someone as popular and beautiful as Tanya would be my friend. Both homecoming and prom queen, she was one of the *hot chicks* I both envied and despised. I could still remember going over to her house, a block over from mine, helping her get dressed for a date with some guy, or sitting around her bedroom fantasizing about how fabulous our lives were going to be once we were finally adults. For me being a wife and mother represented the apex of good living. Tanya, however, had far loftier ambitions for her life. Not only was she going to be a top fashion model ala Beverly Johnson, she and her movie star husband were going to travel the world partying it up with the crème de' la crème of high society.

Since then, our lives had veered in quite different directions. While mine had far exceeded my expectations, Tanya's had been derailed by an unexpected pregnancy that forced her to drop out of college sophomore year. Over time the balance of power had shifted between us. Now, I was the popular girl, and Tanya was the one watching...and resenting me from the sidelines. I almost didn't invite her to take part in my wedding at all, but doing that would have confirmed that our friendship was over. Though she tried not to show it, I sensed that on some level Tanya hated me. No longer the sister-friend who stood in awe of her, I was now a bitter reminder of a life that should have been hers. Knowing that, I still couldn't bring myself to let her go.

"Danni looks fabulous," Eliyse said, noting the mournful look on Tanya's face. "Don't you think so *Taaanya*?"

"She looks wonderful," Tanya said, forcing her lips into a thin smile. "You're going to make a gorgeous bride, Danni."

Eliyse smirked. "Wow, it almost sounded like you meant that."

"Thank you, Tanya," I said, my eyes shooting daggers at my current best friend, as my former one disappeared behind the screen. "Cut it out," I mouthed.

"Did you sleep with Amadeus?" Eliyse mouthed back, ready to return to the subject she was far more interested in discussing.

Slowly, I shook my head in the affirmative.

Gasping, Eliyse clutched her chest. "You slut!" she said in a strained whisper. "What have you done?"

"Not here," I whispered back.

"Where did you—?"

"Not here," I snapped.

"What's that?" Tanya asked.

"Umm...I asked how your mom was doing," I said, cutting my eyes at Eliyse.

Shaking her head in disbelief, Eliyse continued re-applying her lipstick.

"She's fine," Tanya called out from behind the changing screen. "Oh, did I mention that Amadeus is in town?"

Eliyse rolled her eyes. "She already—"

"No you hadn't," I said, a half step from pimp-slapping Eliyse's ass. The last thing I needed was for Tanya to get wind of what went down between her big brother and me. Amadeus was her hero. It was one thing to share him with me on Prom night – an act of pity on Tanya's part – it was another, entirely unacceptable matter all together for him and me to have any connection now.

"Yeah, he's staying at Mom's," Tanya said, emerging from behind the screen.

"How long is he going to be in town?" I asked, trying not to sound too interested.

"He starts a new assignment in Japan in two weeks," Tanya said, tugging at the snug dress.

Before Eliyse could comment on how Tanya looked, Hilda beat her to the punch. "You are a size twelve, yes?" the seamstress asked, baffled as to why Tanya's hips threatened to rip the seams of the three-hundred dollar A-line dress.

Realizing she couldn't afford it, I'd told Tanya that I was treating my two bride's maids to their gowns. For her part, Eliyse not only implored me to make Tanya pay her own way or bounce, she suggested I choose something less attractive for her and Rhonda, my other bride's maid to wear. But, I'd promised myself that I wasn't going to be one of those *bridezillas* who forced her maids to wear butt-ugly dresses replete with big-assed bows to ensure that all eyes remained on her during the wedding. The way I saw it, if I couldn't stand a little competition, then I'd chosen the wrong three women to stand beside me anyway. Rhonda Walker – the sister who I replaced at Channel 5 when she got a network gig in New York – had a shoe-collection that rivaled Imelda Marcos', a face that rivaled Halle' Berry's, and a body that screamed "I work out everyday...*damn it!*" And while Tanya was twenty-five pounds heavier than she was in college, the girl was still a remarkably attractive woman. And, Eliyse with her long legs, creamy smooth skin, and hour-glass figure – complete with a black girl butt -- could wear a paper sack and still snatch focus.

"Just a little water weight," Tanya said, willing her body not to bust out of the dress. "It's my time of the month."

Eliyse smirked. "Water weight my a--"

I shot her a look that stopped her in mid-insult. "Hilda, are you done with me?" I asked, overcome with a burning need to get out of this damn gown. The prospect of marrying Powers was growing less attractive with every passing moment. I couldn't help wondering if I was settling for *good enough* when my soul mate – Amadeus perhaps -- was still out there, looking for me. I had three days to find out. But, right now what I needed to do was get out of this tight, suffocating dress.

"You're done," Hilda said, helping me down from the riser. She turned to Tanya motioning for her to take my place.

Holding my train, Eliyse followed me behind the screen.

"Shhh," I whispered before she could form her lips to speak.

"Call me the instant you get home tonight," Eliyse said, genuinely concerned.

"Someone's telephone is ringing!" Tanya called out.

"I'll get it," Eliyse said.

Closing my eyes, I pinched the bridge of my nose trying to stave off the headache forming. This little *incident* had the potential to send my staid, perfectly manicured life into a complete tail spin if I didn't get a quick handle on my shifting emotions.

"Hi Powers," Eliyse said. "She's right here."

Eyes popping open, I snatched for air as E' handed the phone to me over the top of the screen. Taking a deep breath, I forced my dry lips open. "Hey baby."

"You still at the dress shop?"

"I'm about to leave now."

"Good," Powers said, relieved. "You know how Mom can be..."

A royal bitch was what she could be.

"She wants us there by six o'clock sharp."

"I was hoping to go home and freshen up first," I said, slipping into the pin-striped skirt Amadeus had eased down my thighs with such finesse earlier today. Thank God I'd found a fresh pair of panties in my gym bag, or I'd have been completely out of order.

"I'm sure you look fine," Powers said, his attention elsewhere. "Listen, the mayor's office is ringing my other line. I'll see you there in twenty minutes."

"Okay," I said, my heart sinking further into the emotional abyss.

"Love you."

The tear forming in the corner of my eye, I sighed softly into the phone. "Me too."

Chapter Four

Standing at the Washburn's front door, I smoothed out my suit and took a deep breath. If there was a God in heaven, no one would notice, or comment on the fact that I was ten minutes late. Powers' mother was such a perfectionist. For her there was no such thing as a simple dinner. Everything had to be some lavish production with silver service, place settings and floral centerpieces.

"Miss Morton," the Washburn's longtime housekeeper said as she opened the large door.

"Hi Mable," I said, quickly stepping inside. "What's the temperature in there?"

"A cold front," she said, referring to the lady of the house's current mood.

"Great," I said, shuddering.

"Chin up, young Miss," Mable said, giving my shoulder a gentle squeeze. Summoning up my courage, I followed her into the great room where the Washburn clan was gathered.

"You were great with Jamie Foxx this morning," Mable said, trying to shore up my wavering confidence.

"Thanks," I said, wishing I could fast forward the night by three hours.

"He was flirting with you?"

"Was not," I said, smiling.

"Was too," Mable grinned, then stepped aside as we approached the threshold. "I'll have a martini sent in for you," she said prodding me into the room.

"Make it a double."

Mable winked. "You got it."

"You're late," were the first words out of Lillian Powers' mouth.

And you're a mean old cunt, I thought. "There was an accident on I-75," I said, smiling into her surgically-enhanced face.

"Well, you're here now," Powers' older brother Mitch said, rising from the chair to greet me. "Come give your brother-in-law a hug."

Brightening, I stepped into his bear hug of an embrace. "Hey you."

Extending his arms, Mitch shook his head. "Damn, if only I hadn't introduced you to that knucklehead," he said, looking at Powers. "I could have had you all for myself."

And he was right, at least partly. Mitch was the first Washburn man I'd ever met in person. Three years ago, while I was still the health reporter at Channel 5, I was working on a story about Diabetes treatment and prevention. Eliyse, a field producer at the time, suggested I get in touch with the hot young doctor she'd gone out with a couple of times. Realizing who she was talking about, I jumped at the opportunity to make a *professional* connection with a member of one of Detroit's most prominent families. Spying Mitch as he made his way down the corridor of the hospital all confident and charming, I implored myself that under no circumstances would I allow my name to be added to the growing list of women bedded by the doctor who had more than earned his reputation as the consummate ladies' man.

"Step away from my woman," Powers said, pulling me out of his older brother's arms. "Hey you," he said, kissing me on the cheek.

I smiled softly. "Hey."

"Hello Danielle," Gretchen said, clutching her glass of merlot. I didn't know how long she had been there, but I was certain she'd already been to the bar more than once. There was no denying that she was her mother's child. Six months my senior – we were both thirty-one -- Gretchen had already given birth to two perfect, high-yellow Stepford children – four year old Brianna and two year old Bradford. And while the little ones were proof that she and her architect husband, Derek, had done the deed at least twice, I'd always suspected that the brotha -- way too effeminate for my tastes -- was a latent homosexual. That would explain the permanent scowl on Gretchen's face. Poor thing lived in constant fear that some big-dicked trick was going to turn out her man.

"Hi Gretchen," I said, turning to the aforementioned husband, sitting dazed and confused on the sofa beside her, "Derek."

"Danielle," he said, with manufactured bass in his voice. Who that Negro thought he was fooling – besides Gretchen – was anyone's guess.

"You looked good this morning," Gretchen said, with as much of a smile as she was capable.

"Thanks," I said, nodding gratefully to one of the household staff as he handed me my martini.

"Do you think such a low-cut blouse was an appropriate choice, dear?" Lillian asked, her judgment-drenched eyes focused on my breast. "It's so important for a young woman in your field to be appreciated for more than her physical attributes."

Giving her the strained smile I gave whenever she said some stupid shit like that to me, I thought about how Eliyse might have responded. "Those who can wear curve-hugging tops like this do," she'd say with a smug grin. "Those who can't clutch their pearls and hope to God their husband's affair doesn't become public."

Oh yeah, Congressman Washburn had a mistress, also known as his Chief of Staff. As much as Lillian rode shotgun on my last nerve, I actually pitied her. The poor boy on college scholarship she'd raised to her hand, infusing with her family's money, blue-blood respectability, and blue-chip connections had thanked her for her dogged commitment to him and his career by boinking some thirty-something, waif-thin chick on his staff in D.C. And while everyone in the family knew of the two-year affair, no one ever discussed it. These people were as bad as white, Anglo-Saxon Protestants when it came to sweeping stuff under the carpet. With the possible exception of Mitch, who did whatever the hell he wanted, appearance was everything to the Washburn's. So long as it looked good on the surface, all hell could be breaking off just beneath. In two day's I'd be one of them. God help me.

"There's nothing wrong with Danni's blouse mother," Mitch said, taking my side. For his part, Powers sat in the chair next to Lillian, his balls tucked neatly away so as not to disturb anyone.

"Powers, your father wants to see you in the study," Mable said, standing in the entryway.

"No," Lillian said, wrapping her precisely manicured fingernails around Powers' wrist. She looked over at Mable. "Tell Mr. Washburn to get off the phone with Patterson," she said, referring to the five-term Detroit Mayor, "and come join his family for pre-dinner drinks...*now.*"

Mable nodded, then stepped out of the room.

These little moments were Lillian's way of flexing her muscle with her powerful, philandering husband. It was her not so subtle reminder to him that she still ran the show, at least within the confines of their sprawling home.

As I took my last sip of martini, a uniformed woman appeared from the shadows with a fresh glass. "Mable thought you'd like a second."

"Thank you," I said with an appreciative nod. I swear if it weren't for Mable I wouldn't have been able to get through one of these overly-executed family dinners. Having basically raised Powers and his siblings, Mable was the one person to whom Lillian showed any deference. It was she after all who knew where all the Washburn skeletons were buried.

"I hear I've been summoned," Mitchell said, strutting into the great room.

"Really, Mitchell." Lillian tried to sound miffed, but the look in her eyes gave her away. Despite his *shortcomings*, she loved that man to a fault.

"Our son's next political step is important," he said, accepting the vodka gimlet from the lady who'd just given me my second drink.

"I understand that Mitchell," Lillian said through a tight smile. "But it can wait until morning. This is family time."

Ignoring his wife, Mitchell leaned over to kiss my cheek. "Hello, Sweetheart."

"Hi Mr. Washburn."

"Call me Dad," he said, almost as a demand. "Or, at the very least, Mitchell."

"Alright Mitchell," I said, lowering a hand to my leg to stop it from shaking. That man always made me a little nervous. He seemed to like me – or the idea of me being Powers' wife. But, I always got the feeling with him that I fell just shy of his idea of the ideal mate for his son. Mitchell Washburn's children, with the possible exception of Mitch, had a healthy fear of their father. Sure, Powers loved being in a position to help the masses, but I suspected he wouldn't be so driven to be a political big shot had it not been for his father pushing him so hard.

"By the way, the governor's coming to the wedding," Mitchell said, clearly impressed with himself.

Sitting there in quiet desperation, I wondered how I could possibly survive spending the rest of my days connected to these people.

"Yes, Governor Granholm," Lillian said pleased. "She committed two months ago,"

"Not Granholm," Mitchell said. "I'm talking about Governor Sterling."

The gasp escaping my lips, I turned to Powers, sitting at his mother's side.

Easing forward in her chair, Lillian's paper-thin lips curled into an indulgent smile. "The governor of New Jersey?" Her dream of making our wedding the society event of the year was coming to fruition. "I'll call the wedding planner in the morning to make sure the necessary adjustments are made," she said, the wheels spinning in her head.

"Patterson thinks that we should announce your candidacy for the mayor's office right after you and Danielle return from your honeymoon," Mitchell said to Powers.

Shuddering as the chill raced up my spine, I took a long sip of my drink. In just over a year I could be the wife of Detroit's youngest ever mayor. It was pretty much a fait accompli. Seventy-five year old, Patterson Coleman, one of the most popular and powerful mayors in the city's history would announce that he wasn't running again. Next, he'd throw his rather substantial support behind Powers – who just happened to be the son of one of the current mayor's best friends, who just happened to be one of the most powerful men in Congress. It was such a sick, nepotistic little cycle of which I wasn't so sure I wanted to be a part.

"This wedding is key to setting the ground work," Mitchell said, locking his intense gaze on Powers. "We need to offset any concerns the electorate might have about your youth." His eyes twinkled as he spoke. Simply talking about the chess game that was politics gave that man a boner.

I watched Powers' Adam's apple lift, then lower as he sat there listening obediently to his father outline their plan of attack. While he loved politics as much as Mitchell did, Powers was more of a purist. For him, being Mayor was important because it would afford him the platform from which to effect even greater change. To his father the job was a one-, maybe two-term stop on his son's sure road to Senator or Vice President. If the electorate benefited from Powers' success great, but for Mitchell, such things were secondary to winning and the political clout and influence that came with it.

"It wouldn't hurt if you could be pregnant by Christmas," Mitchell said, turning his attention to me. "You can keep the job until he's elected."

Not bothering to hide my annoyance, I cut my eyes to Powers giving him a *you better check your old man, or I will* glare.

"Dad those are private matters between Danni and me," he said, almost whispering.

"What your father means to say," Lillian said, trying to clean it up, "is that—"

"I said exactly what I meant to say," Mitchell declared, shutting her down. Oh, the sheer arrogance of that man.

Lillian lowered her head and shut her mouth. Gretchen and Derek disappeared into the sofa, grateful not to be in the mix. From the corner of his eye, Mitch glanced over at his younger brother hoping as I did that Powers might stand up to his father, if not for his own sake, then for mine.

Mitchell tried to charm me into submission. "I'm not trying to control your life…"

The hell you aren't! I thought, looking him dead in the eyes. I've tried to be respectful, but this man needed to recognize that I wasn't one of his fucking children. And, I certainly wasn't his functional alcoholic wife. The first time he'd cheated on my ass, I'd have done a Lorena Bobbit on his crown jewels.

"But you must understand that you're marrying into an important family."

"Mr. Washburn," I said, staring him down. "With all due respect—"

Mable appeared from out of nowhere. "Dinner is served."

"We'll talk about this later," Mitchell said, already up from his chair.

Like hell we will, you pompous, arrogant, prick.

When I didn't move from my seat, Powers asked, "You coming?"

Grudgingly, I stood to my feet, fuming as I followed him and his family to the dining room. These yellow folk might have been pretty, but they were a dressed up mess. If Powers didn't mind his daddy telling him when and how to wipe his own ass, that was his business, but I'd be damned if Mitchell Washburn was going to run rough shot over me. I'd call the wedding off before I'd let that shit happen.

Chapter Five

"Now that's an amazing story," I said, still trying to shake off my fumbling of the live interview with singer Kem in the segment prior.

"Wow, I'll say," my co-anchor said, feigning interest neither of us really had. "The resiliency of the human spirit is absolutely incredible."

Barely paying attention to him, I nodded. "Simply amazing."

You were...amazing.

Damn you Amadeus! No matter how hard I tried I couldn't push him out of my thoughts. Last night I hadn't gotten a wink sleep, replaying what had happened at the hotel over and over in my head. As Powers slept peacefully beside me, I tossed and turned, the brushfire between my legs threatening to completely envelope me. By two in the morning I was so worked up that I'd actually tried to get a rise – literally – out of Powers. Still half asleep, he pushed my hand away from his pajama bottoms. "Baby we both have long days," he said, groggily, before turning to his other side.

"We're running short," Eliyse barked into Douglas' and my earpieces. "No happy chat. Go straight to the kicker."

Acting as if our spastic executive news producer wasn't screaming into his ear, Doug maintained his anchorman smile as he turned his head in the direction of the camera with the illuminated red light. "Finally this morning...a story about a man who got more than he bargained for at a local garage sale," he said introducing the piece. "Local five's Trina Gallant has the details."

"We're back in forty-five seconds," Eliyse said, hastily.

Douglas chuckled as he adjusted his earpiece. "I see our leader is in a mood today."

Lost in my own thoughts, I didn't respond, but Eliyse did. "Your mic is still on you prick," she said over the loud speaker. "Just for that I'm taking ten seconds from you..."

What had attracted me most to Powers – besides his cleft chin, broad shoulders and bedroom eyes – was his stability. He wasn't the wild, dangerous type who took a girl's breath away only to leave her broken and bitter in the end. Powers was a kind, patient, loving *man*. The kind a woman could build a life with.

Standing just off set, the stage manager signaled us that we had ten seconds before we came out of the story. Looking past her, I stared off into the middle distance, lost in my self-created drama, and self-inflicted pain.

"Doug, do a quick toss to traffic," Eliyse instructed.

Clearing his throat as the stage manager counted him down from five seconds, Doug lifted his head from the monitor built into the top of the anchor desk, beaming into the camera. "Let's take one final look at traffic with Jennifer Simpson."

"We're short Jen...just do the Lodge, then toss it to weather," Eliyse said as the traffic reporter explained to viewers how an overturned tanker was going to completely screw up their morning commute.

"That's it for traffic," Jennifer said, handing off to weather. "How's it looking out there Andrew?"

"Today is a classic example of April showers bringing May flowers," the meteorologist said with a chuckle.

"Save the funny...twenty seconds," Eliyse snapped. "Kill the school bell temp graphic," she said to the director sitting in the control room beside her.

"Currently, Metro Airport is reporting sixty-eight degrees... Seventy-one at Detroit City," Andrew said, trying to wrap up. "Expect a beautiful sun-filled day with highs reaching the lower..."

"Doug, Danni you got thirty seconds to wrap this puppy up," Eliyse announced.

"Sounds like a great day's in store for us," Doug said, turning to me. When I didn't respond, he nudged my arm gently.

"Danni...talk!"

The sound of Eliyse's shout into my ear snapped me out of my reverie. "Thank you for joining us this morning for Local 5 Morning News," I said, recovering. "For Douglas, Andrew, Jennifer and the rest of the Local 5 Team, I'm Danielle Morton."

"Stay with Local 5 all day for Metro Detroit's most complete news coverage," Doug said as the show's theme music played in the background. "Danni and I will be back in twenty-five minutes with a recap of this morning's headlines."

"But for now let's send you off to New York," I said, grinning into the camera like I didn't have a care in the world, "and the *Today* show with Katie and Matt."

"And we're out," Eliyse said with palpable relief.

Taking a defeated breath, I detached the lavaliere microphone from the lapel of my salmon colored jacket, unhooked the battery pack from my waist and dropped both onto the anchor desk. My personal life had become a giant cluster-fuck. One or two more morning shows like this one and my professional one would be going down the tubes as well.

"You okay?"

I needed to keep my wits about me. It was one slip-up that nobody had to ever know about, certainly not Powers. I lived firmly rooted in the realization that a hundred women would jump at the chance to marry a man like my fiancé. It would be utterly foolish of me to push him -- a good man, who loved me -- away simply because he didn't make my toes curl. This wasn't a soap opera, for goodness sake. Given the choice between passion and true love, the smart sista went for the latter. I was a lucky woman and I needed to start acting more like it and less like some restless freak. Still, I couldn't help but wish Powers gave me butterflies... like Amadeus did.

"Danni?"

I flinched when Douglas touched my shoulder. "I'm sorry... what?"

"I asked if you were okay."

"I'm fine," I said, rising from the anchor desk. Retrieving my scripts with one hand, I reached for the coffee mug with the other. "But I would kill for five straight hours of restful sleep."

"Planning the wedding of the year is no small feat, huh?" Douglas' smile was a knowing one. "I'm sure the station's making it into a ratings opportunity only adds to the stress."

"Got no one to blame for that arrangement, but myself," I said wearily as we made our way out of the studio and down the long corridor leading to the newsroom. "They didn't do it without my permission." Douglas and I had a good relationship, but not so close for me to confide in him that I'd actually been the one – guided by Eliyse -- to suggest the idea of Channel 5 creating a thirty minute special about my wedding.

"Well, if you need any help," Douglas said, taking a seat behind his desk directly across from mine "I'm here for you."

"That's kind of you Doug," I said, lowering my coffee mug beside my computer. "But between Powers' mother and the wedding planner, I've got all the help I could ever want."

"Oh, to be young and in love," he said with a wistful smile. Twenty-five years my senior, Doug had been married to his wife Natalie for twenty years. "Enjoy this time of white-hot passion and sleepless nights." He sighed as he reclined in his chair. "Soon enough the kids, car note, mortgage, and college tuition will crowd passion right out of the equation."

"Thanks, Doug," I said with a sarcastic smirk. "That really makes me want to go...jump off a cliff."

"Don't misunderstand me," Doug said, clarifying. "I'm more in love with Natalie than I was the day we got married. I wouldn't trade my life with her and our three kids for anything in the world." His words were laced with sincerity. "But that *can't keep our hands off each other lust* is long gone...in its place is a deeply rooted love, and a shared history that's far more stimulating."

"Really?" I asked skeptically.

"Absolutely." Doug shook his head in the affirmative. "Think of it as the difference between moonshine and fine wine," he said, somehow sensing my need to hear the wisdom he was imparting. "The former is a cheap high that's easy to come by, but ultimately short-lived. The latter, however is full-bodied and dense," Doug said surely. "And while the buzz might take a little longer to come by, it's a far more satisfying one that tends to linger long after the last sip."

"Well, look at you," I said, genuinely impressed. "Natalie didn't do too bad for herself after all."

"I'll tell her you said so." Doug smiled as he rose to his feet. "You want some more coffee?"

"No, I'm fine thanks," I said, the smile on my face tensing as I spied Eliyse marching toward us. I was certain she was coming over to tear me a new one for my total lack of focus during the show.

"You okay, Danni?"

"Yea," I said, but didn't mean it. "Look, I'm sorry about that last cue."

"Don't sweat it," Eliyse said, sitting down on the edge of my desk. "Let's just agree that you've had better days and be done with it."

"Thank you," I said, covering my mouth as the yawn escaped my lips.

"Not getting enough sleep, are we?"

"No," I said, reaching for my cup of cold coffee.

"I meant to call you last night," Eliyse said pensively. "So we could talk about...what happened."

"Powers spent the night."

"Ah," Eliyse said understanding we couldn't have talked about my roll in the sack with Amadeus even if I wanted to. I didn't want to.

"So do you wanna go someplace and talk now?" she offered. "I got a few minutes before the planning meeting starts."

Taking a pensive breath I glanced around the busy newsroom to make sure nobody was up in my business.

"Danni how did this happen?" Eliyse asked concerned.

Pretty sure that she didn't want to hear how the sensation of Amadeus' tongue against my ear had made my panties fall to my knees of their own accord, I said weakly, "It just happened."

"Sleeping with another man..." Eliyse said, then hesitated. She looked at me intently. "You did sleep with him right?"

The realization made me quiver...and not in the good way. "God help me."

"Okay," Eliyse said, trying to keep her emotions in check. "Then back to my point. Sleeping with a man who is *not* the one you're about to marry doesn't just happen, Danni. You have either lost your mind, or are subconsciously trying to sabotage your relationship with Powers."

I glared at her. "You think I planned to fuck him?"

"That's not what I said," Eliyse answered, matching my hard stare. "But you need to take some responsibility for this shit. Your clothes didn't simply disintegrate as you tripped over your Prada's, just happening to fall on Amadeus' big ole stiff dick."

"Eliyse," I said, distressed by the visual, "do you have to be so graphic?"

"Yes," she said. "Clearly somebody needs to paint you a picture." Eliyse shook her head in frustration. "What the hell, Danni? You have a good man who loves your magically delicious ass, and you bed some old high school flame!"

"Will you lower your voice please?" I asked, feeling like a common skank. "You don't understand what I'm dealing with."

"Oh please explain," Eliyse said, folding her arms. "Please explain to me what you could possibly be dealing with that would cause you to risk your future with a man like Powers."

"You are such a hypocrite E'!"

Eliyse drew back. "Excuse me?"

36

"You take every available opportunity to remind me just how boring, and unexciting Powers is," I said angrily. "I would think you of all people would understand how I'm feeling."

"Don't even try to pin your bullshit on me," Eliyse said, not having it. "I tease you about Powers, but I like him a lot. Besides, I'm not the one who agreed to marry the brotha. You are."

"What if I want more?"

"More what?" Eliyse asked. "More excitement...more spice?"

"Yeah."

"Tell Powers," she said simply. "Instead of stepping out on the man days before your wedding day, step up to the plate and tell him what you need," Eliyse said adamantly. "He might very well surprise you."

"I doubt it."

"But you'll only know for certain if you try," Eliyse said. "I suspect that Powers is capable of giving you more if he had a clue of what that *more* was?"

Speechless, I fell back in the chair, shame washing over me like the waves of a tiding ocean.

"First and foremost though, you need to end this madness with Amadeus," Eliyse said. "You can't fix you and Powers as long as he's in the picture confusing things with his big ole cock."

My face blushed.

"Umm hmm." Eliyse smirked. "I remember what you told me about prom night," she said, giving me the eye. "*Turtleneck* and all."

I couldn't help but laugh. "You can be such a nasty little thing."

"Clearly I ain't the only one," E- said, her lips twisting into a grin. "Who can blame you for not thinking straight? But now it's time to do the right thing here." Eliyse took a beat before laying it down for me. "Yesterday is done and there is *no* reason to mention it to Powers," she said, answering the question before I could pose it. "Call Amadeus and tell him that what happened, while nice, will never happen again. You hear me?"

Taking a deep breath, I nodded. "I hear you."

Just then, one of the production interns approached my desk with the most beautiful bouquet of red roses.

"You shouldn't have!" Eliyse said, snatching the vase out of his hand.

Giving his superior a curious grin, the intern said, "Those just came for you, Ms. Morton."

"Damn," Eliyse said, feigning disappointment.

Taking the vase from her, I lowered them onto the desk. "Thanks."

"You're welcome," the intern said, not moving from where he stood.

"Are you waiting for a tip?" Eliyse asked, shooing him away. "Off you go."

"Oh, sorry," he said, hauling ass.

"Let's see what your fiancé has to say," Eliyse said, reaching for the card.

"To me," I said, attempting to snatch it from her hand.

"Too slow," Eliyse said, moving out of my reach. She opened the envelope, her eyes dancing as she read…

There is nothing I wouldn't do for you…
I'll talk to dad today.
P-

"He really is one of the good guys," Eliyse said, handing me the card. "Don't give him up without a fight, Danni."

The tear welling in the corner of my eye, I nodded as she gripped my trembling hand.

Glancing down at her watch, Eliyse cringed. "Shit, I'm late for the planning meeting," she said, rising from the desk. "I'll check in on you later."

"Okay," I said with a tentative smile. "Thanks E'."

Eliyse gave me a reassuring look. "You got it," she said, then rushed off to her meeting.

Sifting through the mess on my desk, I located my cell phone. It rang the instant I reached for it. When I saw the number on the caller ID I steadied myself.

"I was just about to call you."

"How fortuitous for me," Amadeus said, his deep baritone sparking heat inside me. "I hope you were calling to say you wanted to see me as badly as I do you."

"I'm getting married in three days." I bit down pensively on my bottom lip. "What happened between us yesterday can—"

"Don't," he said, stopping me. "Don't say it."

My eyes darted around the noisy newsroom. "Amadeus, what happened was a mistake."

"I want you so badly, Danni," he said in a sensual growl. "Hold you in my arms...taste you..."

Swallowing the moan rising in my throat, I shifted in my chair, the desire to feel him inside me again almost more than I could stand. While my head implored me not to be a fool, not to risk a lifetime of happiness for an hour of white-hot passion, my body wanted what only Amadeus could give it.

"Amadeus we can't—"

"Please Danni," he said, his voice dipped in yearning. "Baby please."

"Amadeus--"

"I need to see you."

"We can't do this."

"Do what?"

"This."

"Will you at least meet with me so we can talk?"

Exhaling a shaky breath, I considered. What I should have done was gotten the hell off the phone.

"Meet me at the hotel."

"Amadeus."

"Then come to my mom's house."

I didn't respond. I didn't dare.

"All we'll do is talk," Amadeus said. "I promise."

God help me. "Okay."

Chapter Six

 T here are times in each of our lives when even though we know we shouldn't do something, say something, or step into a given situation, we do, say, or step anyway. What I had done yesterday – and was doing at this very moment -- was a classic example or throwing good sense and caution to the wind for the sake of the fleeting, superficial thrill. I could try to justify my reasons for having gone into a hotel room or for sitting here on the sofa currently with a man who I knew had an incredibly powerful effect on me. Be it restlessness, boredom, loneliness, or simply a need to sow some phantom wild oats, the fact remained - I had no business doing what I was doing. And as was usually the case when you did stuff you knew you ought not, you had no one to blame but yourself when the train jumped the tracks, and the shit hit the fan.

"Is there nothing I can say or do to stop you from marrying him?" Amadeus asked, not really wanting me to answer in the affirmative.

Easing over on the sofa, I shook my head no. "I love him," I said, reminded for the first time in days how much I truly did love Powers. "He may not have your raw passion, but he is the man I want to spend the rest of my life with."

Amadeus exhaled a defeated sigh. "Fair enough."

Leaning in closer, he kissed me, the taste of his lips causing my body to warm. Amadeus was one fine black man, but I wasn't suffering from any delusions as to the true nature of my feelings for him. I was *not* in love with him, not even back in high school when I basically stalked the guy. What I felt for him was lust, pure unadulterated, base lust. He was the hero in my dreams; the intoxicating charm, devil-may-care attitude, and spine-tingling confidence in and out of the bedroom. There was an air about him that had always drawn me in like a moth to a flame. Amadeus was beautiful, and smart…and dangerous. What transpired yesterday, as wrong as it was, had been magical. The smooth, but sure way he'd eased himself inside me, the determined knowing of his tongue as it parted my quivering lips, his strong hands, those gorgeous dreads. Sex with Amadeus was as good as it had been in my dreams. Yet, as amazing as he'd made every single inch of my body feel, my heart broke a little bit, just as it had on prom night. But, I was no longer a fat insecure high school girl. I was a grown-assed woman who needed to get a firm grip on reality. Amadeus was a great fantasy, but Powers was real.

Rising from the sofa, Amadeus walked over to the stereo. Slipping in the Luther Vandross CD, he pressed play. Turning to me he extended his hand. "Dance with me."

"Amadeus," I said weakly.

His eyes pleaded with mine. "For old times sake."

A nervous breath escaping my lips, I stood to my feet.

Drawing me into his arms, he hummed the melody of the song sweetly in my ear as we started to dance.

Finally he said, "I wish yesterday could happen again—"

"But, it can't," I said, pulling away.

"I know," he said, pulling me back into his arms. "Making love to you yesterday..." Amadeus hesitated.

"What?" I asked stiffening.

"Thought I heard something," he said, glancing back toward the hall leading to the kitchen. "Just the house settling."

Returning his hand to my back, we resumed dancing. Amadeus sighed as he stared into my eyes. "You are amazing, Ms. Morton."

"You've already told me that," I said, blushing. "Yesterday at the hotel."

"Ah yes," he said, a dirty little smile forming on his beautiful lips. "Well, it bears repeating."

Locked in an embrace far too intimate to be appropriate, we continued dancing, lost in our own world of what *might* have been.

"Sometimes I wonder how things would have turned out had I stayed in Detroit," Amadeus said, a hint of melancholy in his voice. "Maybe I'd be the one marrying you instead of Powers."

Resting my head on his shoulders, I closed my eyes and allowed myself the luxury of imagining that he hadn't left three days after my prom for a summer exchange program in Italy. Something in my gut told me that the two of us would have failed miserably as a couple. The last two weeks notwithstanding, I liked normalcy and routine in my world. Amadeus, on the other hand, was a gypsy at heart. The boredom that was regular folk's lives would have driven him to madness, or at the very least out of my arms. Even in high school he was a restless soul, never able to sit in one place for too long. God love him, Amadeus needed to keep moving. Men like him were happiest when they lived on the periphery, free to go in whatever direction their wild imaginations and boundless energies directed them.

"What happened between us yesterday was wrong," I said, slowly reopening my eyes. "But on some level I'm glad it did."

"Glad enough that perhaps we can go upstairs and make it happen again?" Amadeus asked with a sly grin.

"Not that glad," I said, laughing as I lifted my head from his shoulder. "Being with you has finally allowed me to put it all behind me."

He looked at me curiously.

"I've had a crush on you since the day Tanya brought me to this house," I said, recalling the sweet memory. "But time has come for me to put all those schoolgirl feelings where they belong."

"And where's that?"

"In my past," I said, kissing his cheek. "Take care of yourself Amadeus."

"You too Danni," he responded, correctly sensing that this was to be our final goodbye. Lifting his hand to my cheek, he stroked it gently. "Powers is a lucky man."

Taking a step back, I studied Amadeus' face committing it to my memory. From time to time I'd pull the gorgeous visual from the recesses of my mind if only to remind myself that even something this beautiful couldn't compare to my husband. Not in the ways that mattered most.

"Goodbye Amadeus."

"Goodbye."

Walking out the door, I implored myself not to look back as he stood on the front porch watching me as I got into my car. Starting the engine, I pulled off. Once onto Jefferson Avenue, I reached into my purse pulling out my cell. I couldn't dial the number fast enough.

"Hey beautiful," Powers said the instant he answered.

Clutching my chest I silently thanked God for saving me from myself. "Hey yourself handsome."

"Did you get the roses?"

Fighting back the tears, I nodded. "Umm hmm."

"Is everything okay?"

"It is now," I said, exhaling softly as the weight lifted from my shoulder. "The flowers were absolutely beautiful."

"I love you so much Danielle Morton," Powers said, the genuineness in his voice stopping me cold.

"And I love you."

"Mean it?" he asked, only half-joking.

"Absolutely," I said without hesitation. "I can't wait to be your wife."

"You have no idea how much I needed to hear you say that," Powers said, the relief in his voice telling. "I was starting to wonder if maybe you were having second thoughts about us."

Unable to deny the veracity of his concerns, I didn't respond to them. "How soon can you get out of there tonight?"

"My last meeting with the planning commission should be over by five-thirty," Powers said.

"I'll have dinner waiting for you at six," I said, not bothering to wipe the tear streaming down my cheek as I merged onto I-94.

"You're cooking it?" Powers asked surprised.

"Yes," I said with a playful smirk. "It's time I started taking better care of my husband, which includes making sure he gets at least one home cooked meal a day."

"Do you have any idea how much you mean to me woman?" Powers asked. His exhale was audible. "I want to give you the world Danni."

"You already have," I said, straining to see the road through my tear-stained eyes.

"If there is ever anything you need from me that I'm not giving you," Powers said, placing his heart on his sleeve. "Promise me you'll let me know."

"I will."

Chapter Seven

"That was so good baby," Powers said, savoring the last bite of his filet mignon.

Reaching for the empty plate I smiled, pleased that my man was happy. "I'm glad you liked it."

"Let me help you—"

"No, no," I said, guiding him back into the chair. "Don't you lift a finger." Kissing him on the lips, I cooed, "It's my pleasure to take care of my king."

"What's gotten into you?"

Standing there in skyscraper-high Manolo's and a sheer black teddy, I answered, "Nothing's gotten into me." A devilish grin formed on my painted lips. "Not yet, anyway."

Powers eyed me curiously as I led him into the living room. His eyes blinked wildly as I eased him down onto the sofa. Powers was unsettled by, and – if the bulge in his dress slacks was any indication – thoroughly aroused by my assertiveness.

Kissing him deeply on the mouth, I lowered to my knees between his spread legs.

He swallowed nervously. "Danni what are you--?"

"Shhh," I said, silencing him. "I got this...okay?"

Licking his dry lips, Powers nodded. "'K."

Removing the Bacco Bucci's, I slipped off his socks, rubbing his freshly pedicured feet.

Closing his eyes, Powers leaned back against the sofa, allowing himself to enjoy the stimulation. That's when I made my move. Carefully, I lifted his foot. Easing his big toe into my mouth, I sucked gently but surely.

A gasp escaping his lips, Powers' eyes popped open. From the look on his flushed face I thought he was going to snatch his foot away, demanding an explanation for my new-found freakiness. Instead he closed his eyes again and whispered breathlessly. "Damn, baby."

After giving his other foot equal attention, I lifted myself from the floor. "Be right back with dessert."

His jaw hanging, Powers didn't say a word as he watched me sashay into the kitchen.

My heart beating wildly, I took a deep breath. Steadying my shaking hand, I reached into the refrigerator, removing the chocolate covered strawberries and bottle of Dom.

"So far so good," I said, smiling as I poured the two glasses of champagne.

I had been on pins and needles waiting for Powers to come over this evening. After changing my mind at least four times, I decided to risk my own pride and comfort, and fear of rejection for the sake of our relationship. Tonight, I was going to take Eliyse's advice and show my man -- through words and actions -- how to please me between the sheets. The lack of fire in our bedroom was as much my fault as it was Powers'. I mean come on, how in the world could I expect him to hit my sweet spots if I never told him where they were? That was all about to change. I'd have to take care, of course, not to bruise his fragile male pride, but before this night was through I was going to school my man on how to make me scream. In turn I wasn't going to stop until he'd strained a vocal cord or two as well.

It wasn't until this afternoon when Powers asked me to tell him if I needed something he wasn't giving me that I realized the error of my ways. All this time I'd been lying in the prone position playing good girl, hoping he'd somehow read my mind. Powers was a fiercely intelligent, intuitive man, but the brotha wasn't a freakin' mind reader. How ironic that the solution to my dilemma had been lying next to me the past two years in the form of a wonderful man who wanted nothing more than to give me the world.

"Don't answer that," I called out when I heard the sound of the phone ringing.

"You sure?"

"Very," I said, damned if anyone or anything was going to keep me and my man from fucking each other's brains out tonight.

"You selfish, greedy, two-faced, boogie-assed bitch!"

The cruel words being spewed from my answering machine barely audible from the kitchen, I took a sip of the champagne, plotting my next move in my head. After feeding each other dessert, I'd ease myself between Powers' muscular thighs, pressing my hot flower against his stiff manhood. He might have had the disposition of a saint, but that man had the body of a bad boy. Thanks to a competitive spirit between them, Powers had been joining his brother at the gym thrice weekly since he was in his late twenties. At thirty-two, Powers' body was a broad-shouldered, well-chiseled, butterscotch-colored example of delicious perfection. The thought of finally showing him how to put all that strength and power to work was making me wet.

"Easy Girl," I said, brushing my hand over my excited nipples. "Don't get there too soon."

Oblivious to the fact that my world was about to come completely unglued, I continued plucking rose pedals from the stem, using them to decorate the tray.

"It's not enough that you are about to marry one of the most eligible, popular, nicest men in all of fucking Detroit," Tanya shouted into the machine. "You had to have my brother too?"

Lifting the tray, I strutted toward the kitchen door, stopping short when I heard the shrill voice.

"Yeah, I know you fucked Amadeus at the hotel yesterday," Tanya said angrily. "I overheard the two of you talking about it today as you were dancing cheek to cheek in my mother's..."

"Oh shit!" I gasped.

Ignoring the crash of the glasses and strawberries behind me, I raced toward the living room, hoping for what I wasn't sure. The look on Powers' face as he stared at the telephone said it all.

Leaping toward the sound of Tanya's screeching voice, I snatched the cord from the wall. "Powers, let me explain—"

"What is she talking about?" he asked, not letting me finish.

Words failing me, I began to sob.

"You...you cheated on me?"

The pain in his voice cut me to the quick. I had to try and make him understand. "Powers...it just—"

"Don't say it!" he snapped. "Don't you dare say 'it just happened'." His eyes burned with rage. "Say anything, but that Danielle."

Oh shit, he was using my full name. That was never a good thing. "I'm sorry, baby," I said, moving toward him. "I didn't mean for it to—"

"Do not touch me," Powers growled, slapping my hand away as I reached to touch his shoulder. Looking at me like I was the absolute lowest form of life, he shook his head in stupefied disbelief. "Who are you?"

"I'm the woman who wants to be your wife," I said, desperately. "I can explain this Powers, really—"

"I said, don't touch me!" He shouted, pushing me away with more force than he intended.

Unable to maintain my balance in the come-fuck-me pumps, I went tumbling to the floor.

For a brief moment Powers' disgust with me, shifted to concern. When I lifted myself up against the wall, his anger quickly returned.

"I know what I did was wrong," I said in a shamed whisper.

"Did you ever love me Danielle?"

"Of course I did...do," I said, cringing as I struggled to get up on my feet. "How could you even ask?"

"How could I ask?" Powers laughed hysterically though he found none of this even remotely humorous. "Because you fucked another man three days..." he said, then hesitated. Snatching up his coat and shoes, he headed for the door. "I gotta get out of here."

"Powers please...wait!" I begged, racing after him.

Flinching at the sound of the slamming door, I staggered over to the sofa. Twisting myself into a tight ball, I lay there crying like a baby. For this fine mess, I had no one to blame but myself.

Chapter Eight

"**I**'m gonna whoop your ass!"

"Eliyse, please hang up the—"

"Oh, I'm shaking in my boots," Tanya said with a smirk. "Danni, I suggest you check your girl."

"Why don't you check me?" Eliyse retorted. "I can't believe you are so jealous of Danni that you'd destroy her relationship with Powers—"

"*Hooold* up!" Tanya barked into the phone. "For the record, I ain't jealous of nobody. And, the only person responsible for destroying Danielle's relationship with Powers is Danielle."

Leaning back against the headboard, I grimaced as the truth of Tanya's last comment settled in my stomach like a bad meal. While I have no doubt that she took great pleasure in seeing my life crashing around me, she was spot-on in her assessment of blame. Had I not set this train in motion, there would have been nothing a hating friend, or anyone else could have done to derail it.

"Why would you even leave a message like that on Danni's answering machine, Tanya?" Eliyse asked sharply. "You know Powers spends most of his nights here."

"I don't have to explain my actions to you," Tanya said smugly.

"You are *sooo* transparent."

"Fuck you, Eliyse."

"No, Tanya, fuck you!" Eliyse shot back.

"Ladies please," I said, barely able to muster the strength to whisper the words.

"You betta watch your back," Eliyse said, ignoring my plea. "'Cause the next time I see your *hateration* ass, it's gonna be on and poppin'."

"Bring it bitch!"

Eliyse guffawed. "Oh, it's brought...*be-atch!*"

"I say there's no time like the present," Tanya said. "Why don't you come on over now...I'll leave the front door unlocked to make it nice and convenient for you to whoop my ass."

"I'm on my way," Eliyse said. To know the girl – who on the telephone sounded like a straight-up sista – was to know she had every intention of going.

"Eliyse you are not about—"

"Uh uh Danni," Tanya interrupted me. "Don't stop her. Come on Blondie," she said, daring Eliyse. "But do know that the instant you step foot over my threshold, I'm gonna bust a cap up in your bony white ass...and enjoy doing it."

"Should have known you weren't woman enough," Eliyse said. "Maybe that's why your ex-husband now sleeps with men—"

"Danni!" Tanya screamed at me for telling her secret.

"Eliyse!" I screamed at her for breaking the confidence.

"Go to hell," Tanya snarled. "Both of you."

"You first, you pathetic—" Eliyse stopped short when she heard the sound of the dial tone.

Returning the receiver to its base, I lowered myself in the bed and pulled the covers over my head. I don't know what I expected to accomplish by calling Tanya. Perhaps I was seeking the same thing I'd sought with each of the fifteen unanswered calls I had placed to Powers in the hours since he had stormed out of my apartment: Understanding. Now that it was all said and done, the utter stupidity and selfishness of my actions were crystal clear to me. For two hours of toe-bending good sex, I'd put my entire future at risk. Okay, maybe that was overstating it a bit, but you get my point. If I could do it all over again, I would have thanked Amadeus for calling me at the station to say hello, then graciously declined his offer to have lunch. As was the case with hindsight, it was twenty-twenty, but always a day late and a dollar short.

"That heffa hung up on us!" Eliyse said, fuming as she stepped into my bedroom.

"You shouldn't have picked up the extension, Eliyse."

"Whatever," she said, with a quick wave of her hand. "It's water under the bridge."

Lying on my side, I stared into the dark abyss that was my life. "I am so stupid," I said with a dejected sigh. I wanted to cry, but I had no tears left to shed. "I've lost Powers forever."

"Don't say that," Eliyse said, sitting on the edge of the bed.

I looked at her like she was crazy.

"It ain't over till the fat lady sings," she said confidently. "You are not the first woman to cheat...trust."

"That fact does little to make me feel better."

"Do you still want to be with Powers?"

"It doesn't matter," I said, my lips quivering. "He'll never forgive me."

"Never say never," Eliyse said, rising from the bed. She shook her head as she looked down on me curled in the fetal position. "Get up and get dressed."

"Could you leave now," I said, not budging. "I need to be alone so--"

"So you can wallow in self-pity?" Eliyse asked, not waiting for an answer. "I don't think so." Wrapping her hand around my forearm, she yanked me up from the bed, ushering me toward the closet. "Get dressed."

Too tired to fight, I did as told.

"After we finish flattening Tanya's tires, and pouring sugar in her tank," Eliyse said, pointing at the powder blue jogging suit, "we're going to the bar, get drunk...then come up with a plan."

"A plan for what?" I asked.

Grinning like the crazy bag lady who hung out in front of Harbortown Market, Eliyse said, "For getting Powers back, silly."

Stepping out of the closet, I sighed wearily. "Eliyse—"

"Eliyse nothing," she said, tossing me my sneakers. "What you did was the height of skank-hooch."

"Hey!" I said, having the nerve to be insulted.

"Gotta keep it real," Eliyse said, handing me a baseball cap. "You fucked up, Girlfriend."

"Royally," I said, ready to climb back in bed.

"But that doesn't have to be the end of this story," Eliyse said with an assuredness that actually gave me some hope.

"What do you mean?"

"Fortunately for you, Powers loves your whorish little self."

"You do have a way with words," I said, flashing Eliyse the fakest of smiles.

She chuckled as she checked her drag in the mirror. "The very thing that got you in this mess will get you out of it."

Fastening the laces of my sneakers, I smirked. "And again, you've lost me."

Eliyse headed out of the bedroom. "Powers is but a man," she said as if the statement held the key to my salvation.

Not sure where she was taking me – figuratively or literally -- I followed her to the front door. "What does his being a man have to with anything, E'?"

"Oh, young grasshopper," Eliyse said, strutting toward the elevator. "You must understand that men do most of their important thinking with the little big-men between their legs," she explained.

Watching the numbers light up in descending order, I stood beside my friend, still clueless to what the hell she was talking about.

"I learned a long time ago that few things *can't* be fixed with sex."

"Sex!" I said in shock. If this girl truly thought my fucking Powers was going to make him forgive me for fucking someone else, she was more messed up than me.

"Yes, sex," Eliyse said, waving at the doorman as we passed him. "Men, God love 'em are fairly simple creatures, easily controlled."

I looked at her with incredulous eyes. "Really?"

"Stick your tongue in the right places, show him a few choice tricks between the sheets, and like that," Eliyse said, snapping her fingers. "He's hooked."

Opening the door to E's Mercedes convertible, I felt what little hope I held onto slip into the evening wind. "You cannot be serious?"

Eliyse settled into the driver's seat, unfazed that her pale pink micro-mini was showing all her goodies. "As serious as Whitney on crack."

"Then you need to rent a clue," I said, cutting my eyes. "Sex isn't going to fix this."

"Not that boring old-school, missionary, no-talking, ten minute and out shit you and Powers are used to," E' said, speeding out of the parking lot. "I'm referring to the stick your fingers up his butt, let him hit it from the back, slurp the pole till he shoots like a geyser kind," Eliyse explained without so much as blushing. "It does the trick...then some."

"I'm not about to act like some freak in order to get Powers to forgive me," I said smugly.

"Hmmm," Eliyse said, spying me from the corner of her eye. "Perhaps had you been more willing to let your freak flag fly in your own bed, you wouldn't have had need to go looking for satisfaction in someone else's."

Ouch! Her words stung like a pissed-off bee. Seeing how she was right, I swallowed the nasty words ready to fly out my mouth.

"History bears me out on this," Eliyse said. "Men have fought wars over pussy...*good* pussy that is."

Maybe it was desperation, or hunger, but the girl was actually starting to make sense to me.

"But if you aren't willing to do what it takes to get him back," Eliyse said, shrugging. "Maybe you didn't love him as much as you claimed—"

"I'm willing," I said, cutting her off.

Eliyse eyed me carefully. "You sure?"

Matching her cool stare, I shook my head. "Absolutely."

Chapter Nine

*S*ipping on my merlot, I stared at the clock. Powers was supposed to be here an hour and a half ago. With each moment that passed, my hope for reconciliation faded more. It had taken ten minutes of begging to get him to agree to come over so we could 'talk' about what happened in that hotel room three days ago. Yet, talking was the last thing I was planning to do. Clearly, I wasn't going to win Powers back on the strength of my position. No matter how I might have wished otherwise, there was no getting around or glossing over the truth; four days before I was scheduled to marry one man, I had lay down with another.

As Eliyse had so eloquently stated, utilizing the power that rested between my legs offered the best shot of getting Powers back. Though my best friend had instructed me to greet my fiancé – former fiancé -- at the door wearing nothing but a pair of stiletto pumps and a smile, I had chosen to attire myself in a sexy red negligee. I was desperate, but not that desperate. Not yet, anyway. However, I did take her advice about the pumps, which were squeezing my toes something awful.

Sighing, I shifted my weight on the sofa, trying to accept that my preparations had been for naught. Ten more minutes and I was going to slip out of this ho-gear and slip into a nice hot bubble bath. Crying like a baby, I would drink myself into a pain-numbing stupor. I couldn't even be mad at Powers for standing me up this way. In the grand scheme of things, his act of violation didn't come close to my own.

A breath of frustration slipping through my painted lips, I stood to my sore feet, reaching for the glass of wine. Tossing back what remained of the merlot, I walked into the kitchen and poured myself another round. Getting plastered was the only thing I had to look forward to tonight. Considering that Eliyse and I had drunk ourselves under a table the night before, you'd think liquor would be the last thing I'd want. Opening my bloodshot eyes at three this morning, my hangover made its presence immediately known in the form of a pounding headache. It took every ounce of strength I had to roll over in bed and pick up the phone to call the station. But tonight, I needed the liquid courage that alcohol supplied. If I was going to garner Powers' forgiveness, I would have to put it on him like he'd never had it put on him before. By the time his second orgasm rocked his sweaty body, my little indiscretion wouldn't seem so bad.

Heading out of the kitchen, I stopped in the hall, spying my image in the mirror. Clinging to the glass of wine with one hand, I stared at my image. I looked like a call girl, a high priced one, but a call girl just the same. Smirking, I smoothed out my hair, which fell just past my shoulders. What was it with black men and hair? I wondered. Even Powers, who wasn't terribly hung up on such shallow things, had made his preference for long, flowing locks clear to me when I'd suggested discarding the weave. I had actually considered chopping it all off as a show of defiance, just to make it clear to him that I'd wear my hair – and anything else – as I damn well pleased. But now, I'd gladly let this shit hang to the floor, if doing so would get me back into Powers' good graces.

Startled by the sound of the door bell, I spilled wine on myself. Wiping at the small stain, I took a deep breath.

"Pull it together, girl," I implored myself.

Making my way down the hall as fast as my high heels would allow, I placed the glass on the table, then wrung out my hands in an effort to focus my spastic energy.

"Breathe, Danni…breathe," I said, crossing the living room. On the other side of that door was my future. And, if I had any shot of claiming it, I needed to give the performance of my life.

Opening the door, I gasped. "Amadeus, what are you doing here?"

"I wanted to make sure you were okay," he said, his face contorted in concern. "The station said you'd called in sick this morning."

"I'm fine," I said, my eyes darting around the empty corridor. "Look, this really isn't a good time."

"I know," Amadeus said, misunderstanding. "Tanya told me what happened. I am so sorry."

"It's okay," I said, glancing toward the elevator. Who was I kidding? Powers wasn't coming.

"The last thing I wanted to do was come between you and Powers," Amadeus said, taking a step toward me.

"This isn't your fault," I said, blinking quickly as my eyes watered. "Like your sister said, the only person culpable here is me."

"Baby, don't do this to yourself," Amadeus said, wiping away the tear as it streamed down my face.

A pained moan escaped my lips as his hand stroked my cheek. You'd think I'd learned my lesson, but at that moment I felt so vulnerable and lost, a kind gesture meant the world.

Closing my eyes, I gave over to the comfort of his tender touch. I whispered his name. "Amadeus."

"Amadeus!"

My eyes shot open. "Powers!"

"You son of a bitch!" he shouted, lunging toward Amadeus.

"Powers don't!" I shouted as my estranged fiancé's fisted hand connected with my lover's face.

His eyes bugging, Amadeus lifted his hand to his bloodied lip. Before he could utter a peep, Powers had landed another blow.

Rushing toward the sparring men as they exchanged blows, I tried to separate them.

"Stop it," I said, ducking out of the way of Powers' right hook. "Please stop!"

My cries went unheard as Powers barreled into Amadeus, sending him crashing against the wall. Grimacing, Amadeus tried to block the flurry of punches to his face and midsection. I had never seen Powers this angry or aggressive in my life.

"I will kill you!" Powers shouted, attempting another right hook.

Blocking the punch, Amadeus landed one of his own to Powers' abdomen, sending him stumbling back toward the opposite wall.

"Stop it!" I shouted, tugging at Amadeus' sleeve. He tried to elude me, but I held onto him for dear life.

Shaking off the pain, Powers moved toward Amadeus. "You're a dead man."

"Powers please," I said, inserting myself between them. "Amadeus you need to go."

Amadeus didn't move. "I'm not going to leave you alone with him."

"I'm her fucking fiancé," Powers said, insulted.

"It's okay," I said, pushing Amadeus toward the elevator. "Please...just go."

Exchanging daggers with Powers, he finally turned to leave. "You call me if you need anything—"

"Get the fuck on," Powers growled. "With your dreadlock-wearing ass."

Showing remarkable restraint, Amadeus continued down the hall.

When the elevator doors closed, Powers turned to me. "You must think I'm some kind of punk."

"No, I don't," I said, backing up as he approached. Never had I seen such fire in his eyes. Were I not afraid for my life, I would have been so very turned on.

"What did he do for you, Danni?" Powers asked, taking another threatening step toward me. "Did he eat your pussy?"

My eyes bugged as he pushed me inside the apartment. I didn't know what to make of his behavior. Maybe learning about me and Amadeus had sent him over the edge.

"Is that what you like?"

"Powers let's talk—"

"You like it rough don't you?" he asked, not bothering to close the door as he followed me into the living room. "Is that why you cheated on me?"

"I didn't mean for any of—"

"Shut up," he said, glaring at me.

"Baby, you need to calm—"

Powers grabbed me by the arms. "I said, shut up," he growled. Pressing my back against the entertainment center, he ripped off the negligee.

My heart racing, I snatched for air as he spread my legs apart, forcing his index finger inside me.

"Is that how you like it?"

The pain quickly gave way to pleasure as he slid another angry finger into my wet vagina. "Powers...oooh..."

A cool grin spread across his lips as he pulled out of me. Taking a step back, he studied me as I stood before him naked, afraid, and strangely aroused. Unfastening his jeans, he kicked off his sneakers. Lifting the t-shirt over his head, he stepped out of the clothes.

"Get on your knees."

Without a hint of resistance, I did as he instructed. I probably shouldn't have been, but I was actually enjoying being controlled this way.

"Suck it like you sucked Amadeus'."

It took everything I had not to climax right then and there. Angry sex – according to Eliyse anyway – was the best kind.

"That's it," Powers moaned as he grabbed my bobbing head, guiding it up and down his rock hard shaft. "Suck it...yeah Baby, suck that pole."

With a raised brow, I continued working him with my tongue and lips. Where in the world did Powers learn to speak like this? I wondered. For a man who was the definition of a black, anal-retentive conservative, he was talking like a straight-up thug. Color me strange, but I kind of liked it.

His legs starting to buckle, Powers pulled away.

"Was that okay—?"

"Shhh," he said, looking down on me with a combination of lust and disgust. "Don't talk. All you need to concentrate on is being a good fuck."

Motioning me to my feet, Powers shoved me into the dining room. With one sweeping motion he cleared off the table. While I could have done without my crystal candle holders and gorgeous china plates being sacrificed, I was as anxious as he was to get the show on the road. Still, there was something dangerous about what was happening here. Part of me wanted to demand answers from Powers before we took this any further, garner some kind of assurance that this wasn't going to get too crazy, too far off center. The greater part of me, however wanted him to handle me, without regard to social graces or good taste.

Lifting me onto the table, Powers forced my legs apart. "Come closer to the edge," his gruff voice demanded.

Unable to stifle the squeal, I held onto the sides of the table, bracing myself as he sought out my clit with his eager tongue. Had I'd known the muscle between his lips was this expert, I would have been begging him to go downtown on the regular. With my mouth hanging open, and my legs spread eagle, I tried to recall why we hadn't tasted each other before. Powers and I had never even broached the subject of oral sex prior. We were like two boring characters in a terribly boring play; him the straight-laced politician, and me the good girl who could count her past sexual partners on one hand. Without realizing it, we'd boxed ourselves into a corner, neither leaving the other room to be anything else.

"You like that?"

"Yea...yes," I stammered as he continued suckling my stiffened clit.

"That's it," Powers said, squeezing my thighs as he buried his head deeper. "Moan, damn it."

And moan I did. For the next ten minutes I cried out in pleasure, until the raging orgasm stole my breath. When my sweat drenched body stopped rocking, Powers stood to his feet. The sight of his erect penis bobbing against his six-pack abs brought me back to the brink of ecstasy.

"You are so—"

"I told you not to talk, didn't I?" Powers asked roughly.

Nodding my head in the affirmative, I swallowed my words.

He motioned for me to climb off the table, then instructed, "Turn around."

Looking at him curiously, I was about to ask why, but caught myself. In silence, I did as told.

"Lift your leg up," Powers said, his breath heavy on my neck. "Grip the table."

I cried out in agony as he forced himself inside me. The intense pain shot through me like fire. Everything in me wanted to tell him to stop, but I couldn't form my lips to speak.

"Did he hit it like this?" Powers asked, pumping into my virgin backside. "Huh, Danni, did he?"

Sure he didn't expect me to answer, I continued squealing like an excited pig as I lay hunched over the table, struggling to get my mental arms around what was happening to me. My fiancé was strumming my ass like a violin, but didn't want me to talk or look at him while he did so. We'd have to discuss some things before our next go round, but if this was any indication of what our sex life was going to be during our marriage, I was game.

Bracing his legs against the table, Powers pumped harder, each thrust more ferocious, more demanding than the last. "Whose are these?" he asked cupping my breasts tightly.

"*Oooh*...shit..."

"Answer me!" Powers demanded. "Whose titties are these?"

"You...yours...yours baby," I stuttered. God help me, but I was actually enjoying this.

His penis stretching me to my limit, Powers increased his pace. "Whose ass is this, hmm?"

"It's...oh shit!" I gasped as he moved in and out of me like a mad man on a mission. This shit was blowing my mind. What the hell!

"Powers, I'm 'bout to—"

Before I could finish the thought, he wrapped his hands around my waist. "Son of a bitch!" He cried out, his body seizing as he erupted inside me.

Collapsing on top of me, Powers caught his breath. Pulling out, he shook the residue of his excitement onto my freshly polished hardwood floor, then slapped my sore ass.

I turned to face him, unsettled by the cruel grin on his face.

"Did you like that?" he asked.

"Yes," I said with a tentative smile. "Very much." We could talk about areas for improvement tomorrow.

"Remember it," Powers said, the coldness returning to his eyes. "Cause it's the last time you'll be getting any from me."

My eyes widened. Surely I had misheard him. There was no way he was playing me like this.

"Think your girl Tanya might want to give this a go?" Powers asked, stroking his semi-hard penis.

"I sure would," Tanya said, walking into the dining room. As if it were her right, she kissed Powers full on the lips. "Umm," she cooed. "Can't wait to taste the rest."

Jaw hanging to the floor, I stood there horrified as my backstabbing friend and my former fiancé headed out of the room hand in hand. "Powers wait," I said, racing after him. "Don't do this!"

I continued pleading with him as he dressed. "Powers, we can work this out. Please don't leave me."

Tanya stood waiting at the door, a shit-eating grin spread across her face. "Let's not be a spoiled sport Danielle," she said.

"Shut the fuck up!" I barked at her.

"Snappish," Tanya said with an amused chuckle. She was clearly taking great pleasure in this.

"Powers please," I said, reaching for his arm. "You have to give us another chance."

"You had your chance," he said, snatching out of my grasp. "Now if you'll excuse me, Tanya and I need to be going now."

I followed him to the door. "Powers don't leave me!" I cried out. "Don't leave me!"

****

"Powers please don't leave me!"

"Danni," the voice called out. "Baby wake up."

Fighting my way back to consciousness, I slowly opened my eyes thanking the heavens when I saw his beautiful face staring down at me.

"Powers," I said, reaching to touch him. "Oh, thank God."

"It's okay, Baby," he said, stroking my flushed cheek.

"You didn't leave me?"

"No," Powers said confused. "I've been right by your side all night."

Clutching my pounding chest, I exhaled. "Then it was just a dream."

"Looks like it was one hell of a dream at that," Powers said, wiping the moisture from my brow. He leaned back against the headboard, pulling me into his arms. "You wanna tell me about it?"

"I don't even remember," I lied.

"You were begging me not to leave you," Powers said. "What was that about?"

"I don't know," I said, glancing over at the alarm clock. "Like I said, I don't remember the dream."

"If you say so," he said, not buying it, but letting me off the hook.

"What I do remember is that I'm marrying the man of my dreams in four days," I said, kissing him on the lips.

"Which means you better dump me soon," Powers said laughing. "Before you run out of time."

"Don't say stuff like that!" I said, hitting him in the arm.

"Ah, baby I'm just kidding," Powers said, kissing my forehead.

"Well stop," I said, reaching over to turn off the alarm clock.

"You love me?" Powers grinned, drawing me back into his embrace.

"With all my heart," I said seriously. "Never forget that."

"I won't," Powers said. He kissed me again, then lifted himself from the bed. "Better get in the shower."

"I'll make coffee," I said, smiling as I watched him walk into the bathroom.

"Hey, Danni," Powers said, poking his head out the door.

"Hmm?"

"I can't wait to make you my wife."

The sincere look on his face was enough to make me fall in love with him all over again.

"Me too," I said and meant it from the very bottom of my heart.

How I loved that man. In a matter of days I would pledge my commitment to Powers before God. I had no intention of breaking my word.

When I heard the shower running, I snatched up the telephone. The dream may not have been real, but the lessons learned surely would be.

"Amadeus, hi it's Danni," I said, certain I was doing the right thing. "Listen, I'm going to have to cancel lunch today."

EPILOGUE

"*L*et's take a final look at weather," Doug said, twisting in his chair. "This is a day for the record books, huh Andrew?"

"That's right Douglas…"

"You ready for this, Danni?" Eliyse asked, speaking into my earpiece.

No I wasn't. But in thirty seconds, I'd have to do it just the same.

"Ready," I said, shaking my head in the affirmative.

Doug winked at me. "I'm right by your side."

"I know," I said, softly.

"Sunny skies as far as the eye can see," Andrew said, standing in front of the blue screen. "Today's highs should reach the mid- to upper-eighties, with light and variable winds…"

"Ten seconds guys," Eliyse advised. "Jenny we're going to cut final traffic so we can ummm…" she said, trying not to get choked up. "We gotta give our Danni a proper send off."

Standing on the traffic set, at the opposite side of the studio, Jenny smiled at me. "Absolutely," she mouthed.

Saying goodbye to these people was going to be tough. My reasons for leaving the show however helped to bolster my resolve. God willing, I'd get through the next seven minutes without falling apart.

"So get out there and enjoy this wonderful day," Andrew said, wrapping up. "Back to you Danni."

Taking a deep breath, I stared into the camera. This was it.

"Finally this morning, I have the bittersweet task of saying goodbye," I said, the tears I'd implored myself not to cry already welling in my eyes. "Today will be my last day co-anchoring *Local 5 Today* with this remarkable gentleman sitting beside me…"

Douglas reached over, covering my hand with his.

"As much as I have appreciated and cherished the opportunity to bring you the news every morning," I said to the camera. "The strong desire to spend more time with my growing family has necessitated my making some adjustments."

Jennifer and Andrew made their way across the studio, taking seats at the main news desk with me and Douglas.

"With my husband's new responsibilities," I said, glancing down at my expanding belly, "and the new arrivals..."

The general manager, news director, along with much of the production staff for the morning show began filing into the studio as I continued.

"But I'm not leaving the Local 5 family," I said, brightly. "After my maternity leave is completed, I plan to return to the station I love to co-anchor the weekend editions of *Local 5 News*."

Staring into the sad faces of the people I've started my day with for the past half decade, I tried to remain upbeat. "My colleague, Maddy Stevens will be joining the *Local 5 Today* team on Monday. I have no doubt she's going to enjoy working with these talented folks as much as I have."

"Danni, I know we promised not to make a big deal out of this," Douglas said, with a guilty grin. "But we couldn't let you get away from us without taking one final look at your time as my partner in crime."

"The Robin to his Batman," Jennifer chimed in.

Andrew laughed. "The Beavis to his But--."

"Hey!" Douglas and I said in unison.

"What he meant to say," Jennifer said, laughing, "is that you two made an incredible team." Reading from the TelePrompTer, she cued the video retrospective. "When it comes to morning television no one does it like Danni Washburn."

"Roll tape," Eliyse said, sniffing. "Back in three minutes guys."

"Three minutes," I said in a stunned whisper. In television three minutes was an eternity of time usually reserved for deaths of presidents, or mass murders.

"Danni, watch the screen," Eliyse said, clearly up to no good. "This is gonna be fun."

Spying the silly grins on the rest of the morning team's faces, I lowered my eyes to the monitor built into the anchor desk, watching the piece as it played. "Oh Lord," I said, nervously. "What warm embarrassment have you people crafted?"

"Danielle Washburn," Douglas said playfully. "This is your life."

"Two years ago when Danni married, then City Council President, Powers Washburn, Local 5 was there," the narrator said.

"Eliyse," I said, my heart doing a back flip. "You better not have—"

"Hush," she said, trying to sound serious. "We're getting to the good part."

I sucked on my teeth as the footage of my wedding played. "Eliyse you are *sooo* gonna get it for what I think you're about to do to—"

"Wait for it," Eliyse said excitedly. "Here it comes..."

Covering my face with my hands, I peeked through my fingers. "No," I said, cringing.

"And she's down!" Eliyse said, just as I went tumbling to the floor of the church with the grace of a drunken elephant.

"Dead executive producer walking," I said laughing.

Of course dropping to my knees at my wedding couldn't have been a dream. No, I had to do that for real, with cameras rolling no less. My mortification changed to exuberance when I learned two weeks later the cause of my unsteadiness: I was five weeks pregnant with Powers, Jr.

"Back in twenty seconds guys," Eliyse warned.

Doing a quick check of my lipstick in the small mirror Douglas and I shared during the show, I handed it over to him. In a lot of ways he and I were like an old married couple. It was going to be weird not calling him every night to coordinate clothing, or laughing at his bad jokes every morning as we shared our first cup of coffee together in our make-up chairs.

"A two-time Emmy award winner, Danni Washburn is one of the jewels in Local 5's crown..." The narrator said.

"Corny," Eliyse growled.

Beaming, I continued looking at the screen. "You guys."

"We love you lady," Andrew said, kissing my cheek.

"I love you too."

"Quick group hug?" Jennifer suggested.

"Yes, please," I said, cooing as they gathered around me.

"Ten seconds," Eliyse said.

Barley back in his seat, Douglas adjusted his jacket as the red light atop camera three illuminated. "For the past five years I have had the unparallel pleasure of working with one of the best journalists in the business," he said, turning to me.

"The pleasure has been all mine," I said, swallowing the lump in my throat. "I'll miss you guys something awful, but like everyone else in Detroit I'll be watching you every morning over breakfast with my family."

"We wanted to give you a little going away present," Douglas said, smiling. "Along with a few things for the twins."

I followed his eyes as they eased toward the studio door, stunned when I saw my two favorite men walking onto the set looking just a handsome as they pleased.

"Good morning Mr. Mayor," Douglas said, rising to shake Powers' hand as he stepped onto the main set.

Letting go of his daddy's hand, Junior raced toward me. *"Mommeeee!"* he said excitedly as he climbed into my lap. "These are for you."

"Thank you sweetie," I said, accepting the roses. At that moment I wasn't the anchor in the tenth largest market in the country, but a wife and mother who adored her husband and son.

"Take my seat," Andrew said, rising from the chair next to mine.

"Good morning," I said, blushing as my husband sat down beside me, kissing me softly on the cheek.

"Good morning beautiful," Powers said.

Good God, I loved me some him!

"Are you surprised?" Junior asked, demanding my attention as he settled in my arms. "Daddy said you would be surprised."

"Yes, I am Honey," I said, for a moment forgetting about the cameras, or the fact that we were on live television. "But pleasantly so."

Clutching her chest, Jennifer exhaled a wistful sigh as she looked on.

"We've got a few other surprises for you this morning," Douglas said, motioning for the stage manager to bring in the large sheet cake. Behind her, three production assistants followed carrying a bassinet and baby stroller built for two, both emblazoned with the Local 5 logo.

"You guys!" I gushed. "This is too much."

"Nothing is too much for our Danni," Douglas said sincerely.

"I couldn't have asked for a better send off than this," I said, fanning my flushed face with the hand not holding onto Junior. "Thank you so much."

No longer able to hold back my emotion, I let the tears stream down my cheeks. "You have no idea," I said, struggling to get the words out as I looked at Douglas, "how much I have loved working with you."

"Don't you make me cry, Danni," he said with a nervous chuckle.

"Oh God," Eliyse said, balling in the control room. "This is great fucking television!"

Junior, looked up at me, his little face wrinkled with concern. "Are you okay, Mommie?"

"I'm wonderful, Sweetie," I said, running my fingers through his curly mop of hair.

"Then why are you crying?"

"Because I'm so happy."

"Oh shit!" Eliyse said, realizing the time. "Thirty seconds guys."

"Okay, everybody we've still got a show to finish here," I said, turning to Douglas.

Taking Junior from my arms, Powers rose from his chair. "Stay," I said, stopping him.

"That's all for *Local 5 News Today*," I said into the camera. "We thank you for starting your morning with us."

"For Andrew, Jennifer," Doug said, then smiled. "The Mayor, Powers Junior—"

"That's me daddy!" Junior said excitedly.

"Shhh," Powers said, holding onto our son.

"And my partner Danielle Washburn," Doug said, reaching for my hand once again. "I'm Douglas Anderson."

"Thank you for five great years Detroit," I said warmly. "I'll see again...*soon*."

Doug swallowed. "The *Today* show is next."

"Cue music," I heard the director say into my earpiece. "Camera one stay on Danni and her family."

Junior watched with a bemused grin as the staff and crew gathered around us. Powers handed me a handkerchief.

"Thank you baby."

He whispered to me. "Thank you."

"We're clear!" Eliyse said. "Great show everybody."

Gazing at my husband and son, I marveled at my good fortune. I had a career I enjoyed, and a family I adored. This was indeed the life of my dreams. Only it wasn't a dream. My life was very real, and for it I thanked God every chance I got. Still, every once in a while I thought about how things might have turned out had I gone to lunch with Amadeus. Thankfully, for me I'd learned my lesson by way of conscience and not consequence. After all, only a fool would put her hand over a blazing fire simply to prove what she knew all along – she'd get burned. Danielle Washburn was nobody's fool.

PROMISE ME

Darrious D. Hilmon

Prologue

Drawing my arms tighter across my chest, I glanced down at my crossed legs, ensuring I wasn't exposing more of the goodies than I'd intended. While I felt a bit embarrassed sitting on the blanket-covered floor, naked as a jay bird, I also felt oddly invigorated – and thanks to a few hits of Harris' joint – high as a kite. It wasn't my style to be so uninhibited. If my mother knew I was in some boy's studio apartment posing in the buff, she'd have my bare ass for a midnight snack.

Portia Belcher had been very clear with my baby sister, Julia and me about what it meant to be a black woman in America. Our very survival depended upon staying focused and clear-headed in order to successfully maneuver a lifetime's worth of tricky emotional and psychological terrain. For a black woman, black men were both her greatest gift, and most deadly vice. According to my mom, it was more than okay to love him, but the smart sista never lost sight of the monumental necessity that was shoring up the invisible foundation – one that didn't depend on love, emotional support, or a man's paycheck -- on which she and her children could sustain should her black prince ever leave. And the chances were good that sooner or later the brotha would venture away in search of that *something* that continued to elude him.

It wasn't until after my father walked out on my family shortly before my seventh birthday, that I came to truly appreciate, and respect my mother's wisdom. Following her advice had kept my heart from being broken. It had also made it nearly impossible for me to ever truly love a man. That was until I met Harris Sifuentes.

"Tilt your head just a little to the left for me."

"Is this okay?" I said, doing as instructed.

"Ah, Thalia," Harris said in a sensual growl, his eyes drinking in my naked form. "You're perfect."

Oh how I so loved the sound of that man's voice. It was melodic, mesmerizing almost. And the way he said my name – *Thaaalia* – was orgasm-inducing.

"You are so beautiful," Harris said, working feverishly to capture my image on the canvas. A wistful smile formed on his hair dusted face as he took a step back to study the painting. "Absolutely exquisite."

My cheeks flushed as I sat there watching him watching me. It was the height of flattery that a man like Harris found me so captivating. Truth be told, it was his fine caramel colored self who deserved to be immortalized -- preferably naked in all his delicious glory. I'd never actually seen Harris in the buff, but something in my gut told me his body was a work of art. Just the sight of him taking a bare-footed step in his ripped jeans and paint-stained wifebeater was enough to make me wet. His lean, naturally muscular body moved with a dancer-like fluidity. Harris was the kind of man that made other men nervous when they were around him. He was only five-feet-nine, but had a self-assured air about him that suggested good things indeed came in small packages. And if that twinkle in his hazel eyes didn't make a woman weak in the knees, the snow-white come-hither smile would.

Carefully I shifted my aching butt. I didn't want to break his flow, but there was only so much longer I'd be able to sit like this.

Harris snapped out of his artistic haze long enough to ask, "You okay?"

"I'm fine," I said, forcing a smile as my legs started to cramp.

"Just let me finish your torso," he said, his voice pleading for my indulgence. "Then we can take a break...okay?"

"Okay."

I studied him intently as he returned his attention to the canvas. The way his long fingers wrapped themselves around the paintbrush, the wrinkle in his brow, the intensity in his eyes; I loved everything about that man. Lord knows I'd tried so hard to resist Harris that first night we double-dated with my sister and her dick-du-jour. But without even trying too hard, he'd pulled me into his zone. By the time he kissed me goodnight, ever-so softly on my forehead, I knew I was in trouble. But, I didn't care. Most of the guys I'd dated prior had only feigned interest in my mind, all the while silently charting the quickest route to my panties. Harris was different. He was genuinely interested in hearing my thoughts and opinions. In the two-months we'd dated, I'd shared things with him I hadn't even told my sister. For Harris, the litmus test for every choice was "will doing it make you happy...will it bring value and joy to your life." He was the type of man my mother had deemed most dangerous: one who dared to dream.

"Beautiful," Harris said, staring across the room at me. "I am so glad to know you Thalia...so glad."

And with those words the ship sailed, the fat lady sang. I was in love with Harris Sifuentes, a fact that both scared and delighted me. That a man could so utterly take my breath away had come as a surprise. That he could do it so consistently was a miracle. Harris made me feel more alive than I'd ever felt before. With him I was never quite sure what he would do or say next, mainly because Harris wasn't sure himself. Wherever the universe wanted to take him was where he wanted to go, far more interested in the journey than the ultimate destination.

"Can we take that break?" I asked with a guilty grin. As wonderful as it was watching him transfixed in his world, my ass was killing me.

"Ah...sorry," Harris said, quickly lowering the brush. He looked over at me, his eyes filling with concern. "I've made you sit too long--"

"It's okay," I said, not wanting him to feel badly. Harris was a sensitive man who took great pains to respect those sharing his space.

"No it isn't," he said, making his way over to me. "It's just when I get the privilege of painting something...someone as exquisite as you, I can't seem to pull myself away..." Harris hesitated. "You thirsty?"

Before I could respond, he was already in the kitchen ready to fulfill my request. "More red wine?"

A sigh escaped my lips as I watched him bouncing around like an over-sugared five-year-old. He was a quirky, odd, beautiful man, and I loved him. God help me – especially when momma found out – I loved Harris with every single fiber of my being.

"That would be great."

Balancing the two wine glasses – formerly mayonnaise jars – Harris walked toward me, lowering carefully onto the blanket beside me. "For you my lady," he said handing me the merlot.

"Thank you," I said, taking a long sip.

Harris jumped up to his feet again, racing toward the steamer-trunk atop which sat the half-smoked joint.

It was then that it hit me that I was laying around this man's home wearing nothing but blushed cheeks and a smile.

"No!" Harris cried out when he saw me reaching for the blanket to cover myself.

"What?" I asked with a sheepish grin. "You're not painting right now."

"That doesn't make me appreciate your raw, curvaceous form any less," Harris said, the building bulge in his faded jeans belying his innocent smile.

"I feel weird," I said, turning beet red as I sat there locked in his gaze.

"Would it help if I were naked too?" Harris asked.

"Oh good *Lawd* yes!" I wanted to shout out. But, before I could utter a word, the wife-beater was on the floor. My eyes widened as he unsnapped the top button of his jeans. "Harris...Harris what are you—?"

"I don't want you to feel uncomfortable...*ever.*"

My jaw fell to the floor when I saw his body – far better than the one in my dreams. Without the least bit of shame he stood there his long, perfectly shaped penis saluting proudly. I couldn't be sure what was more tantalizing, his chest, sculptured and perfectly symmetrical, his taught six-pack abs that rippled in time with his breathing, his hairy track-runner's legs, or the massive slab of beef hanging between them.

"You are..." I stammered as he approached. "You are..."

"In love with an amazing, stupendous, intelligent, regal woman," Harris said, lowering to the floor beside me.

Snatching for air as he took my hand, placing it on his chest, I racked my brain in search of my good – you shouldn't go there with this man – sense, drawing an utter and complete blank. We were as different as night and day and yet I couldn't imagine going back to the orderly, mundane snore that was my life before him.

"My heart is yours," Harris said, placing a soft kiss on my quivering lips.

His sexy, musky sent filled my nostrils, making me lightheaded and giddy. I don't think I'd ever smelled anything more glorious in my life. The touch of his knowing fingers to my flushed cheeks sent quakes of ecstasy through me so powerful it literally took my breath away. Good God, I wanted this man inside me in the worst way. I could hear the echo of my mother's voice in my head imploring me to run away before his love could take control of me, engulfing me in its addictive flame. The sound of my heart screamed louder though, beseeching me to give in, give up...give over to him.

"I love you Thalia," Harris said simply.

A wave of panic overcame me. Head racing, heart pounding, I fought not to hyperventilate. Did I dare tell this man that I was in love with him as well? "I'm still having trouble deciding between the fashion design internship in New York," I blurted out, "and the management training program at the bank."

Pulling back, Harris gave me a curious look, but didn't say a word. He simply held my hand as I teetered at the edge of the emotional cliff.

"My mom thinks I should take the job with the bank here in Detroit," I said, wiping the moisture from my brow.

Harris lit the joint, listening intently as I rambled on. He took a hit, then handed it to me.

"What do you think?" I asked, struggling not to choke on the smoke entering my lungs.

Pondering, Harris took the joint back. Finally, he looked me straight in the eye. "I think you should do what your heart tells you," he said, pointing to my chest.

"Mom thinks a career in fashion is a fool's paradise," I said, desperate not to listen to a thing my heart was saying.

"Listen to your heart," Harris repeated. "Do what you love. The money will follow...or it won't."

"Or it won't?" I said with an incredulously raised brow.

Harris chuckled lightly as he lowered me back onto the blanket. "If you're living authentically," he said, kissing each of my aroused nipples. "The universe will supply you with all you need."

A gasp escaped my lips as I felt his manhood expand to its full eight-plus inches against my inner thigh. I had a sneaking suspicion that Harris would prove as talented a lover as he was an artist.

"You're what I need," I whispered.

"You've already got me," Harris said, spreading my limbs as he prepared to enter my body. "May I make love to you?" he asked as if unsure of my answer.

Shaking my head in the affirmative, I gave up, and gave in. As Harris worked my body like a perfectly tuned Stradivarius, I sensed that my life was about to change. Nine months later I'd be certain of it.

CHAPTER ONE

*P*ounding the gavel against the kitchen table, I called the meeting to order. "As you both know, we are here today..." I said, hesitating when I noticed that my brother was still playing with his stupid Gameboy. "Umm, excuse me..."

"Hey!" he yelped as I snatched the toy out of his hand.

"I'm trying to have a meeting here," I said, glaring at him.

Snatching the game back from me, Thomas growled, "I can listen to you and play Tetras."

"Tommy this is important," I said. He may have thought so, but multitasking was not his strength. He was a one thing at a time kinda guy. "We only have four weeks to stop this travesty from taking place. You need to focus."

Sitting beside me, my best friend, Becca gazed at Thomas. Poor thing was so in lust with my brother she couldn't think straight.

Ignoring the both of them, I continued. "We need to put Operation: DBG--"

Thomas looked at me like I was speaking a foreign tongue. "Operation what?"

"Operation Doug-Be-Gone," I clarified. "We have to come up with a plan to get that man out of our lives before it's too late."

Fondling his Gameboy as if it was his date, Thomas plopped his big feet onto the table. "Why do you hate Doug so much?"

Becca's head snapped in my direction.

"I don't hate Doug," I said, swallowing my disdain. "But he's in the way."

"Of what?" Thomas asked, still not grasping the severity of our current situation. I swear the male gender could be so stupid sometimes.

"Of Mom and Dad getting back together," I said, rolling my eyes at the bribe in his hand. "And it doesn't help matters when you let Doug buy you off with cheap gifts."

Thomas smirked as he stuck the Gameboy in his pocket. "You're just mad he didn't buy you one."

"For your information he offered to buy me an Ipod," I said, smugly. "But I said no...like you should have."

"Yea right," Thomas said, guffawing. "Doug wants to buy me stuff...I'll take it."

"Judas," I snarled.

"Who 'dat?" Thomas asked, completely missing the poetic irony of the comparison. Sometimes it was hard to remember that he was actually a year older than me. Sadly, my brother was only of normal intelligence, and a man – or at least one in the making. With such limitations, it was unfair of me to expect too much from him.

"How could you pick Doug over your own father?" I asked, my stare dressing him down. "Don't you love Daddy?"

Thomas sunk in his chair. "Yea, but—"

"But nothing," I snapped. "The more you make Doug feel welcomed in our father's home—"

"Come on Hailey," Thomas interrupted. "Daddy ain't lived in this house in forever."

Becca gave me a *he's got ya' there* look. She was my girl and all, but sometimes I just wanted to slap her silly.

"So what," I said annoyed. As far as I was concerned it didn't matter that it had been six years, two weeks, and five days since Daddy lived in this house. It was still *his* home. The day Mom kicked him out was easily the very worst one of my life. When I asked her why she would hurt Daddy that way, all Momma said was, "I'm doing what I must in order to protect you and your brother." To this day she hasn't told me the real reason she divorced Daddy, though from what I could gather from eavesdropping on her and Aunt Julia's conversations, it had something to do with his taking drugs.

"So long as Doug don't try to walk up in this piece running things," Thomas said with an arrogant smirk. "It's all gravy to me."

"It's all gravy!" I said, floored by my brother's devil-may-care attitude. "You are so simple sometimes—"

"You simple," he said, brushing his dirty white sock against my arm.

"Whatever," I said, slapping his foot away.

Thomas squealed as his chair went tumbling backward. Before he'd even hit the floor, Becca was already on her feet rushing to his aid.

"Are you okay?"

Ignoring Becca, Thomas glared at me.

"I didn't mean to push you that hard," I said, remembering that while I might have been smarter, he was bigger.

"You better be glad today is your birthday," Thomas said, slowly retaking his seat.

"Sorry," I said in a guilty whisper.

Thomas reached down to retrieve his Gameboy. Unfortunately it wasn't broken. "Like it or not, Momma divorced Daddy," he said.

My brother's blunt truth stung a bit, but I remained undaunted. Assuming Mom really didn't have any choice but to divorce our father six years ago, things were different now. Harris Sifuentes was clean and sober, had been for the past four and a half years. For the life of me I couldn't understand why my mother hadn't taken him back yet. Sometimes that woman's practicality – anal retentiveness, according to Aunt Julia -- got in the way of her happiness.

"Momma's in love with Doug now--"

"No she isn't!" I interjected, not daring to let Thomas finish the cringe-inducing thought. Mom couldn't be in love with Doug because as surely as I was brilliant, she was still head-over-hills for Daddy. She may have been in denial about her true feelings, but that didn't make them any less real. I saw it in her eyes when she stole glances at Daddy whenever he came to pick up me and Thomas. Saw it in the blush of her cheeks whenever her true love touched her hand, or kissed her forehead goodbye. Mom claimed that she and my father were just being civil for me and Thomas' sake, but I knew the truth. Mom was a woman in love -- and not with Doug.

"He seems like a pretty decent guy," Thomas said.

"That's because he's trying to seal the deal," I said, growing increasingly more frustrated with my brother's London fog-like denseness. Turning to Becca for support I implored, "Will you tell him how much of a hell life is with your step father."

Before she could respond, my head snapped back toward Thomas. "Judge Sampson was all sugar and spice when he was trying to get Becca's mom to marry him. Then just like that," I said, snapping my fingers. "He became a monster. Isn't that right Becca?"

"He can be a little strict some—"

"And tell Thomas about how horrible the Judge's children are to you," I said, cutting her off. I swear to God that girl was little more than a babbling idiot whenever Thomas was within ten feet of her. "Tell him how you have to let Blythe sleep in your room whenever she comes over."

A look of bemusement colored Thomas' face as he sat there tugging absentmindedly at the peach-fuzz growing under his chin. "But, Doug doesn't have any kids—"

"And why is that?" I asked, trying not to upchuck my lunch as Becca continued staring all dreamy-eyed at my brother. "Why doesn't a man in his early forties have any kids?"

Thomas shifted in his chair, barely paying attention.

"Don't you find it strange that Doug has never been married?" I pressed.

"Not really," Thomas said, his eyes easing over toward the window. It was obvious that he wanted this to end so he could get back out into the summer sun for yet another dumb game of b-ball with his boys.

"Hello?" I said, snapping my fingers to shake Thomas out of his sun-induced daze. "Will you focus please?"

"Look Hailey, I know how badly you wish Mom and Dad were back together," Thomas said, rising from the chair. "But there is nothing you can do to make them if they don't want to—"

"But they do want to!" I said desperately.

"So why is Momma marrying Doug next month?" Thomas asked, heading toward the back door. "Look, I gotta get to the park. You gonna be all right here alone for an hour or so."

"Yes," I said in a defeated sigh. "Go on and play with the other idiots."

Not bothering to be offended, Thomas snatched up the basketball from the floor – another bribe from *Douuug*. "See ya," he said, already out the door.

"It's really not so bad having a step-father," Becca said.

"I'm quite happy with the real father I already have," I said, rising from the chair to answer the telephone. "Hello?"

"Why so glum young lady?"

"Hey, Mom."

"This is your special day," she said. "You should be on top of the world."

And I will be just as soon as my entire family is back under one roof.

"I'm fine," I said. "How's work?"

"It's work," Mom said with a slight chuckle. "Where's your big brother?"

I smirked. "Outside playing with the other children."

"Did you tell him I said to be ready by five-thirty?"

"Yes, Ma'am."

"We don't want to be late getting to the restaurant," Mom said. "Doug's put a lot of effort into making your birthday dinner special."

Thankfully my mother couldn't see the sour look on my face through the phone or else she'd have popped me in my pouting mouth. "Is Daddy coming tonight?"

There was a moment of loud silence, before Mom finally responded. "He's...umm...no he's not," she said, stammering.

"But I thought you said it was going to be a *family* dinner?"

"Yes, but—"

"Aunt Julia and Uncle Kyle are coming, right?"

"Umm hmm."

"And Grandma."

"Yes, Hailey," Mom said, not sure where I was going with this.

"Then why can't Daddy?" I asked. "He's family too."

Mom exhaled an exacerbated sigh. "Hailey, you can celebrate your birthday with Harris tomorrow when he picks you and Thomas up for the weekend."

"But my birthday is today."

"Hailey," Mom said in that tone of hers.

"Fine," I said, my eyes rolling back in my head.

"I'll be home to pick you and your brother up at five-thirty."

Holding the phone from my ear like it was a germ I didn't want to catch, I sucked on my teeth – though not so loudly that Mom could hear me, of course.

"You still there, Sweetie?"

"Umm hmm," I said in a bored monotone. "Five-thirty...got it."

"Okay, I gotta go," Mom said. "Love you."

Without responding I hung up the phone. Seeing how it was my birthday and all, I figured this would be the day to do something bold. Tomorrow I'd go back to being a good girl.

"I wish she'd stop trying to force that *man* down our throats," I said, turning to Becca.

"Maybe you should just try to make the best of it," she said.

"Maybe..." I said, hesitating as the thought popped into my head. "Or, maybe not."

"Hailey...what are you up to?" Becca asked as I picked up the receiver.

Not answering her, I dialed the number I knew by heart.

"Hello?"

"Hi Daddy," I said, a devious smile forming on my lips. "You busy?"

CHAPTER TWO

I stared at the cell phone in disbelief before stuffing it back into my purse. My daughter had better be glad it was her birthday, or I'd be halfway home to tap her hide for hanging up on me without so much as a goodbye. I loved Hailey something awful, but, sometimes that little girl pushed me right to the edge. Her 150 IQ would lead her to do great things someday. That was, if she could manage to get through her childhood without making me kill her.

"Sorry, I'm late," Julia said dashing toward the table faster than any seven months pregnant woman should. "The damned maintenance man managed to blow every freakin' fuse in the gallery...again."

"You might want to consider replacing him," I said to my baby sister as she settled into her chair.

"Mr. Johnson?" she asked, making a face. "I could never fire that man. He's like family."

"Family that sets fires in the trash can," I said sarcastically.

"That fire wasn't his fault," Julia said, then laughed. "Not technically, anyway."

I shook my head laughing at my sister's interesting way of seeing things. I loved the girl to death, but Julia Taggart was a *flower*. In so many ways she reminded me of my ex-husband, Harris. The both of them were dreamers, determined to see the world through pastel-colored hues. Fortunately for Julia, she'd inherited enough of my mother's practical sensibility to keep from completely getting lost in her idealism. Harris had no such practicality.

"So how's life for First Standard Bank's new Vice President of Small Business Development?" Julia asked, beaming like a proud parent.

"It's a lot of work," I said with a sigh. "But I'm managing to keep up."

"Keep up," Julia said disbelievingly. "You my darling sister never simply keep up."

"I assure you, staying above water is the extent of my ambition right about now," I said, smiling at the waiter as he placed my glass of iced-tea on the table. "Thank you."

"May I start you off with a drink as well?" he asked, turning to Julia.

"Yes," she said with a straight face. "Let me get a chocolatini... heavy on the 'tini."

The waiter's eyes bugged as they latched onto Julia's big stomach. She sat there looking at the poor boy as if nothing was the least bit peculiar about her request.

"She'll have an iced-tea as well," I said, letting the red-faced server off the hook.

"Heavy on the sugar," Julia said, giving him a playful wink.

The waiter laughed nervously.

"I had you there didn't I?"

"Oh, yea," he said, exhaling an audible sigh of relief. "I'll be right back with your non-alcoholic drink."

"You need Jesus woman," I said, cutting my eyes at Julia.

"And a good lay," she said, waving her hand. "But I digress."

Removing the napkin from its gold holder, Julia stuffed it into her lap. "If you're having so much trouble keeping up," she said, reaching for the bread. "Maybe you should consider postponing--"

"Don't finish that thought," I said, interrupting her. "Come hell or high, Doug and I are getting married in four weeks."

"What's the rush?" Julia asked, chewing away on the pumpernickel. "With the new job and two teen children, perhaps—"

"Perhaps, I should be grateful for my blessings," I said, cutting her off again. "The timing of everything may not be the greatest, but I can and *will* find a way to make it all work."

"Why won't you even consider postponing the wedding?" Julia eyed me incredulously. "If Doug really is the man for you, what's waiting a few months gonna hurt?"

"Julia—"

"Just until things smooth out a bit," she said, studying me closely. "I'm sure Doug would understand...*considering.*"

"Considering what?" I asked, regretting the words as soon as they escaped my lips.

"How Hailey feels—"

"Let me stop you right there," I said, my finger zipping into the air. "Bright as she might be, Hailey is only twelve—"

"Thirteen," Julia corrected.

"She is still a child...and a daddy's girl to boot," I said, trying not to get too defensive. Reaching for my glass of iced-tea, I took a sip. "Doug is a good man, who isn't put off by the fact that I have two kids. He treats both Hailey and Thomas like his own."

The look on Julia's face as she wiped her mouth with the napkin made it clear she wasn't buying what I was attempting to sell. "So you're telling me Doug actually makes you happy?" she asked, pointedly. "I mean really happy?"

"Yes," I said with more resolve than I actually felt. Doug did make me happy, well, sort of happy. I mean, I wasn't head-over-hills, slap my own ass happy. But, I was content.

"Do you love him?"

"I care deeply for Doug," I said, averting my eyes from my sister's questioning ones. "He's a good, solid man. He has a great job...strong finances."

Grimacing like she'd just smelled horse poop, Julia dropped her napkin onto the table. "Oh my God," she said, horrified. "You sound like you're describing the benefits of a business merger, not two people coming together in marriage."

"Why are you so against my marrying...?" I asked, stopping short when the waiter approached.

"Thank you," Julia said, accepting her drink from him, but not taking her eyes off of me.

"Are you ladies ready to place your orders?"

"Umm hmm," Julia said, finally turning her attention to the menu. "Let me have the..."

Lord, I wish I had followed my first mind and declined my *buttinsky* sister's invitation to lunch. Had I eaten at my desk, I could have been more productive, and free from having to defend, for the millionth time, my decision to marry Doug. It was impossible for Julia to be objective about him. Like Hailey, her loyalties lay firmly with Harris. She was the one who'd introduced me to the man I would marry – and divorce – some fifteen years ago. Harris and Julia were taking an impressionist art class together over at the Center for Creative Studies. When she suggested I meet the young artist, I balked at first, but finally gave in to her incessant assurances that Harris was like no other man she'd ever met before. God help me, Julia had been right. The moment I laid eyes on him I was hooked, and instantly hornier than a bitch in heat. That man was and remains an absolutely magnificent sight to behold. Thank heaven I was finally getting over him. It was high time too, seeing how it had been six years since we divorced. Doug Johnson was the man in my life now, whether my sister and daughter liked it or not.

"And for you, Miss?"

"Earth to Thalia," Julia said.

"Oh, sorry," I said, shaking off my thoughts. "I'll have a small Caesar salad."

Julia looked at me, waiting for me to add something more substantial. Pregnant women thought everyone should be eating like a pig just because they were.

"And another glass of iced-tea," I said, handing the menu to the waiter.

Once the server was gone, Julia took a leisurely sip of water before asking, "Why are you marrying a man you're not in love with?"

Gripping the napkin, I forced down the scream tickling my throat. Julia and Hailey were working my last good nerve about this. I don't know what made either think they knew what I needed better than I did.

"And before you reach across the table and pimp-slap me," Julia said, smoothly. "Remember two things...one, I'm pregnant and two, I know you."

I rolled my eyes, but didn't argue the veracity of her words. Julia was not only my younger sibling, but also my closest friend. She knew me better than anyone. Personality-wise, we were as different as night and day. Where I was practical to the point of being anal retentive, Julia was a free-spirit who flew through life by the seat of her pants. We were a good balance for one another. She kept me from taking everything too seriously, and I offered her a nice, stiff kick in the butt when she wasn't taking things seriously enough.

"When was the last time you and Doug did the deed?"

My face turned beet red. "Excuse me?"

"You ain't deaf," Julia said, unfazed by the fact that I was choking on my tea. "When was the last time that man put the dick on you?"

"Doug and I have elected to stop having sex until we're married."

Now, Julia was the one choking. "That proves my point right there," she said eagerly.

"What point is that?"

"You're not into Doug," Julia said, wiping the tea from her chin. "Not the way you are...*were* into Harris."

"In case you hadn't noticed, my former and future husbands are two very different men." Thank God for that.

Julia shook her head adamantly. "Oh, that they are."

"Why do you dislike Doug so much?" I asked, becoming irritated with her. Julia always had a soft spot for my ex. Even after the divorce was final she continued working with Harris. In two weeks she was hosting an exhibition of his new work at the gallery she owned. But, did I make a fuss about them remaining so damn close? No, because I would never be so arrogant as to demand that she pick a side. So long as Julia didn't tell Harris my business, or share too much of his with me, I let them be. But, now the heffa was crossing the line...big time.

"I like Doug just fine," Julia said with a slight shrug of the shoulder. "He's a tad on the dull side..." She rolled her eyes. "Who am I kidding? The man is boring as hell. And the two of you together is like watching paint dry."

"Bite me," I snarled.

Julia smirked as she took a bite of her burger. "Doug should be doing that."

"You need to stop," I said with an uneasy chuckle.

"And you need to be with a man who's got some flava'."

"*Flava',*" I said, eyeing her curiously. "When did you start talking like a fifteen year old?"

Ignoring my question, Julia continued trying to make a point I had no intention of hearing. "You need someone exciting, and passionate, a man who's sexy and talented...a little dangerous..."

A smile spread across my lips as I listened to my sister paint the picture. She wasn't going to get any argument out of me. If the brother she was describing showed up on my doorstep, I certainly wouldn't kick him to the curb. Problem was that man only existed in the movies. My world was firmly rooted in reality.

"You need someone who'll draw you out of that straight-laced shell," Julia said, pointing at my navy pin-striped pant suit. "And those boring-assed clothes."

I slapped her hand away playfully. "Shut up."

"I'm serious," Julia said. "You need a man with the power and charisma to push you out of your comfort zone. A man just like..."

Holding my breath, I prayed she wasn't about to say his name.

"Harris."

I exhaled. So much for prayers.

"You think he's all that," I said, struggling to sound light-hearted. "Then you have him. The two of you are more alike than he and I ever were."

"One," Julia said, holding up her index finger. "I got a man—"

"I love Kyle," I said, referring to her husband. "But he's far more like Doug than the man you just described."

"And that's why we work so well together."

My brow furrowed. "Come again?"

"The very reason why your husband—"

"Ex," I corrected.

"Technicality," Julia said. "The very reason why Harris and I would never have worked is the very reason why Kyle and I work so well." She leaned back in the chair. "It's about balance," Julia explained. "Two high strung people would eat each other alive inside a week. Much the same way two boring...I mean *low-key* people coupling up risked lulling each other into a coma."

A wistful smile spread across my sister's face. "You and Harris? The two of you were magic together."

I rolled my eyes, not bothering to respond. Whatever magic Harris and I might have had together disappeared in a puff of smoke, just like much of our savings when he spent it all on drugs behind my back. Never would I put myself, or my children, in that kind of emotional and financial jeopardy again.

"You can try and deny your true feelings all you want, but you and I both know that Harris is the love of your life."

"Was," I corrected. "Then he tore my heart to shreds...or have you conveniently forgotten that part?"

"I remember exactly what happened," Julia said. "If you recall, I was right there holding your hand through the storm. I loved my brother-in-law something fierce, but when he couldn't get his shit together I was the one insisting that you divorce him."

She wasn't lying. When Harris hit rock bottom, it was Julia who loaned me the money to pay the five months late mortgage, and Julia who helped me pack Harris' shit while he was off getting high when he was supposed to be at work.

"But things are different now," Julia said, beseeching me to see things in a softer light. "Harris has shaken off the monkey. He's drug free and--"

"And I'm happy for him," I said, quickly. "But that doesn't change a damn thing."

"You still love him."

"So what if I do?" I asked, the anger I'd kept in check for years resurfacing. "That doesn't mean I'm going to be foolish enough to go back to him."

"Where's your sense of forgiveness?" Julia asked, looking at me as if I were some cruel, heartless woman. "Why can't you give Harris another chance?"

"Why should I?" I asked, almost shouting. "I loved Harris more than I thought I was capable of loving any man, and he broke my heart!"

Julia drew back in her chair, surprised by the intensity of my outburst.

"I will never, ever give Harris, or any man a chance to hurt me that deeply again!"

Noticing the eyes of the other patrons in the restaurant lingering on our table, I took a calming breath. Attempting to reach for my glass, I couldn't steady my hands enough to grasp it. "Damn it," I said, in an angry whisper.

"Thalia, I'm sorry," Julia said softly. "I just want what's best for you."

"Harris isn't it," I said as much for her sake as my own. "I need to get on with my life...my future."

Julia squeezed my hand. "Be careful that you don't trample on your future, trying so hard to outrun your past."

"Doug is a good man, Julia," I said a hint of desperation in my voice. "He's solid and hardworking. And he loves me."

"But are you in love with him?"

"I care for him."

"That wasn't my question, Thalia," Julia said. "Are you in love with Doug?"

Forcing my eyes up from the plate, I looked at my sister. "I'm a thirty-five year old divorcee with two teenaged children," I said as a matter of fact.

"You still haven't answered my question."

"I'm not going to," I said resolutely. "Next month I am going to marry a good man. I need you to support me in my decision, Julia."

"But—"

"No buts," I said, cutting her off. "You are my sister. And I am asking...imploring you to support me."

A look of disappointment colored Julia's face.

"Can you do that for me?" I asked, ignoring my ringing cell.

"Get your phone," was Julia's response.

"Hello?" I answered, forcing a smile to my face when I heard his voice. "Doug, hi Darling."

Julia sat there watching me for any hint of deception.

"That sounds wonderful," I said too brightly. "I'm sure Hailey will love it..."

Sucking on her teeth, Julia pushed her plate away. I didn't care that she was upset, or disappointed, or whatever the hell else she might have been. I expected her to suck it up, and get with the program.

"I'm picking the kids up at five-thirty," I said, enduring my sister's dagger stare from across the table. "We should be at Dave and Buster's by six....Julia? Of course, she's coming," I said, giving her the eye. "Sweetie, everything's going to be perfect. Look I need to go..."

My entire body stiffened when Doug said those three words.

"Me too," I said, maintaining my perfectly painted-on smile. "Bye."

Julia chuckled as I closed the phone.

"What?"

"Me too," she said, unimpressed. "Oh yeah, that's hot."

"I need to get back to the office," I said. "Thank you for lunch."

"You should know that Harris still loves—"

"Julia, don't," I said, rising from the table.

"Fine," she said with a dismissive wave of the hand. "It's your life."

"Thank you for finally remembering that," I said, leaning over to kiss her on the cheek. "See you tonight," I said, then headed for the door.

CHAPTER THREE

*T*homas' eyes danced with excitement as he gazed out from the glass-enclosed private room. "This place is da' bomb!" he proclaimed.

My grandmother and I both turned in his direction.

"Boy," Grammy said, cutting her eyes at Thomas, "your parents spend far too much on your private school education for you to massacre the King's English that way."

His lips curling into an embarrassed grin, Thomas pulled out her chair. "Sorry, Gram."

Taking a seat, she said, "Let's try it again."

"This place is slammin'," Thomas said, then quickly corrected himself. "*Slamming*."

"Better," Gram said, not taking her eyes off of my brother. "But just barely."

Relieved, Thomas raced around the table.

"Will you watch it?" I snapped as he stole the chair I was about to take. "There's more than one you know."

"But I got dibbs--" Thomas said, stopping cold when he felt Gram re-lock him in her gaze. "I mean, I've selected this particular chair," he said giving her a wink.

Shaking her head, Gram settled back in her chair, satisfied that her work – for the moment anyway – was done. To know my grandmother was to know you didn't use Ebonics in her presence. Having just retired from a 25-year stint as an eighth grade English teacher, Portia Belcher took personal offense to the misuse, misplacement, or mispronunciation of words. She might not be able to force the entire world to respect the language, but she'd make damn sure her own grandchildren did.

"Hey black people!" Aunt Julia said, making her way into the room with Uncle Kyle only steps behind her. If he wasn't my uncle I'd have the biggest crush on that man. He was – as Gram would say – one tall drink of water on a hot summer day. At six-foot-four, Kyle had the smoothest, darkest skin. Where Daddy, who was very light-skinned, bordered on pretty, Uncle Kyle was more ruggedly handsome.

Waddling her way over to me sitting beside my stupid brother, Aunt Julia kissed my cheek. "Happy birthday, Sweetie."

"Thanks, Auntie," I said with a smile.

"Let me take that," Doug said, retrieving the wrapped gift from Uncle Kyle's hand and placing it with the others. Trying to be everything to everybody, he rushed over to pull out Mom's chair for her. "Allow me."

I rolled my eyes – discreetly of course – as I sat there watching Doug at work.

"Thank you," Mom said, giving him a smile that was a little too warm for my taste. That man had to go.

"When's the grub coming?" Thomas asked, anxious to woof down dinner so he could get out to the game floor of Dave and Buster's.

Gram shuddered, but didn't bother to correct him.

That *Douuug* would select this loud, electronics-infested, game emporium to host my birthday dinner further proved that the man didn't get me at all. While my knuckleheaded big brother might have been in hog heaven here, I'd have preferred dinner – at a real restaurant – and a play.

"Calm yourself," Mom said, giving Thomas the eye kids the world over had learned to fear.

"Are you expecting someone," Julia said when she noticed me staring at my watch.

"Just checking the time," I said, not wanting to let the cat out of the bag until it was too late for Mom to stuff it back in.

"Can I go play a--?"

"After we eat and give Hailey her gifts," Mom said, cutting Thomas off at the pass.

Exhaling a defeated sigh, my brother turned to Uncle Kyle. "Don't try and sneak out of here before I whip you in a game of Skeeball old man."

"Oh, I see the young fella's feeling his oats today," Uncle Kyle said, up for the challenge. He leaned in closer so Mom, Gram, and Julia couldn't hear him. "Let's make it interesting—"

"No cash bets," Julia said.

"Shoot," Kyle and Thomas said in unison.

"Best two out of three," Kyle said, setting the rules of engagement. "If I win you come into the body shop this weekend and help me with inventory."

"Fine," Thomas said with an arrogant smirk. "But, if I win, you have to buy me those new pair of Jordan's I've been eyeing."

"Bet," Kyle said, extending his hand.

90

Taking the bet, Thomas glanced over at Doug, who was all up in Mom's grill. "You want a piece of this action?"

Laughing, Doug raised his hands. "I'll pass on this one."

After what felt like an eternity of uncomfortable silence, Mom turned to Doug. "This is very nice," she said, then looked across the table at me. When I didn't utter a solitary word, she prompted. "Isn't this nice Hailey?"

"Umm hmm," I said, flashing Doug a wan smile. "Thank you."

"You're very welcome," he said, cheesing like a fat cat.

Julia lowered her head to hide the fact that she was chuckling. She knew how I felt about that man. Truth be told, I think she felt the same.

"I wanted your special day to be perfect," Daddy-wannabe said.

Thankfully, the manager appeared at the door motioning for Doug before I was forced to respond with, "Only my father can make things perfect."

Once he was out of the room, Mom shot me a look. "Be nice," she said tersely.

"I am."

"She is," Julia said.

Mom rolled her eyes at her sister. "You too."

Gram stared at Julia's stomach "How is my grandson doing?" she asked, deftly shifting gears.

The very mention of his son brought a prideful smile to Uncle Kyle's' face. He was going to be such a great father, just like my dad.

"I know I wish he'd come on out already," Julia said, feigning impatience.

"Divine order," Gram said, smiling.

"My boy will show his face when he's good and ready," Kyle said firmly. Clearly, he'd never had to carry around a large kicking fetus in his stomach for nine months.

Reading my mind, Aunt Julia, smirked. "Easy to say when you're not playing host carrier," she said, punching him in the shoulder.

"I love you," Kyle said, kissing her on the cheek.

"Umm hmm," Julia said, trying not to smile, but failing.

Mom sighed softly as she looked at her sister and brother in-law. She could have had the same good love they shared, if she'd get over herself and take my father back.

"That's the third time you've looked at that watch in as many minutes," Gram said, her brow rising in suspicion. "What are you up--?"

"Harris," Mom said in a horrified whisper.

"Hi everybody."

My heart leaping into my throat, I twisted my body in the direction of that glorious voice. "Daddy!" I cried out, leaping up from the chair. Racing into his arms, I kissed him.

Dropping the gift onto the table in just a knick of time, Daddy lifted me into the air. "Happy birthday, Baby Genius," he sang out. "Sorry I'm late."

"That's okay, Daddy," I said happy to see him.

Looking as if she had just seen a ghost, Mom swallowed. "Harris, what are you—?"

"I invited him," I said, quickly.

Mom's glare made the hairs on the back of my neck stand. "But I told you—"

"Is something the matter?" Dad interrupted, thoroughly confused by his former wife's reaction. They were no longer officially a couple, but Mom was usually far happier to see him than her current scowl suggested.

Julia and Kyle exchanged uneasy glances as Gram looked on with a bemused expression on her face. A trouble-loving grin spreading across his face, Thomas settled back in his chair eager to see how this little drama would play out.

"I explained to your daughter," Mom said to Daddy as she continued glaring at me, "that it wouldn't be appropriate for you to come tonight—"

"To a party for my own daughter?" Dad said, his eyes widening in shock.

"No," Mom said hastily. "I meant to a party thrown in her honor...by Doug."

Inching behind Daddy, I held my breath as Mom approached us.

"Ah," Dad said, realizing what he'd just walked into. Turning to face me, he said, "Not cool, Hailey Marie...not cool at all."

"I didn't think Doug would mind," I said, innocently. Man, did I hate it when Daddy was disappointed in me. He always got that look in his eyes that made me feel worse than any words ever could.

"It doesn't matter what Doug..." Mom said, stopping short when the fiancé in question stepped back into the private dining room.

"Harris?" Doug said, stunned to see Daddy standing there looking hella good in his jeans and white linen shirt, that gorgeous hair of his pulled back into a ponytail. "I didn't realize you were joining us."

"How are you Doug?" Dad asked, extending his hand to the enemy.

Mom glowered in my direction. I looked away. She was going to kill me for doing this, but to have my daddy here would be well worth the punishment. Besides, it was patently unfair of her not to let him come to his own daughter's birthday party. She should be the one ashamed of her actions, not me.

"I can't stay," Dad said, his eyes easing toward Mom. "Just wanted to drop off Hailey's gift so she'd have it on her birthday."

"Thank you, Daddy," I said more as an apology than a signal of appreciation.

"Thank you, Harris," Mom said, exhaling a discreet sigh of relief.

"Well," Daddy said, inching back toward the door. "I'll be on my way."

"Nonsense," Doug exclaimed, reaching for Dad's arm and guiding him back into the room. "It's sacrilege for the birthday girl not to have her father at her party," he said, sounding strangely okay with Daddy being there.

Julia cocked her head to the side, taken aback by what she was witnessing.

"Is that...okay with you?" Dad asked Mom.

Forcing her tight lips into a smile, she nodded. "Sure."

"Great!" Doug said, his kindness – real or manufactured – making it harder for me to dislike the guy. While I remained steadfast in my belief that he wasn't right for Mom, he was proving to be a pretty decent man.

Following Dad and Doug to the table, Mom grabbed me by the upper arm. "We'll talk about this later," she said through a painted-on smile.

"Hi Mom Belcher," Dad said, leaning over to kiss Gram on the cheek.

"Harris," she said, unable to stop the blush from coloring her face. "Nice to see you."

Rising from his chair, Thomas pumped chests with Daddy. It was some strange male-bonding thing the two had been doing for years. "Sup Pops?"

Grams cleared her throat...loudly.

Catching her none too subtle drift, my brother cleaned it up. "I mean, hello father," he said in an overly affected tone. "How are you this fine day?"

Daddy chuckled as he squeezed his son's shoulder. "King's English?"

"Umm hmm," Thomas said, trying to whisper. "You know how she is--"

"She's not deaf," Gram said, finishing his sentence. "That's what she is."

A wistful look on her face, Mom stared at father and son as they stood side by side. Thomas was the spitting image of his sperm donor, albeit taller and two shades darker. No matter how far my mother may have wanted to run, Daddy's spirit, and genes refused to be outdistanced.

Making his way over to Julia, Dad placed his hand on her stomach. "How much bigger do you plan to get?" he asked with mock concern.

"Forget you, Man," Aunt Julia said, slapping his hands away. She and my father had a good relationship. Apparently, it had been my auntie who'd introduced Daddy to my mom in the first place. Thankfully, Julia had stuck by his side even after his own wife kicked him to the curb like day old trash.

"Ah...where's my gift?" Julia said, eyeing daddy's empty hands.

"In the car," Daddy said with a sardonic chuckle. He turned to Uncle Kyle. "How's the living, my man?"

"It's all good," Kyle said, giving Dad some dap. "How you doin'?"

"Blessed man," Dad said, glancing toward Thomas and me. "Absolutely blessed."

"Here, sit by me Daddy," I said, pulling out the empty chair between Thomas and me.

"Julia tells me that your new exhibition is going to be the talk of the town," Kyle said.

"I don't know about that," Dad said, being far too humble. The man was talented as all get out. And, if the pieces I'd seen at his home studio were any indication, his new exhibition would have the crowds cheering his name, and other artists cursing it.

"Don't know my ass..." Julia said, catching herself when she felt Gram's glare. "Spare us all that false modesty," she continued, making a point of looking across the table at Mom. "Harris' new pieces are some of the most brilliant, intimate, emotion-drenched work I've seen in my entire life."

"Stop exaggerating," Dad said, blushing.

While I sat bursting with pride as Aunt Julia went on about my daddy, Mom squirmed uncomfortably in her chair, avoiding her sister's taunting gaze at all costs.

"I'm still waiting to see the lead piece though," Julia said, turning her attention back to Dad. "When might that be Mister Artist?"

"Soon," he said.

"The exhibition opens in two weeks," Julia said.

"You've got a new show going up?" Doug said unaware that my father's *Emotions* series was set to be shown at Aunt Julia's art gallery.

Mom swallowed nervously as Daddy and Doug both looked her way for some sort of explanation. She didn't utter a peep.

"You're welcome to join us for the opening night party," Julia said with a cool grin. "Thalia and the kids are coming," she said, flashing Mom a wide grin. "Isn't that right Thalia?"

"Umm hmm," Mom said, giving her pushy sister a look.

"Absolutely," Doug said, smiling. Why that man didn't get the fact that my mother would never care for him like she did my father was beyond me. Denial was a sonofayouknowwhat.

"I'm a bit of an art aficionado myself," Doug said, puffing out his bony chest.

Aunt Julia and I both gave him disbelieving looks. That anal-retentive, *so boring he makes me sleepy* man wouldn't know real art if it bit him on his flat behind.

"Is that a fact?" Dad asked, leaning forward in his chair.

"Sure am," Doug said, proudly. "Just last week I bought a piece I saw at the furniture store when I was there picking up a new chair for my home office."

Aghast, Julia clutched the non-existent pearls around her neck. "You do realize that just because something comes with a frame around it doesn't make it art?" she asked, her voice dripping with haughty disdain.

Mom cut her eyes at Julia. Gram did everything in her power not to burst out laughing as she sat there. Realizing, he'd just stuck his foot so far down his throat it was sticking out his butt, the smug grin on Doug's face faded, much like his chances of stealing my mom from my dad.

"Are you ready to place your orders?" the waiter asked, appearing from out of nowhere.

"Yes," Mom said swiftly.

Thomas snatched up the menu sitting on the table before him. "Let me have a—"

"Ladies first," Dad said, discretely reaching for his son's arm.

"Sorry," Thomas said embarrassed.

After everyone finished placing their orders, Mom -- desperate to keep Julia from resuming her verbal spanking of Doug -- turned to me. "Why don't you open your gifts while we wait for the food to arrive?"

"Good," Thomas said, eager to speed through this painful exercise in tense civility.

"Okay," I said, happy to inventory my bounty.

Rising from the chair, I went over to the table that held my gifts. Lifting the small box with silver wrapping, I looked over at Mom, smiling. "Whatcha get me?" I asked, shaking the package.

Relaxing a bit, she smiled. "Open it and see."

My eyes bugging, I held up the gold necklace with diamond studded cross. "Thank you, Mommy," I said, rushing over to give her a kiss.

"You're welcome, Honey."

Dad got up from the table. "Here, let me help you with that," he said, taking the necklace from me and placing it around my neck.

A bittersweet smile formed on Mom's face as she watched. Noticing, Doug took a discreet breath, trying not to be hurt by the love he saw in his fiancée's eyes...for her ex-husband.

Back at the table, I reached for the box Dad had bought. It was longer than Mom's gift, but equally compact. Barely able to contain my excitement, I ripped off the technicolored wrapping paper, squealing in delight. "An iPod!"

Maybe I was mistaken, but I could have sworn I'd heard a defeated sigh escape Doug's tightened lips. He was probably just jealous that Daddy had gotten me the very thing he'd offered to buy me a couple weeks ago. I'd refused Doug's bribe, but would gladly accept the gift from my father.

"I already programmed every Jill Scott song I could get my hands on into that puppy," Daddy said, knowing how much I loved the singer/poet. Like me, Jill was a deep sister with a lot to say about the state of things. She could write a whole album about my mother trying to outrun the sound of her own heartbeat.

"Thank you Daddy!" I said, going over to kiss him, once again.

"I'll give you your other gift tomorrow," he said with a wink.

"Not the laptop?" I asked, almost screaming

He smiled that wonderful smile of his. "You'll have to wait and see."

Squeezing Doug's hand as it rested on the table, Mom said, "Why don't you open Doug's—"

"No," he said, cutting her off. "I...umm...it's the wrong...I'll take it back...and umm get you something else."

"I'm sure Hailey will love whatever you bought her," Mom said, trying to assure him.

"Looks like Harris and I had the same idea when it came to Hailey's gift," Doug said with a forced half-grin.

Now, I was no fan of Doug Johnson's, but even I felt a bit sorry for the guy sitting there looking all hurt and put-upon. But, I'd get right over it, I sure would. In war – and this was very much a war – casualties were inevitable.

"I'll take it," Thomas said, moving toward the unwanted gift.

I stepped right out of his way.

"You will do no such thing," Mom said.

"It's okay," Doug said, waving Thomas on. He turned to me, the Doogie Howser smile returning to his face. "How 'bout you and me go shopping..."

Dad's jaw-clenched, but he remained silent. Julia gave him a knowing glance, but kept her lips sealed as well.

"You can have anything you want," Doug said, his earnestness almost endearing.

"No thanks," I said, holding up my new iPod. "I have everything I want..."

Doug fell back in his chair. Mom looked as if she was about to jump out of hers.

Fine, I'll give the man a little love. Forcing my lips into a smile, I said, "Your hosting this dinner for me is gift enough." It took everything I had not to choke on the words that came out of my mouth next.

"Thank you."

"You're very welcome," Doug said, buying my totally manufactured kindness like the colossal doofus that he was.

Mom gave me a grateful smile as I went back to opening my gifts. Let's hope she remembered my kind gesture when dolling out my punishment later.

As for Doug, the only thing I wanted from that man was for him to step aside so Mom and Dad could reconcile. And, when I wanted something badly enough I usually got it.

CHAPTER FOUR

*T*he instant we stepped through the back door, Thomas made a b-line for the stairs. "I'm gonna put these in your room," he said, holding up the bag containing Hailey's gifts.

"Thanks," Hailey said, careful not to make direct eye contact with me. I'd deal with her in a moment, but first I needed to find out what my overly helpful son was up to.

"And then you're going straight to bed, right?" I asked, eyeing him as he turned from the stairs.

Giving me that Casanova smile he always gave when he wanted something, Thomas said, "I was gonna play a few games of Tetras first."

Like his father, Thomas Sifuentes could talk the panties off a lesbian nun if he was so inclined. While I remained immune to his – and Harris' – wily charms, Thomas had come to appreciate, and fully exploit the profound power his cute face, bedroom eyes, and shit-eating grin afforded him with the neighborhood girls now sniffing around our door like stray pussies in search of catnip.

"Come on *Maaa*," Thomas said, pouring it on thick. "I'm not even tired."

Okay, I'll admit it. I wasn't completely immune to my son...or his father. "You can play for thirty minutes, then I want you in bed," I said, resisting the urge to add, "With both hands above the covers."

I learned the *hard* way – pun intended – that Thomas, while still an essentially problem-free child, was growing into a man, despite my valiant efforts to keep him my innocent, little boy. As I had on any number of occasions prior, I'd walked into his bedroom without knocking about three weeks ago, in order to liberate his dirty laundry from the floor. Lying across his bed, buck-naked, *Hustler* magazine in one hand, his fully-aroused member in the other, my little big-man was satisfying his male urges. A loud, horrified gasp escaped my lips as I dropped the basket, almost tripping over myself to get out of the room. I'd covered my eyes, but unfortunately not before noting that my son shared more than just his father's charisma. Harris had since had the *conversation* with Thomas, who was taking great pride – and pleasure – in his new found *ability*. Lack of shame, or inhibition were but two of the myriad other traits he and his dad shared.

"I mean it Thomas, you've got thirty minutes," I said, glancing down at my watch.

"How 'bout an hour?" he countered, somehow assuming this was a negotiation.

"Thomas," I said in a tone that should have implied he was pushing it.

And, yet he pressed on. "School's out Mom," he said. "Let a brotha enjoy his summer vacation."

"You're right," I said, shaking my head as if his point had been made successfully. Taking another look at my watch, I pondered, then smiled at Thomas. "In that case you've got thirty minutes—"

He looked at me curiously. "That's the same—"

"You wanna make it, ten?" I asked, still smiling.

"Fine," he said, accepting his partial victory.

"I'll be up to check in exactly, thirty..." I said, hesitating as I took another look at my watch. "Twenty-nine minutes."

Already racing up the stairs, Thomas called back. "Knock first!"

"I'm gonna head up as well," Hailey said, trying to ease by me.

"Not so fast," I said, catching her arm.

"But I'm really tired."

"This won't take long," I said, motioning toward the kitchen table. "Have a seat young lady."

"I'll stand," Hailey said.

Pulling out the chair, I gave her the eye. "Sit."

Grudgingly sitting down, my defiant daughter stared off into the middle distance. She could make this hard if she wanted to.

Taking a seat beside her I asked, "What do you have to say for yourself?"

"About what?"

"You know what I'm talking about," I said in no mood. "Why would you do something so hurtful?"

Hailey didn't blink. "I didn't realize that inviting *my* Daddy to *my* birthday party was hurtful," she said in that haughty, *I'm smarter than you* tone, that made me want to slap her little behind into next week. "When you said it was a family dinner I assumed that included my—"

"No you didn't," I said, shutting her down, "I specifically told you that Harris wasn't to be invited."

Hailey shrugged her shoulders. "I disagreed."

I counted to five in my head before responding. "I don't believe I ever asked for your opinion, Hailey."

"Are you telling me that Daddy can no longer be a part of my life now that Doug's in the picture?" Hailey asked, daring me to say yes.

"That's not what I'm saying," I said, irritated, "and you damned well know it."

"Then why is my inviting Daddy such a big deal?"

"Because I told you not to invite him." What part of this was the child missing?

"Technically, you never said—"

"Don't," I snapped. "Do not try and outwit me little girl...you will lose."

Her eyes rolling back in her head, Hailey exhaled a bored sigh.

"I know exactly what you were attempting to accomplish by inviting Harris tonight," I said. "But, it's not going to work."

The smirk on Hailey's face suggested she believed otherwise.

"I'm not going to tolerate anymore of your little tricks Hailey Marie Sifuentes, do you here me?" I asked, staring her down. "Doug and I are getting married—"

"Why, would you do something like that," Hailey asked, sounding genuinely confused, "when it's so obvious that you're still in love with Daddy?"

"Hailey—"

"Don't even try and deny it, Mom," she said, talking to me as if I was the thirteen year old. "I can see it in your eyes every time the two of you are in the same room."

"You need to remember your place, Hailey," I said, doing my level-best not to go ballistic on her smart little behind.

"How do you feel about Daddy?"

"That's not your concern."

"I disagree."

"Hailey I don't give a damn what you agree or disagree with," I said, my finger pointed in her smug little face. "Contrary to what you believe, this is not some kind of democracy where you have the right to assert your every opinion."

"So, what?" Hailey asked, frowning. "I'm supposed to sit idly by as you make the biggest mistake of your life..."

My eyes damn near popped out of my head as I listened to my child. This little heffa must have lost her ever lovin' mind talking to me this way.

"Not to mention hurt Daddy—"

"Enough!" I shouted at her.

Hailey flinched.

"Who in the hell do you think you are talking to, little girl?" I asked, thoroughly outdone. "You might have an IQ of 150—"

"152," Hailey corrected.

"Whatever," I snarled. "The fact remains that you are still only twelve—"

"Thirteen."

"Don't' interrupt me again, Hailey," I demanded. "There are some things, intelligence notwithstanding, you are simply too young to understand."

"I understand completely," she said, simply. "You're afraid."

"Excuse me," I said, one half-step away from ignoring Oprah's advice not to whip my child's smart ass.

"You're afraid to admit to yourself that you still love Daddy."

Hailey's words knocked the wind out of me. Falling back in the chair, I looked away for fear she'd see confirmation of her assertion in my eyes.

Reaching for my trembling hand, Hailey stroked it. "He's better now Momma...I promise," she said, the sincerity in her voice heartbreaking. "Daddy won't hurt you again."

Rising from the table, I walked over to the refrigerator. Opening the door, I blocked Hailey's view of my flushed face. "Go on up and get ready for bed," I said, discreetly wiping the tear from my eye.

"Mom—"

"Bed, Hailey," I said, keeping my back to her. "Now."

"Goodnight," she said, making her way toward the stairs. "Mom?"

"Umm, hmm," I said, sniffing.

"I love you."

Exhaling a sigh, I turned around to face her. "I love you too."

Watching Hailey as she disappeared up the stairs, I clutched my pounding chest. My daughter was a handful, but she would forever own a piece of my heart. Just like her father.

CHAPTER FIVE

"*I*'ll get it!"

Barreling down the stairs, I made my way to the door, smiling brightly as I flung it open.

"Hey there Baby Genius."

"Hey Daddy," I said, kissing him on the cheek.

"Where's your mom?" Dad asked, glancing around the living room.

"I'm right here," she said, heading in from the hall. "Hailey, could you give your father and me a few minutes?"

My brow rising in suspicion, I asked her, "Is everything okay?"

"Everything's fine," Mom said, her words doing little to reassure me. "Why don't you go finish getting ready?" Ushering me toward the stairs, she gave me a gentle swat across the backside. "Your dad will be all yours and Thomas' in five minutes."

Still not trusting her, I made my way upstairs. After stepping loudly enough to be heard down the hall toward my room, I tiptoed back to the edge of the stairs.

"What's up?" Dad asked, taking a seat on the sofa.

Vacillating a bit, Mom took a seat in the chair, placing her hands tentatively in her lap. "It's about what happened last night."

"I wasn't in on it," Dad said quickly.

"Harris, I'm not blaming you," Mom said, reassuring him.

Dad exhaled a relieved sigh. "Our daughter can be a bit headstrong sometimes."

Mom smirked. "Tell me about it."

"It's gonna take a little time for Hailey to get used to the idea of you and Doug..." Dad said, hesitating. Apparently, he was having as much trouble getting his mental arms around Mom's impending nuptials as I was.

"I realize that," Mom said, averting her eyes from Dad's. "But in a month Doug and I are getting married..."

Adjusting myself at the top of the stairs, I stared at my parents wondering how it was possible for two people so perfectly suited for one another not to be together. What was it that made it so impossible for the them to reconnect? Sure, it was fear, but pride and ego played their parts as well. My mother was too stubborn to give into her feelings, and Dad was too proud to beg her for another chance. Adults were supposed to be smarter than kids, but sometimes they truly missed the forest for the trees.

"Harris," Mom said, "I need your help here."

"How?" Dad asked ready, and willing to please the woman he loved. "Tell me what you need, Baby....Thalia."

From my vantage point it was a bit difficult to be sure, but I was fairly certain my mother was blushing.

"I need you to help me to make Hailey understand that the two of us will never be..."

Daddy stiffened as Mom spoke.

"Help me discourage her from holding onto the fantasy that you and I are going to someday reconcile—"

"Would that be such a bad idea?"

Mom's jaw fell into her lap. "Would...what...huh?" she asked, stammering like she did whenever Daddy got too close emotionally.

"Us, reuniting," Dad said, reaching for her hand. *"Thaaalia..."*

The sound of her name from his lips, made Mom shudder – in delight, I was betting.

"I'm not the same man I was six years ago."

Pulling her hand from his, Mom jumped up from the chair. "Harris, I'm getting married in less than a month," she said, trying to convince herself. "What are you...what...?" Mom rubbed the back of her neck pensively.

"I said that Hailey was having a hard time getting used to the idea of you and Doug," Dad said, rising to his feet. He made his way over to Mom. "Truth is, I'm having trouble getting used to it as well."

Stepping back until the wall stopped her, Mom's eyes widened as if she were watching a car wreck unfold before her. "Don't even."

"In the back of my mind, I'd always thought you and I would get back together someday," Dad said, taking a step toward her.

Pushing past him, Mom darted to the other side of the room. "Harris, don't do this," she said in a desperate voice. "Please don't do this to me."

"I'm not trying to do anything," Daddy said, approaching, "except be honest with you about my feelings." Cupping Mom's face in his hands, he gazed into her eyes. "Thalia, I still lo—"

"Don't!" Mom said, slapping his hand away. Marching back to the side of the room she'd just deserted, she took a shaky breath. Lowering her voice, she glared over at Daddy, not moving from where he stood. "For the sake of our children, you and I have...up until now anyway, have managed to maintain good relations," Mom said, her tone a warning. "Please don't fuck it all up by pulling some shit like this on me."

"I'm not pulling anything," Daddy said, insulted. The vein in his temple throbbing, he wrung his hands in an attempt to shake off the negative energy. "Do you still love me, Thalia?"

Mom turned her back to him. While Daddy couldn't see the tears burning her eyes I could.

"Tell me you don't love me," Daddy said, his voice cracking. "And I'll...I'll give up."

Shutting her eyes tightly, Mom said, "I don't love you, Harris."

Covering my mouth to stifle the gasp, I shook my head in stunned disbelief.

Daddy looked utterly crestfallen. "Fair enough," he said, moving to get out of the house before his emotions got the better of him. "Tell Hailey and Thomas I'm waiting in the car."

Mom flinched at the sound of the door closing behind him.

My father may have taken her at her word, but I could see the pain in my mother's eyes as she uttered the lie. A thin smile forming on my lips, I walked back down the hall, more certain than ever that Thalia and Harris Sifuentes belonged together. And I was just the *Baby Genius* to make it happen.

CHAPTER SIX

"**Y**ou, okay?" Doug asked, gently squeezing my shoulder with one hand while steering his Saab sedan down the highway with the other.

"Umm hmm," I said with a painted-on half smile. "Just a little tired is all."

Accepting the excuse for my sullen behavior, Doug continued driving. "That was a pretty good movie, don't you think?"

Staring out the window, I nodded. "Umm hmm."

To tell the truth, I had absolutely no idea if *The Mad Season* was a masterpiece, or a piece of crap. For the past two hours I'd sat in the dark theater replaying snippets of my history with Harris in my head while the film played out on screen. Every so often the sound of Doug's laugh, sigh, or chuckle would break my trance, but I'd soon return to the Technicolor, stereophonic world inside my head.

"Angel Hart was amazing," Doug said, commenting on the television turned movie star. "Good to see a *black* movie that's more than a slap stick farce..."

Not really hearing a word my fiancé was saying, my thoughts returned to my ex-husband, and the night that ultimately served as the beginning of the end of our love affair...

"Harris, are you in here?" I asked, pushing open the slightly ajar bathroom door. Gasping, I stared at him. "You told me you weren't going to do that again."

On his knees before the closed toilet, Harris wiped the white residue from his nose hastily. "I just needed a little pick me up."

Shaking my head in disbelief, I marched out of the bathroom. "I don't believe you," I said, angry and disappointed.

Struggling to his feet, Harris followed me into our bedroom. "Come on Thalia," he said. "It's no big deal."

"No big deal!" I exclaimed, spinning around to face him. "Harris you are doing drugs!"

"Don't go getting all dramatic," he said, plopping down on the edge of

106

the bed. *"I'm just...just trying to take the edge off."*

My brow raised, I asked snappishly, "Take the edge off what?"

Harris freed himself from the shirt and tie, tossing them to the floor. "My life."

"What kind of bullshit is that Harris?" I asked not feeling his little self-pity party one bit. We were adults for goodness sake. Sometimes it was necessary to make sacrifices for the good of our family.

"I realize that working for the pharmaceutical company may not be your idea..." I said, hesitating. Perhaps a softer approach was in order.

"Harris I understand how much it hurts to put your dreams of being a full-fledged artist on the back burner—"

"It wasn't a dream," he said, interrupting. "I was a full-fledged artist."

"But you weren't making any money—"

Harris jumped up from the bed. "That's all life's about to you, isn't it?"

Caught off guard by his outburst, I took a step back. Harris rarely flashed anger, but had been doing so with alarming frequency the past couple of weeks.

"Fuck my dream, right?" Harris approached, his glazed eyes fixed on me. "I thought you were different," he said sharply. "But you're just like every other woman I've dated. All you care about are material things. You don't give a damn about my happiness and actualization."

"That's unfair and you know it!" I shot back. "I am not some gold-digger, Harris. But if your definition of 'different' implies that I'm willing to go without food, shelter, and basic necessities while you pursue some pie-in-the-sky dream," I said, my words sharp as daggers, "then, no I'm not different than most women."

Disgusted, Harris stomped back into the bathroom. Careful to keep a safe distance, I followed him.

"I didn't purposely set out to kill your dream Harris," I said, trying to make him see that I wasn't the soul stealing bitch his eyes made clear he believed me to be. "But we've got two kids, a mortgage and college to think

about. That's our reality."

"Fine," Harris said, returning to his spot on the floor. "I'll keep putting on the monkey suit like a good little soldier, if that's what you want."

"What about the drugs, Harris?" I asked, eyeing the two lines of cocaine sitting on my toilet.

"I work for a drug company," he said with mocking sincerity. "It would be hypocritical of me not to get acquainted with the product, don't you think?"

Shooting him a look that would make all the demons in Hell tremble, I said, "Katz Pharmaceuticals sells diabetes and high-blood pressure medication, Harris."

"Well I say it's high-time they diversify," he said, chuckling as he lowered his head toward the coke. "I'm simply doing a little research and development on their behalf."

"What about Thomas and Hailey?" I asked, hoping his love for his children was greater than his lust for the shit he was snorting into his body.

"I'll be careful."

It was at that moment that I finally allowed myself to see the severity of the situation. Even if Harris had come to hate me enough to destroy me by destroying himself, Thomas and Hailey remained the Alpha and Omega of his world. If he wouldn't break this habit for his children's sake, there was little hope of saving him.

"That's not good enough."

"Nothing ever is with you," Harris said, readying to sniff up the last line of white powder.

"Harris, no," I said, moving toward him. "You will not do this in our house."

"Move Thalia," Harris said, blocking me with his body.

"I will not let you do this to yourself!"

"Stop it Thalia!" Harris shouted as we struggled for ownership of the plastic vial. Desperate to keep me away from his expensive mood enhancer, my husband gave me a hard shove, sending me flying across the room.

A high pitched squeal pushed past my lips as my head slammed against the opposite wall.

Instantly sober, Harris rushed to my aid. "Baby...I'm sorry," he said, sincerely. "I didn't—"

"Don't touch me!" I shouted, jerking away.

"Thalia, I didn't mean to push you."

Grimacing, I pulled myself up from the floor. "But you did," I said, a little less in love with him than I was only ten minutes ago. Heartbroken, but resolved, I turned to leave. "And it's the last time you ever will."

"Thalia?"

The sound of Doug's voice brought me out of my own head. "I'm sorry," I said, shaking off the dark memory. "What'd you say, Honey?"

"We're here," he said, eyeing me curiously.

Turning to see the house that Harris and I went into debt purchasing seven years ago, I sighed.

Doug was about to remove the key from the ignition, but I reached for his hand to stop him. "I have the most awful headache," I said. "Maybe I should be alone tonight."

"Of course," Doug said, careful not to sound too hurt.

"You understand, don't you?"

Kissing my cheek, Doug smiled. "Absolutely."

"Don't get out," I said, before he could get out of the car. "I can see myself to the door."

"Okay."

Feeling Doug's eyes on me as I walked up the driveway, I turned to wave goodbye as I reached the door, then quickly stepped inside. Standing in the darkness, I exhaled a dejected breath. This was not the way things were supposed to go down. How dare Harris do this to me. He had no right to say those words. To plunge a dagger into my barely healed heart just weeks before I was to marry Doug was unconscionable. Selfish, that's what he was. Harris knew as well I did that he didn't want me. Male ego was the motivator of his actions today, not love.

"Damn you, Harris," I said in an angry whisper.

Flipping on the lamp, I tossed my purse onto the sofa, then headed for the kitchen. I needed a drink. Reaching for the bottle of wine sitting on the countertop, I stopped short. Tonight I needed something stronger.

Bottle of Belvedere in hand, I sat down at the kitchen table. Pouring myself a full glass, I downed the vodka, grimacing as it burned a path through my chest. As I listened to the sound of the humming refrigerator, I tried to block out the noisy clutter inside my head. But, it was no use. No matter how hard I tried, the conflicting emotions demanded to be heard.

With my drink in hand, I rose from the table, making my way over to the telephone. I needed the support and empathy that only one woman could give me.

"Hello?"

Tears welled up in my eyes the instant I heard her voice. "Hey, Ma."

"Thalia?" Mom asked concerned. "Is everything okay?"

"Umm hmm," I said, biting down on my bottom lip. "I just wanted to hear your voice."

"That's sweet," Mom said, not buying it. "I thought you were going to see a movie with Doug."

"We did," I said, taking another sip of the liquor. "I just got home."

There was a moment of uncomfortable silence.

"Is Doug there too?" Mom asked, well aware that the kids were staying with their father for the weekend.

"He...umm...he wasn't feeling so well," I said, proving just how piss-poor a liar I was. "He didn't want to risk getting me sick."

"How caring of him," Mom said smoothly.

After another round of uncomfortable silence, she asked, "How much longer are we going to do this before you tell me what's really going on?"

Blinking as the tears streamed down my cheek, I slid down the wall to the floor. "Oh Momma," I said, sobbing like a baby. "Oooh, damn him."

"Damn who?"

Wiping at my stained face, I tried to compose myself. "Harris."

"Ah," Mom said, able to fill in the blanks without knowing a single detail.

"That sonofabitch..." I said, catching myself when I remembered who was on the other end of this phone. "That *man* had the nerve to come over here today and try to tell me that he was still in love with me."

"Harris?"

"Yes Harris," I said, the very mention of his name making my blood boil. "He claims that in his dumb head he always believed we'd get back together. Can you believe that?"

"Yes," Mom answered.

That stopped me cold.

"I'd assumed the same."

My eyes just about popped out of my head. "What?"

"That was until you announced your engagement to Doug five months ago," Mom clarified.

"Ma' how could you have even thought such a thing?" I asked, staggered. "You of all people?"

Exhaling softly, Mom said, "I fear I may have done you a disservice when you were growing up."

"How's that?" I asked with a raised brow.

"In my efforts to protect you and your sister, I'm afraid I may have robbed you of the ability to fully love a man," Mom said.

"No," I said, defending her actions. "You taught us how to protect ourselves."

"Maybe I taught you too well."

"What are you saying to me Momma?"

"Men are a funky mess sometimes," she said with an ironic chuckle. "They are imperfect, selfish, thick-headed..."

I shook my head in complete agreement.

"And even though the chances were pretty good he'd one day break it into a million pieces, it's unfair for a woman to love her man with anything less than her full and complete heart."

Well I'll be damned! After all these years this woman was changing her tune. For my entire marriage to Harris, I struggled not to give into the demanding urge inside me, imploring me to love him fully, completely...fearlessly. Now my mother was telling me the approach, one she'd aggressively encouraged, was flawed. Ain't that 'bout a bitch?

"Do you still love him?"

Sensing that truth was gaining on me, I leapt to my feet, leaving the empty glass where it sat on the floor. My eyes darting about the kitchen in search of what, I wasn't sure, I licked my dry lips. I didn't dare answer Mom's question. I didn't want to.

"Thalia?"

The phone still at my ear, I rushed out of the kitchen and down the hall. Back in the living room, I stared at the photos taken of

Hailey and Thomas; miracles created by way of my union with Harris Sifuentes. What if I was to blame for what happened? Perhaps Harris wouldn't have lost his way had I loved him more, lowered the walls surrounding my heart, allowing him safe refuge there. Maybe had I not demanded he be someone other than the wonderful, artistic, sensitive man that he was when I'd met him, Harris wouldn't have felt the need to turn *to* drugs, and *away* from me. I'd never know the answer for sure, but the thought that I might have played even a minor role in breaking that beautiful man's spirit was enough to make me cry.

"You don't have to answer me," Mom said, letting me off the hook. "But before you walk down that aisle with Douglas, you need to answer it for yourself."

"Ma," I said, barely able to hold back the next round of tears, "I need to go."

"Okay," she said softly. "Thalia?"

"Hmm?"

"Everything has a way of working itself out in the end," Mom said, her words bringing me little comfort. "Just close your eyes and listen to what your heart is trying to tell you."

"Goodbye Ma," I said, then hung up the phone.

CHAPTER SEVEN

*T*here were any number of things I loved about spending the weekend's with my father, but preparing Sunday breakfast was at the top of the list. While my brother snored upstairs like a drunken fat man with a sinus infection, Daddy and I laughed, talked, danced and sang – the man couldn't hold a note, God love him – while flipping hotcakes, scrambling eggs, and stirring cheese grits. It was our own special private time, and I relished it.

"Baby will you hand me the pepper?"

Retrieving the seasoning from the counter behind me, I handed it to Dad. "Here, you go."

"Thank you, Ma'am," he said with a smile.

"You're very welcome, Sir," I said, smiling back at him.

While Dad continued making the veggie omelets – he wasn't big on meat – I pulled down the plates from the cabinet, and began setting the small table in the corner of the kitchen. When we all lived under the same roof, my father was adamant about the family having breakfast together. He believed that taking the time to connect with the people you love *before* you stepped out into the world fortified not only the body, but the spirit as well.

Once the table was set, I hopped back onto the stool, studying the open 3,500 square-foot loft Daddy had called home since Mom had put him out of ours. With the exception of the living room area – sofa, coffee table, bookshelf, two directors' chairs, and an entertainment center – Dad had turned most of the first floor into his art studio.

Paint brushes sticking out of large glass jars sat in the corner, while unused canvas boards lay stacked atop the three work tables, and against the brick walls. Situated in a semi-circle, works in varying stages of completion sat on easels. While most were uncovered, one in particular was hidden beneath a paint-stained cloth. Daddy had been clear with Thomas and me that the piece in question was not to be seen by anyone, including his children, before it was shown at his exhibition.

When Mom started letting him take my brother and me on alternating weekends, Daddy had the second floor of the loft separated into four equal sized rooms. Three served as bedrooms, while the fourth room served as Dad's office. In there, he graded student projects, and prepared lesson plans for the impressionist art class he taught over at the Center for Creative Studies. The man's desk was a cluttered mess, but he claimed it was "organized chaos that made artistic sense." Whatever that meant.

I watched Daddy, humming lightly as he folded the omelet in the skillet. He was the picture of happiness. Despite all he'd been through, my father remained as gentle spirited and kind-hearted as ever. Sometimes though, I wish he would be a little less *whatever the universe decides* and a little more *grab the bull by the horns.* I firmly believed that were he to give Mom a gentle, but testosterone-drenched nudge, she'd break down and finally admit her true feelings for him.

"What?" Daddy asked, realizing I was staring at him. "Do I have a boog?" he asked swiping at his nose.

"*Nooo*, Daddy," I said, making a face.

Correctly sensing I was about to hit him with something uncomfortable, he sighed. "What's on your mind Hailey Marie?"

"I was just wondering if you were planning on coming to Mom and Doug's wedding."

"I don't think that would be such a good idea," Dad said, focusing his attention on the pot of cheese grits as if they held the secret to the universe.

"You love Mom, don't you?" I asked, already certain of the answer.

"It's not that simple," Dad said, not answering the question posed.

"Yes it is," I said. "You either love Mom or you don't."

Shifting his weight nervously as he stood at the stove barefoot and thoroughly uncomfortable, Daddy said, "Yes, I love your mother."

"Then why haven't you asked to come back home?"

"It's complicated."

"You adults make things a lot more complicated than they need to be," I said with a smirk. "If you love Mom and she loves you...I don't see the problem."

Dad wiped the building moisture from his brow. "Thalia doesn't love me."

"Yes she does."

Turning off the stove, Daddy motioned for me to sit with him at the table. "Hailey, I know how much you want your Mom and me to get back together, but I'm afraid it's not going to happen."

I stared at him blankly as he spoke. Mom's performance the other day might have fooled my father, but I wasn't buying it.

"Doug seems like a nice guy—"

"But he's not you, Daddy," I said, interrupting.

"But he is the man your mother wants to marry," he said. "Doug's the one she loves, not me."

"Not true."

"Hailey—"

"Daddy, listen to me," I said, damned if I'd let him give up on the love of his life without a fight. "I don't care what Momma said Friday..."

His brow rose incredulously, but thankfully he resisted the urge to ask me how I knew what Mom had said.

"She is still in love with you Daddy."

"Listen to me Hailey," he said, taking my hand. "I blew my chances with your Mom. And, as hard as it might be, I have to accept...and *respect* the fact that she's moving on with her life." Daddy looked me dead in the eye. "And so do you."

"If you knew that Mom was still in love with you would you fight for her?"

"Hailey come on now," Daddy said, certain I was being an unrealistic child. "Enough is enough."

"Answer my question."

Daddy studied me carefully, a thin smile spreading across his face. "What do you know, Baby Genius?"

"Nothing," I said with a cool grin. "And you still haven't answered the question."

Daring to allow for the possibilities, Dad said, "I'd fight to the death."

I could have jumped across the table and wrapped my arms around that glorious man's neck. Instead, I fixed my eyes on his. "Ask her again Daddy. And this time make her look you in the eyes when she answers."

Dad took a moment to digest my words, before calmly rising from the table. He placed a tender kiss on my forehead. "Go wake your brother up," he said, thanking me with his eyes. "Breakfast is ready."

"Yes, sir," I said, confident that my work here was done.

CHAPTER EIGHT

*E*nduring the stolen glances, and tentative smiles of the patrons inside Taggart Gallery, I thought about the always put-upon father in that campy old TV show *Soap*. Whenever he felt the walls closing in on him, he'd snap his fingers, certain that doing so would make him invisible to the world. Like him, my efforts to disappear tonight had failed. Instead, I stood with my back pressed against the wall, wishing I could be anywhere else but here.

Don't misunderstand me. I wasn't hating on my ex-husband. In fact, I was genuinely happy for Harris and his skyrocketing success. He'd worked hard to get to this place in his life; overcoming addiction and the personal demons that almost swallowed him whole. Watching as he spiraled out of control, I feared he would never break free of the chains that bound him. But he'd done it, and I was both relieved and happy for him. Even as he was breaking my heart, never once did I wish for him anything less than grand happiness and utter peace of mind. Sometimes though, witnessing from the sidelines as my former husband stepped proudly into his own, was a real bitch.

"Why are you holed up in this corner?" Julia asked, handing me a glass of champagne. "The jazz trio isn't looking for a fourth," she said, nodding at the band.

"Leave me alone, fat lady," I said, inching away from the spot I'd held for most of the hour since my arrival. "Have you seen Thomas and Hailey?" I asked, realizing I'd not seen the two in more than ten minutes – an eternity in *parent* time.

"They're in the new wing checking out more of Harris' exhibition," Julia said, fixing her gaze on me.

"What?" I asked certain that the shit-eating grin on my sister's face suggested she was up to no damn good.

"Nothing," Julia said, feigning innocence as she prodded me deeper inside the gallery. "So what do you think?"

"Amazing," I said in awe as we came to a stop in front of the painting titled *Baby Genius*.

"Beautiful, isn't it?" Julia said, studying the piece.

"Umm hmm," I said, pushing down the emotion bubbling just beneath the surface. The oil on canvas of a little girl – Hailey – sleeping on her father's chest was breathtaking. Julia had been on-point in her assertion that this was some of Harris' most intimate work. The passion he had for his craft reeked from every painting in the place, each one tugging at my heart; all bitter reminders of what I'd gained...and lost in the past fifteen years.

"You have to take a look at this one," Julia said, leading me toward the opposite wall.

Of its own accord, the laugh rose from a place deep inside me as I laid eyes on *Boys Will Be Boys* -- a charcoal drawing of a father and son roughhousing. Shaking my head, I allowed my mind to wander back to any of the countless occasions I'd had to get on Thomas and his father about wrestling in the house. Curled into a ball, his eyes filled with hysterical glee, my son would squeal with delight as his daddy tickled him until he was about to pee his pants. There was no denying that a certain energy and *joie de vivre* left our home the day I kicked Harris out of it.

Feeling the eyes on me, I turned to see an old man watching me intently from across the room. Grinning from ear to ear, he lifted his glass into the air as if saluting me. I turned back to Julia. "I thought I was just being paranoid," I said, "but now I'm sure of it."

"Sure of what?"

"People are staring at me." Leaning closer to Julia I asked, "Is my drag okay?"

"You look wonderful," she said smoothly. "Like a work of art, even."

"Julia, what's going—?"

"Wonder what those two are talking about," she said, cutting me off.

Following her eyes, I gasped inwardly when I saw Doug and Harris. My initial instinct was to rush over to separate the two, demanding that they never ever speak again, but I couldn't have made my feet move if I wanted to.

"You think they're comparing notes?" Julia asked.

"Not funny," I said, spying my future and ex-husband as they stood there slapping backs, talking and laughing like old friends. When Harris had extended the invitation to Doug, I got a sinking feeling in the pit of my stomach. "This is just the kind of shit I was trying to avoid."

Julia's brow furrowed. "Did you really expect that Doug and Harris would never have a conversation?"

As far as I was concerned Doug and Harris were oil and water. There was no reason they needed to be mixed. Sure I knew that their paths were bound to cross, but anything more involved than a civil *hello* and quick nod of the head as Harris was picking up, or returning our children was too damned involved for me.

"Has Harris been working out?"

Resisting Julia's efforts to get a rise out of me, I said, "I wouldn't know."

"He's definitely been in the gym."

"I assure you I hadn't notice," I said, forcing my eyes off of Harris's proud backside.

Julia chuckled lightly. "Then that would make you the only woman up in this joint that hasn't."

I had absolutely no intention of admitting it to my nosey-assed baby sister, but I was painfully aware of how terribly good Harris looked, and the attention it was garnering from every artsy fartsy hootchie sniffing around behind him. While he no longer had the power to make my panties wet, I had to give Harris his props for being one of the most exquisite creatures God had ever created. With three buttons undone, that *clinging to every inch* DKNY shirt left little doubt that his chest was even more chiseled than I'd remembered it -- if that was possible. And, those Kenneth Cole slacks were hugging his hair-dusted, caramel-colored ass just right. The first time I saw Harris unclothed, I just about had an orgasm. That he was so damn comfortable in his own skin only made him that much more delectable. I knew for a fact that Doug had a good five inches on my ex, but somehow standing side by side, Harris appeared the taller man.

Julia gave me a coy smile as if reading my dirty thoughts. "Do you miss it?"

"Do I miss what?"

"What I can only imagine was glorious sex with Harris."

Blushing, I took a sip of the champagne. When it came to the sex that Harris used to put on me, glorious was an understatement. Even at our worst, the lovemaking never missed the mark. I could still remember the first time we'd made love like it was yesterday. The very touch of his hand to my cheek made me shudder in ecstasy. Standing before me, his uncut manhood a magnificent sight to behold, Harris reeked of intoxicatingly masculine energy. With his tongue, fingers, and even his toes, he'd worked every square inch of my body like a violin. When I didn't think a man could love me better, Harris slipped himself inside me. Staring into my eyes as he pressed his flesh into mine, I knew all I needed to know. I was the woman he loved.

"You never gave me details," Julia said. "But seeing how the very first time he put it on you your ass got pregnant—"

"Where is your husband?" I asked cutting her off.

"He's around here somewhere..." Julia said, then hesitated. "We've been spotted."

"Oh shit," I said, flinching when I noticed Harris and Doug looking in our direction. "We are not going over there."

"Don't be silly," Julia said through a bright smile. "Your husband and fiancé are waving us over, we can't just ignore them."

"It's *ex*-husband," I corrected. "Tell them I had to go to the restroom," I said, preparing to head for the nearest exit.

Thwarting my getaway, Julia wrapped her hand around my forearm. "Just breathe," she said, edging me forward. "This is going to be—"

"Painful," I said, finishing her sentence.

Julia chuckled as we continued making our way toward my waking nightmare. "For you, yes," she said, freeing the glass of champagne from the server's tray as he passed us. Handing me the drink she cooed, "But oh so entertaining for me."

"I hate you," I growled as we approached Doug and Harris.

Unfazed, Julia eased between them. "What are you two gentlemen talking about?"

"Thalia, actually," Doug said, looking at me.

Good God somebody just shoot me now.

"Me?" I asked, suppressing the scream in my throat. "What about me?"

"Just how great a human being you are," Harris said with an effortless smile. Damn him for being so fucking sweet.

"You're her!" a woman exclaimed rushing toward us. My head twisting, I looked behind me to see who she was talking about. "Absolutely exquisite," she said, totally invading my personal space.

I took a step back, unsettled by her enthusiasm.

Julia glanced over at Harris as if they shared some secret insight into why this crazy lady was all up in my face like this.

"Miss, I have no idea—"

Before I could finish my thought, Hailey and Thomas raced toward us. "Mom have you seen it?"

Taking my eyes off the woman, I turned to my daughter. "Seen what, Sweetie?"

"Ma, I didn't know you had it in you," Thomas said, impressed. "You were hot!"

My head snapped in Harris and Julia's direction. "What are they talking about?" I asked, now certain the two of them were up to something.

Shifting his weight nervously from one leg to the other, Harris lowered his head. Julia flashed me a self-satisfied grin, but didn't say jack. For his part, Doug just stood there looking confused.

"The painting Daddy did of you," Hailey said, filling in the blanks. "You look so beautiful."

"Take me to it."

More than happy to oblige, Hailey and Thomas took either of my hands leading me toward the back of the gallery. Increasing my pace toward the scene of the crime, I could feel my heart racing like a locomotive. When they noticed me approaching, the crowd of people gathered around the back wall, parted like the Red Sea. The looks on their faces – a combination of appreciation and deference – made my blood run cold. What had Harris done?

I gasped. "Oh my God!"

"You look so happy," Hailey said, releasing her hold of my clammy hand.

The tear blurring my vision, I stared at the painting, instantly overcome with the memories of me and Harris in his tiny little studio apartment. I tried to look away from the image of my naked self, but couldn't.

"This is the coolest painting in the entire exhibition," Thomas said proudly.

Frozen where I stood, I was transported in time. In my mind's eye I could see Harris, painting feverishly as I sat on that blanket feeling more alive and desirable than I'd ever felt before. In the air I could smell the scent of jasmine. Playing in the background, Luther Vandross' pitch-perfect voice wrapped itself around me like a glove. Recalling how wonderful Harris felt inside me as we made love sent a spark of energy up my spine. That was the night we'd created our son. Since, there had been a deeply-rooted bond between Harris and I that, despite my best efforts, had proven unbreakable.

"Daddy loves you so much."

"Hailey please," I said, perilously close to coming completely undone. "Not now."

"I don't think you should be showing your boobs like that," Thomas said with a slight frown. "But it's a sharp painting."

"Wow."

Startled, I spun around to see Doug standing behind us. His jaw scraping the hardwood floor, he stared at the painting, utterly mesmerized by it.

"Doug, I had no idea Harris was going to show this," I said, feeling the need to explain. "I'd only posed for him once...I didn't even know he'd finished it."

"I'm glad he did," Doug said, his eyes still glued to the painting. "You are...*ethereal*."

I glared at Harris and Julia as they approached. "Why didn't either of you tell me about this?" That my ex-husband with my sister's help, had put my deepest self on display for the entire world to see like this was off-putting to say the very least. And, yet, despite the violation, I couldn't help but marvel at the result of Harris' talented hands. Damn that man. Damn him. Damn him. Damn him!

"Please don't be mad," Harris said, giving me that look he gave whenever he'd done something to upset me.

"I'm not mad," I said. And that's what scared me. What I was feeling for Harris at that moment was anything but anger or disappointment.

Doug stepped closer to the painting, leaning in to read the placard beside it. "*Love of My Life*," he read aloud.

My legs buckling beneath me, I looked at Harris. The love I saw in his eyes was so unsettling, I quickly turned away.

"Interesting title," Doug said, smiling at Harris. "Incredible piece of work."

Harris swallowed. "Thanks."

"I don't see a price," Doug said to Julia. "How much is it?"

"It's not for sale."

Doug turned to Harris. "Why is that?" He asked, finally starting to catch on.

Returning my fiancé's hard stare, Harris said, "That painting has special meaning—"

"What Harris means to say," Julia said, inserting herself into the shirking space between the two men, "is that the piece is already sold."

Doug walked back over to the painting in search of the red dot signifying it was already purchased. Seeing none, he turned back to Harris. "I'll give you ten thousand for it."

The vein in his forehead throbbing, Harris snarled, "I already told you—"

"Harris," I said carefully. "Please reconsider."

Looking at me with hurt-filled eyes, Harris turned to Doug. Extending his hand, he said, "You got yourself a deal."

"Wonderful," Doug said, visibly relieved.

"Great," Julia said, giving Harris a look of empathy. "If you'll come with me," she said, motioning for Doug to follow her to the office, "we can take care of the paperwork."

His omnipresent smile returning, Doug gave me a peck on the cheek, "Be right back."

"Okay, Sweetie."

My fiancé might have been a bit on the nerdy side, but he was nobody's fool. Like me, Doug recognized the importance of what had just transpired. By allowing him to buy *Love of My Life*, Harris had finally come to accept the truth; what he and I had was no more.

"Well, I better get back up front," Harris said, preparing to leave.

"Harris?"

"You're welcome," he said, once again reading my thoughts.

As the love of my life walked away, I turned back to the painting. I sighed as I stared at the woman in the picture. Never again would I be as happy...or as deeply in love as she.

CHAPTER NINE

*F*eeling every bit like a thirteen-year-old on the verge of madness, I stalked around the electronics store as Doug suggested any number of items he falsely assumed might tickle my fancy. I'd told the man like a million times already that he didn't need to buy me another birthday gift, but he refused to hear me. The geeky home wrecker was bound and determined to buy me off. What he failed to realize was that my favor – much like my mother's heart -- wasn't for sale.

"What about this one?" Doug asked, pointing at the over-priced mini-DVD player.

Pushing down the bitterness his very existence inspired in me, I spied the gadget. "I like it," I said, tossing the dog a bone.

"Do you want to get it?" Doug asked hopefully.

Fine, if it'll help bring an end to this misery. "Yes," I said with as much enthusiasm as I could manufacture considering that one; I didn't want a freakin' DVD player, and two; I was talking to the man who was about to destroy my family.

Smiling brightly, Doug exclaimed, "Wonderful!"

Rolling my eyes at his back, I followed Daddy-wanna-be as he carried the bribe up to the check out counter. Watching the doofus complete the purchase, it became clear to me what had to be done. If left to their own devices, my mother and father would allow this travesty of a marriage to take place. Well, I for one had had enough of the madness.

Falsely assuming he'd made some kind of progress with me, Doug strutted out of the store. I wanted to kick him in the butt as he stepped out into the mall, but resisted the urge – barely.

"How's about we get a bite to eat?" he suggested.

"How's about you catch a clue and get lost so my mom and dad can do the damned thang!" I wanted to shout. "Okay," I said instead.

Making our way toward the food court, I formulated a plan of attack in my head. Until now, I'd taken the passive aggressive approach with Doug, but he'd been too dense to take the hint. And, seeing how God had been just out of earshot each of the myriad occasions I'd flung a prayer up to the heavens, perhaps it was time for me to take a more direct approach to the problem.

Slipping into the booth, Doug looked up at me. "Well, aren't you going to have a seat?" he asked with a nervous chuckle.

"Oh sorry," I said, sitting down.

"I don't know about you," Doug said, acting like we were Gucci girlfriends, "but I'm famished."

A cruel smirk formed on my lips as I spied him from across the table. Let's see what kind of appetite he'd have after I force-fed him some knowledge.

"What can I do you for?" the waitress said, sashaying her fast self over to the booth.

"Ladies first," Doug said, the genuine smile on his face, taking some of the venom out of my sails. Man, I wanted so badly to hate him, but God help the little bugger, he really was a decent guy...who just happened to be in love with a woman in love with someone else. Breaking Doug's heart wasn't going to be as much fun as I'd first imagined. But, break his heart I must. And, break his heart I would.

"Just a salad for me," I said, not bothering to open the menu. "And a Diet Sprite."

Doug gave me a careful look. "You aren't watching your weight are you?"

"No," I said, struck by the sincere concern in his voice.

"Good," he said. "Because you are perfect just as you are."

The waitress flashed her gold-plated teeth. "That's right," she said, adding a finger snap for good, ghetto-fabulous measure. "You listen to your father—"

"He's not my father," I blurted out.

Both Doug and the over-friendly server drew back.

"Sorry," I said, realizing that I might have come off as a little defensive.

Wondering what familial drama she'd just stepped into, the waitress quickly took Doug's order, then got the heck out of dodge.

"Listen, Hailey," Doug said, weighing his words carefully. "I want you to know that it's not my intent to take your father's place."

And, that was good for him, seeing how he couldn't if he tried.

"I do hope though that you and I might develop a friendship," Doug said. "If you'd just give me a chance you'd see I'm not such a bad guy..."

As I sat there listening to Doug try to get me to buy into a future I knew would never come to pass, I actually found myself feeling sorry for the man. For all of the bitching and moaning I'd done, I had no doubt that, were Doug to marry my mom, he would try his hardest to be a good husband, diligently working to forge some semblance of a bond with Thomas and me. I truly wished for him the love he was looking for one day. Just not with my mother. She belonged to my dad.

"Things are going to be a little weird in the beginning," Doug said, still selling the dream. "But in time we'll all get more comfortable—"

"You're a lawyer for Pete's sake," I said, interrupting. Though I wanted to slowly stick the knife through his chest so he'd have some shot of recovery, sometimes it was best to just plunge that puppy right in there, consequences be damned.

"Yes," Doug answered, not sure where I was going.

"Then how can you continue ignoring the facts that are right before your very eyes," I said, glowering at him.

Squirming a bit, Doug said, "I'm not sure I follow you, Hailey."

"And, I'm sure you do," I shot back. "You know she's in love with him, yet you refuse to step aside."

"Hailey, I don't think this is an appropriate conversation for you and me to be having," Doug said, beads of sweat forming over his wrinkled brow.

"Let's take a look at the facts counselor," I said, pressing forward before I lost my nerve. "The energy between them is undeniable..."

Doug reached for the handkerchief, wiping his face. "Hailey--"

"You had to have noticed it at Dave and Buster's...certainly the other night at the gallery," I said, locking him in my sights. "Good God man, he titled the nude painting of her *Love of My Life*."

That hit home with him.

"What I don't understand is why you're subjecting yourself to this," I said, reminding myself that this had to be done as I observed the crestfallen look on Doug's face.

Reaching across the table I stopped just short of touching his fisted hand as it rested atop the table. "I think you're a good guy, I really do," I said, and meant it. "But you're not the man my mother's in love with. For her sake and the sake of our family please, Doug, please get out of the way."

Just then, the waitress appeared with our orders.

"Fettuccine for you," she said, placing the plate in front of Doug.

"Thank you," he said, mustering a smile.

The server turned to me. "And a salad for you," she said in a tone suggesting she wasn't sure she liked me. She wasn't alone. I wasn't sure I liked myself much at that moment. Despite my reasons, I felt horrible about what I'd just done to Doug. And when he told Mom, God only knew what she was going to do to me.

As soon as the waitress was gone, I said, "Doug I'm not trying to hurt—"

"I'll take what you said under advisement," he said, cutting me off. "In the meantime how 'bout we just enjoy our lunch."

Genuinely sorry for the pain I saw in his eyes, I nodded obediently. "Okay."

****

For the past two hours I'd been sitting on the sofa staring at *Love of My Life*, resting on the floor beside the fireplace. If it were true that a picture could say a thousand words, then the one Harris had painted was screaming them at me. Since it had been delivered yesterday, my ex-husband's love song on canvas had been monopolizing my thoughts. And, while I tried mightily not to, I found myself reminiscing about my life with Harris, yearning for just a sliver of the passion, and happiness...and love we'd once shared.

The sound of the bell broke my concentration. Exhaling wearily, I rose from the sofa, making my way to the door. My heart jumped the moment I saw his face, but that was nothing new. Harris had been having that effect on me since the very first time I laid eyes on him fifteen years ago.

"What are you doing here?" I asked, fighting not to melt from the heat of his gaze. "The kids aren't home—"

"Good," Harris said, stepping over the threshold. "We should have this conversation alone."

My eyes followed him as he walked into the living room. The intensity of his energy as he planted himself in front of the painting made my pulse quicken.

"What conversation is that?" I asked tentatively.

"Do you still love me, Thalia?"

Oh sweet Mother of Jesus, help me. "Harris we've already covered this."

"I want to cover it again."

I stepped back quickly as he approached. "Let's not—"

"I still love you," Harris said, not letting me finish. "I never stopped loving you."

Struggling not to hyperventilate, I took a quick breath. "Harris what we had—"

"Was magical," he said. "And beautiful...and passionate..."

With every step he took toward me, I took one away, until my back was against the wall.

"You were...you are the love of my life," Harris said, reaching to stroke my flushed cheek. "I know I messed up bad, but if you could just—"

"Don't Harris," I said, feeling myself slipping back under his spell. "Don't do this."

"I love you," he said, now so close to me I could taste his mint-tinged breath.

"Why are you doing this?" I asked haplessly.

"Because I love you," Harris said, his soft lips brushing against mine. "I love you so much it hurts, Thalia."

"Please don't."

Harris drew me into his embrace. "Oh, *Thaaalia*—"

"Don't say my name like that," I said, trying to pull away. "Don't touch me. Don't—"

"Don't what?" Harris asked, refusing to let me go – physically or otherwise. "Don't love you? Thalia Sifuentes, I can't *not* love you."

My fragile heart aching, I pleaded with him to release me. "Harris I beg of you, don't do this."

"Thalia, I love you," he said succinctly. "I've loved you from the very first moment I laid eyes on you. We can make this work. Please give me...give us another chance."

"You need to go," I said, praying he wouldn't.

Cupping my chin with his hand, Harris looked me squarely in the eye. "Tell me again that you don't love me, and I will," he said, not allowing me to turn away. "Look me in the eyes and tell me you don't love me, Thalia, and I'll leave you alone for good."

I tried to form my lips to speak the lie, but my heart wouldn't allow it. Tears streaming down my face, I broke down. "God help me I do. I still love you, you sonofabitch....I love you."

Without saying another word, Harris lifted me into his arms, carrying me across the living room. He kissed me hungrily on the mouth, then lowered me carefully onto the floor. Lifting my t-shirt over my head, he suckled each of my throbbing nipples. He unfastened my jeans, easing them down my trembling thighs.

As Harris' head disappeared between my legs, I gazed at the painting, a blissful moan escaping my lips. Once again, I was as happy as the woman looking back at me.

CHAPTER TEN

"*T*hat's it, isn't it?" Julia asked giving me the big eyes. "You've gone mad!"

Ignoring my sister's histrionics, I continued applying the powder to my face.

"You have gone coo-coo for Cocoa Puffs crazy, haven't you?"

"I assure you I am of completely sound mind," I said, tucking back the curly lock that had escaped from behind my ear.

"Then what in the hell are you doing?"

Eyeing Julia through the mirror like she was the one who'd gone crazy, I said sardonically, "Getting ready for my wedding...duh."

"Oh my God!" she exclaimed. "You really are going to go through with this, aren't you?" Before I could answer in the affirmative, my sister said, "After telling Harris you still loved him...then fucking the man—"

"Language," I said, snappishly. Taking a calming breath, I continued getting ready. "Try to remember we're in a church, please."

"Ugh!" Julia threw up her hands in frustration. "You don't want to be happy, do you?"

Ignoring her, I stood from the table, making my way across the room as if all was well with my world. It didn't matter that my heart was beating a mile a minute, my head pounding like a drum, and my stomach churning like a butter maker. Once I walked down that aisle, everything would be okay. Julia, Hailey...and Harris would have no choice but to finally accept my choice.

"Don't you dare put that on," Julia said, snatching the crème-colored, silk Chanel two-piece out of my hands.

Cutting my eyes at her, I said, "*Julia*...give me my clothes." My patience with this girl was running quite thin.

"No," she said, sounding every bit the insolent five year old, "not until you come to your senses."

Taking a step toward her, I growled, "I will tackle your pregnant behind to the floor if you don't—"

"Fine, here," Julia said, tossing the suit at me. "You do realize that you are making the biggest mistake of your life, don't you?"

"Maybe I am," I said, stepping into the knee-length skirt, "but it's my life and therefore my mistake to make."

"Harris has pulled his life back together...and then some," Julia said, trying to reason with me – a colossal waste of her time seeing how my mind was made up.

"And, I'm happy for Harris,' I said, repositioning my breasts as I buttoned the beaded jacket.

"Then why won't you give the brother a chance?"

"I already gave him a chance."

"Give him another," Julia said adamantly. "Thalia you will never love Doug or any man for that matter, the way you love Harris."

"From your lips to God's ears," I said, smirking as I reached for my lipstick.

Julia cocked her head at me. "And just what is that supposed to mean?"

"I loved Harris with every fiber of my being," I said, feeling my jaw clenching as I spoke. "My nose...and legs wide open, I loved that man. And what did I get for my troubles?" I asked, lowering my tube of MAC Fresh Moroccan back onto the table, "a broken heart, that's what."

"Blah-blah-blah...blah, blah," Julia said, following me as I went to retrieve my shoes. "You aren't the first person to ever get her heart broken. Besides, it healed didn't it?"

"Just barely," I said, recalling the many days and nights after Harris moved out that I'd lain curled in the fetal position in an empty bed in so much pain I couldn't see straight. Were it not for Thomas and Hailey, I might have never resurfaced from the abyss of emotional despair. I couldn't risk putting my heart in that kind a danger again. While I cared deeply for Doug, I was confident that I'd never fall so deeply in love with him that I'd lose myself. With Harris it was all but guaranteed that I would.

"Thalia, I realize that you're scared," Julia said, standing between me and the full-length mirror hanging on the closed door. "But we both know that you belong with Harris."

"Julia—"

"You cannot marry Doug today."

"Listen to me," I said, speaking slowly and succinctly because I had no intention of saying it again. "I *am* getting married to Doug today, and there is nothing you or anyone else can say, or do to stop me."

"How can you marry--?"

"Enough!" I barked. "I am through having this discussion with you. Now if you can't support me in my decision, then perhaps you shouldn't—"

The knock at the door interrupted me.

My eyes still locked on my sister's I yelled out, "Come in!"

Tentatively, Doug poked his head inside the room.

"Hey Sweetie" I said, brightening.

Stepping inside, Doug looked at Julia standing there with a scowl on her face, and her ass on her shoulders. "Could I get a minute alone with Thalia?"

"Be my guest," she said, heading for the door. "She's all yours. God help you."

Watching my sister as she marched out of the room, Doug turned back to me.

"Is something the matter?" I asked, noting the pensive look on his freshly shaven face.

"Let's sit down," Doug said, guiding me toward the sofa.

My imagination getting the best of me, I swallowed the dry lump in my throat. "Doug, please tell me what's the matter?"

Sitting down beside me, he took a deep breath. "I love you so much Thalia. The thought of being your husband..." Doug said, then hesitated. "I wanted so desperately to make you my wife that I ignored the fact that you were in love with another man—"

"Doug—"

"Shhh," he said, placing a finger to my lips. "Let me finish."

The tears welling in my eyes, I sat there frozen as he continued.

"I thought I could do it, but I can't," Doug said, shaking his head. "I don't want to be the *good enough* guy. What I want more than anything is for a woman to look at me the way you look at Harris."

Snatching for air, I fell back against the sofa. With everything in me I wanted to assure him that he had misread the signs, gotten it all wrong. But, we both knew he hadn't. And, I respected Doug too much to insult his intelligence by suggesting otherwise.

"If I'm lucky, one day I'll find my soul mate," Doug said, squeezing my hand. "But you? You have the unbelievably good fortune of having already found yours..."

I sat there in stupefied silence as my soon to be ex-fiancé killed me softly with his words.

"If there is any chance that you and Harris can make a go of it again, you have to take it," he said, insistently, "if not for your own sake, then for Hailey and Thomas'."

Placing a kiss on my cheek, Doug got up to leave. "Be happy, Thalia." he said, offering me a final, bittersweet smile. "You deserve it."

Alone, I lowered my head in my hand, bracing as the walls continued to close in around me. No matter how hard I'd tried to outrun it, the truth had finally caught up with me.

"Hey."

Quickly, I lifted my head.

"Harris?" I asked, shocked to see him standing there. "What are you doing here?"

"Doug, called me this morning," he said, taking a seat on the sofa beside me.

"Great," I said with a weary shake of the head. "Just great."

"I'm sorry."

"Are you?" I asked, cutting my eyes at him.

"Of course I am," Harris said. "Seeing you hurt brings me no pleasure—"

"Yet, you hurt me just the same."

Harris' eyes lowered. "And I'll never forgive myself for doing so."

"I loved you so much Harris--"

"And I broke your heart," he said, finishing my thought. "I'm so sorry Thalia." His voice cracked as he spoke. "Not a day goes by that I don't ask myself how I could have allowed anything to put your love for me at risk."

Reaching for my hand, Harris raised it to his chest. "I'm lost without it. I'm lost without *you*."

I closed my eyes. May God have mercy on my soul. Despite everything we'd been through, I still loved Harris Sifuentes in a way so strong it was all I could do to remember to take a breath in his presence.

"Never will I love another woman as hard or as deeply as I love you," Harris said, getting down on one knee. "Thalia, give me the privilege of loving you again and I won't let you down."

Once again, I'd found myself standing at the edge of the emotional cliff. And while I wasn't at all certain I could survive another heartbreak at Harris' hands, I was sure I didn't want to live another day of my life apart from the only man I'd ever loved.

"Promise me?"

Without blinking, Harris looked me straight in the eye. "I Promise."

And with those words, I took the leap, knowing in my heart that Harris would always be there to catch me.

GET RIGHT

Javaki Hilmon

Chapter One

*M*ontana sampled the chocolate Tuxedo strawberries, and the bottle of chilled Cristal that awaited her. In the intimate room lit with tea candles, she exhaled softly as she listened to the soothing sounds of her favorite Vivid Voices Nature-Volume 18 CD.

Leisurely, she slid out of her plush terry cloth robe, positioning herself face down on the table.

"Oh Pete, I'm in desperate need of your Grand Sampler."

"Tell Petey all about it," the man said with a familiar sigh.

"Planning for my wedding is going to be absolutely exhausting." Montana exhaled the tension from her body. "So many things to think about," she said, trying to sound as if orchestrating, and starring in, the wedding of the season would be a chore. "From picking the right caterer, to selecting a band...it's simply too much."

Pete chuckled as he searched the cabinets for the green tea oil Montana always insisted upon. "I know how hard it's going to be for you to spend so much money in so little time."

"Touché," Montana said, lifting herself up slightly from the table in order to take another sip of champagne. "You have no idea how much I needed you today."

Smiling, Pete lowered his hands to her bare back. "I'll have all that tension worked out of you in no time."

Montana smiled. "You always do."

Having been a VIP member of Oasis Spa for the past two years, Montana and her two best friends came in the second Friday of each month for a day of pampering and rejuvenation. It was a luxury well worth the expense.

A soft moan escaped Montana's lips as the warm oil spilled down the sides of her shoulders. Pete's hands were absolutely magical. If he wasn't so obviously gay, she might have been tempted to work her magic on him.

"I'll start with the Swedish and work my way to the Deep Tissue," Pete said, running his fingers gently along Montana's spine in long, vertical strokes.

"Wonderful," she cooed.

For the next hour, Montana fell in and out of sleep as Pete massaged, kneaded and prodded her willing body. The sound of clicking glasses jolted her into full consciousness. Reopening her eyes, Montana asked, "Are you heffas trying to steal my champagne?"

"No," Tracy and Lisa lied in perfect unison.

"Liars," Montana said with a sleepy chuckle.

"You're all set, Love," Pete said, swatting her gently on the rear.

Montana exhaled, luxuriantly. "Thank you, Darling."

"From the look on your face I can tell the massage was excellent," Lisa said, taking a seat in the chair.

"That Pete is indeed a master with his hands," Tracy said with a devilish grin.

"Is he ever," Montana said, extending her neck to stretch her newly refreshed muscles. "I wish I could have him work me over every day."

"Don't let David hear you say that," Lisa said, devouring the last of the strawberries. "You know how he gets."

"You ladies just come up in here and make yourself at home," Montana said, smirking as Tracy licked the chocolate from her fingers.

"We're all like sisters in here," Lisa said, winking at her. "Share and share alike."

"So long as that *sharing* doesn't involve a man," Montana chuckled as she climbed down from the table, "what's mine is yours."

Lisa snapped her fingers. "I know that's right."

"I'm all for the sisterhood," Montana said, reaching for her robe. "But I ain't no fool."

She loved her two best friends, but Lisa and Tracy were still women, and as such they could never be trusted completely. Having shared an apartment with Lisa their junior and senior years at UNLV, Montana knew the girl was capable of doing some downright raggedy shit to get what, or who, she wanted. It was the main reason Montana had befriended her in the first place. With her long hair, longer legs, and blemish-free café au lait skin, Lisa strutted around campus like she was the baddest bitch. When Tracy transferred in from community college, Montana and Lisa took quick notice of the 5'10" stunner, who could pass for Lisa's sister, quickly deciding to invite her into the clique. While not nearly as enterprising as Montana and Lisa, Tracy was smarter than her Betty Boop appearance suggested.

"It's time for a severely past due exfoliation," Montana said, spying her reflection in the mirror. A dark-skinned beauty with a perfect coke bottle figure, she took great care in maintaining her appearance. Her very livelihood depended on it. Without a job to speak of, unless you counted the fifteen hours she offered volunteering marketing services to the local United Way office, Montana's financial well being was in direct relation to her ability to catch and keep a man's eye.

"Good God," Montana said, studying her face intently. "Look at these pores?"

"What's that?" Lisa asked, pointing at Montana's hand.

"What's what?" Montana asked, playing dumb.

Lisa cut her eyes. "I know he didn't ask you to marry him."

Montana smiled coyly, but didn't say a word.

"Heffa, you better say something!" Lisa demanded.

"Well..." Montana, said pausing to make the moment more dramatic.

Tracy and Lisa both leaned in. "Well?" they asked in one eager voice.

"I'm getting married!" Montana squealed.

"Oh my God!" Tracy squealed back. "I can't believe you didn't tell us."

"I was going to, but you vultures attacked me before I could get it out," Montana said, staring down at the diamond that covered nearly three of her slender fingers.

"You lucky bitch," Lisa said with a tinge of jealousy in her voice.

Montana flashed her envious girlfriend a cool grin. "I am, aren't I?"

Since their college days she and Lisa had been quietly competing against one another for gold-digger supremacy. It was all Montana could do not to jump off a bridge when Lisa beat her to the altar by marrying former NBA player/part-time actor Robert Foxworth. With her impending nuptials to David, a man both disgustingly rich, and white – Montana was once again in the lead.

"I'm so happy for you," Tracy said, and actually meant it.

Montana held court on the dark blue velvet loveseat while Tracy and Lisa sat like obedient children on either side of her.

"Remember I told you that David was taking me on a midnight cruise on the yacht last night?"

Both women nodded in unison.

"Well, it wasn't just to show me how to sail," Montana said, winking at her captive audience. "After a beautiful candlelit dinner, catered by the one and only Chef Pascal..."

Lisa's eye twitched, but she maintained the forced smile on her face as Montana continued.

"David got down on one knee, and asked me if I would do him the honor of accepting his hand in marriage," Montana said, blushing at the slightly exaggerated memory. She waved her hand in the air. "Then, he slipped this puppy on my finger."

"That's got to be the biggest engagement diamond, I've ever seen," Tracy said impressed.

"The whole evening was absolutely perfect," Montana said, not bothering to add that she'd threatened to leave David if he hadn't popped the question by Thanksgiving. "Like a fairytale really."

"Sounds like it," Lisa said.

"We're so happy for you," Tracy said sincerely. "Oooh! We have to go shopping for your wedding dress!"

Montana's smiled widened as she spied the look of utter envy on Lisa's face. "I was thinking something in pearl white."

"I'll call the planner that arranged my wedding a few years ago," Tracy offered.

Montana rose from the sofa. "Thanks, Sweetie," she said, making her way to the door. "Let's talk it over during our facials, shall we?"

Making their way into another room down the sterile white hall, the three women settled in the black, leather chairs.

"So how does it feel to *finally* be Mrs. Michaels?" Lisa asked.

"I'm still *Miss* James as of today," Montana answered, enjoying how poorly the color of *envious green* looked on Lisa.

"Oh please," Lisa said with a smirk. "You were Mrs. David Michaels the moment he bought you that Corvette."

"That car is so cool," Tracy said, turning to Montana. "Why don't you drive it anymore?"

"Perhaps because David bought her that shiny new Mercedes," Lisa said with an ironic chuckle.

Choke on it Bitch, Montana thought as she smiled at Lisa. Feeling every bit the diva that she was, the soon-to-be bride extended her chair back, awaiting her therapeutic steam.

An older woman stepped into the room, making her way over to Montana. "I see you have new blemish," she said, examining Montana's face. "We can fix."

"Pay special attention to the forehead and chin area, Geneva," Montana said. "I've been extra oily there lately."

"Of course," the woman replied.

"This is exactly what I needed," Tracy said, settling into her chair. "That husband of mine has been driving me crazy."

Montana fought the urge to add, "And is about the most boring, ill-shaped man I've ever met." Jonathan Morgan should wake up every morning kissing the ass of heaven for his good fortune. In a world that made sense, Montana believed there was no way in hell someone like Tracy would have married a geeky looking accountant of her own free will. With her looks, she could have easily scored a pro athlete, or rapper. One of Lisa's husband's former teammates had been trying to get with Tracy from the moment he first met her after a game at the Forum. But Miss Goody-Two-Shoes wasn't interested in the six foot seven mountain of muscle with big feet, and an even bigger income. God bless her, Tracy chose to follow her heart, instead of the money.

"Well my Robert has been especially good to me lately," Lisa said, desperate to retake the lead. "I don't think there's a greater man on earth."

When he's sober, that is, Montana thought to herself. On more than one occasion she'd been witness to the former Lakers' guard making a complete ass of himself. Last month, during the annual dinner for Big Brothers Big Sisters, the charity where Montana volunteered, Robert tripped down the stairs, landing face-first onto a tray of dirty dishes. The look on Lisa's mortified face was priceless. The whole thing would have been hilarious, had it not been so pathetic.

"No man's perfect," Montana said to Tracy, but for Lisa's benefit. "Not even David."

"Oh please," Lisa said disbelievingly. "What's not perfect about David? He's rich, gorgeous, smart, rich." She laughed. "Did I say rich already?"

Tracy chuckled through the green mask that covered her face. "I believe you did."

"Well it bears repeating," Lisa said, smiling at Montana. "I'm happy for you girl...really."

"Thanks," Montana said sincerely.

"I wish my husband was more like him," Lisa said, then caught herself. "Well, Robert is rich."

"Yea," Tracy said as the attendant raised her chair, "but he's getting one heck of a pot belly on him."

"You need to cut out all those home cooked meals, and make him take you out to dinner every once in a while," Montana said.

Lisa rolled her eyes. "Just because you can't cook--"

"Don't go there," Montana interrupted. "Our maid cooks very well, thank you."

"I've seen that so-called *maid*," Lisa said, giving Montana a teasing grin. "You might wanna make sure David's dinner is all that little hussy's serving up."

"The way I see it, if David's going to cheat on me with another woman, then he's going to cheat," Montana said with an unfazed shrug of her shoulders. "I refuse to spend my time keeping up with his comings and goings... especially if there's a sale at Macy's."

Lisa laughed. "Okay!"

The one thing Montana did better than anything else was spend money, more precisely David's money. For the protection of his multi-million dollar fortune, he'd recently placed her on a monthly allowance of ten thousand dollars.

"Ladies, you've got to try this...what's this called, Dear?" Lisa asked the young woman doing her facial.

"I'm giving you the Chromatic Face Lift Facial," the woman answered. "It adds moisture, balance, and skin reconditioning."

"Well, whatever it does, it feels delightful," Lisa said, closing her eyes. She moaned softly. "I feel twenty years younger already," she said, quickly adding, "shut up Tracy."

"What?" Tracy asked, feigning innocence.

"I don't know how I'd survive without these monthly retreats," Montana said with a sigh.

"You're all set Ma'am."

"Thank you, Geneva," Montana said, nodding to the attendant.

Rising from the chair, she sashayed over to the mirror to check out her freshly exfoliated face. "Gorgeous," she cooed.

Lisa stood to her feet. "Love thy self," she said, chuckling as she gathered up her things.

Tracy pouted as her facial came to an end. "It can't be time to go already?"

"You can stay," Montana said, heading for the door, "but I've got a new fiancé to get home to." Turning, she smiled at the three worker bees. "Wonderful job, ladies," she said. "We'll see you same time next month."

One of the clerks stood waiting for Montana as she stepped out into the hall. "Ms. James, may I speak with you for a moment?"

"Of course, John," Montana said, feeling fresh as morning dew. Her bright glow faded when she noticed the strained look on his face. "Is there a problem?"

"We're having a bit of trouble verifying your credit card information," he said apologetically.

Montana let out a small chuckle. "That's because I recently moved into my fiancé's mansion," she said, smoothly. "I don't think you have my new address on file."

"Of course," John said through a tight smile.

"I'll talk to you as soon as I'm dressed."

"Thank you Ms. James," he said, quickly backing out of her way.

Ignoring the questioning eyes of Tracy and Lisa, Montana strutted into the changing room.

"What was that all about," Lisa asked.

"Nothing at all," Montana said, slipping out of her robe. "They just need to get my new address."

As she dressed, Montana's calm gave way to uncertainty. Something in her gut warned of trouble on the horizon. Stepping into her pink Candies sneakers, she zipped up her duffle bag and made a b-line for the exit.

"Are you going to wait for us?" Lisa asked, hastily fastening her bra.

"Take your time," Montana said, opening the door. "I'll be at the front desk."

Rushing down the hall, Montana forced her lips into an easy-breezy smile. Never let them see you sweat was the motto she lived by.

"Hello Ms. James," the clerk said as she approached the front desk.

"Apparently, I need to update my information with you," Montana said, already bored with the mundane activity.

"Umm...yes," the clerk said, clearly nervous. "Perhaps another credit card--"

"You just need to input my new address," Montana said, interrupting.

Sliding the piece of paper across the countertop, she turned to leave. "I'll see you the same time next month."

"One moment please, Ms. James," the attendant said.

"What else do you need?" Montana said, failing miserably to hide her growing irritation with the overly-aggressive blonde.

The clerk matched Montana's cold tone. "We need to get another form of payment--"

"Excuse me," Montana said, about to tear the girl a new one. "Who in the hell do you think you're talking to like that?"

"What's going on?" Lisa asked, rushing toward the counter.

"The credit card we have on file for you won't accept the charges," the clerk said stiffly.

"What's wrong?" Tracy asked as she approached.

"Nothing's wrong," Montana said, cutting her eyes at Lisa before she could utter a peep. Turning back to the clerk, she instructed, "Get your manager out here."

The clerk snatched up the receiver, whispering into it. Within seconds an older gentleman appeared from the back office.

Montana didn't give him a chance to say hello. "I don't appreciate being harassed by your staff," she said, aiming her finger at the clerk. "Don't think for a minute that I won't hesitate to take my business elsewhere if this kind of treatment continues."

"I assure you that it is no one's intent to harass you," the manager assured with rehearsed sincerity. "But as Becca stated," he said, glancing at the clerk standing beside him, "your credit card has been declined."

Lisa and Tracy exchanged pensive glances.

His lips forming into a pale smile, the manager looked Montana dead in the eyes. "We'll need another form of payment for today's services," he said, handing her a copy of the invoice that totaled just over twenty-five hundred dollars.

Montana slapped the bill onto the counter, then reached into her purse. Retrieving the black AMEX card, she tossed it at the clerk. "Try this."

Now beat red, Becca punched the numbers into the computer. A few moments later, she looked at Montana, pleased. "This card is also denied, Miss James."

Pissed beyond words, Montana sucked on her teeth. "I suggest you check your damn system." She cut her eyes to the manager. "Or get someone over here who can handle entering numbers correctly."

"Perhaps you have insufficient funds in your accounts," Becca said, showing her claws. "We do accept cash if you'd prefer."

Montana took a threatening step toward the snooty clerk. "I'd prefer to —"

Discreetly gripping her by the arm, Lisa whispered, "Down girl."

"Would you like to try another card?" the manager asked.

"I can't believe this shit!" Montana shouted at him. "You incompetent—!"

"Miss James," the manager said, shutting her down. "I'm going to have to insist that you calm down."

"Or what?" Montana asked.

"Could you just bill her for today?" Lisa asked, trying to diffuse the situation. "Until she can straighten out the confusion with her credit card—"

"We billed Miss James for last month's services when her credit card company refused to accept the charges then," the manager said, not letting Lisa finish. "We'll either need a credit card that works...or cash."

"You've got to be fucking kidding---!"

Before Montana could finish the rant, Lisa pulled out her credit card, handing it to Becca. "Try this one."

"Hell no!" Montana barked, snatching Lisa's card out of the clerk's hands. "They are going to fix this mess, right here and now!"

"Let Lisa go ahead and take care of the bill," Tracy said, stroking Montana's trembling arm. "I'm sure one call to your credit card company will get this straightened out in a jiffy."

"Fine," Montana said, embarrassed. She turned on her heels. "I'll be outside."

Not stopping until she reached the parking lot, Montana fell back against the hood of David's Range Rover, unable to believe what she'd just been forced to endure. How dare they make it look like she couldn't afford to be at a place like Oasis? David could buy her the dump, if she'd wanted.

"Don't worry about it, girl," Lisa said as she and Tracy approached.

"I'm not worried," Montana said, trying to hide her growing fear that something was terribly wrong. "David will take care of this."

"I'm sure it's just a minor system glitch, or something," Tracy said, opening the passenger side door.

"Well my card worked fine," Lisa said, smugly.

"What are you trying to say?" Montana asked sharply.

Lisa didn't flinch. "I'm saying that you need to call the bank yourself, and not wait for David to handle it."

"The credit cards are all in his name, so he has to take care of it," Montana said, climbing into the driver's seat of a vehicle she didn't own. At that moment, it dawned on her just how few of the things in her shiny world of superficial thrills were in her name.

"Lisa, I'll get your money back to you by tomorrow."

"I'm not worried about the money," Lisa said, from the back seat.

"I'm just saying," Montana said. "I don't want you to think--"

"The only thing I think is that you should be handling your own money, not David," Lisa said. "You know men will spend and spend and not tell us anything until we check in behind them. They're like children that way."

"We have more than enough money to pay for things like this," Montana said. "I'm sure the bank made another of their many errors."

"Let's hope you're right," Lisa said, unconvinced.

Speeding down the highway, Montana struggled to keep her building anxiety in check. Lisa was right. She needed to know exactly what was going on with *David's* money, and she needed to know now.

Chapter Two

David stared down at the empty glass he'd been fondling for the last ten minutes. Taking a quick glance at his watch, he waved the waitress over.

"Yes handsome," she said with a wide, inviting smile. "What can I get you?"

"Give...me...a...doub...double shot of vodka," David said, his words slurred from the six drinks he'd already downed.

"Is that all?" she asked, bending down further so that he could get a closer look.

His eyes lingering on the server's more than ample breasts, David grinned. "Unless you're offering up something that's not on the menu."

Catching his none too subtle drift, the waitress winked. "You'd be surprised what you could get by being a good boy."

David let out a devilish chuckle. "We'll talk."

Once she was out of sight, he turned his attention back to the game. Counting up his few remaining poker chips, David took another look at his watch. It was three in the afternoon. He'd been at the poker table for almost four hours now, just long enough for him to free his wallet of close to a quarter of a million dollars. Having promised Montana that he'd be home at a decent hour tonight, he needed to make up his losses quickly. He'd recovered from greater deficits before. Sooner or later, Lady Luck had no choice but to smile in his direction.

Some people – including his own parents, who'd cut him off from the family's wealth five years earlier – would suggest that David Michaels had an addictive personality, best serviced by intensive therapy. David however chose to see his predilection for women, booze and games of chance as three interrelated hobbies that helped relieve his stress, not dangerous obsessions that could leave him broke and brokenhearted. He'd won – and lost -- millions letting it ride in some of Vegas' best casinos. For David, the combination of a big win, good liquor, and great pussy was one potent cocktail, indeed.

"Here you are, Cutie," the waitress said, brushing against him as she lowered the drink.

Licking his lips, David tossed a twenty on the table, then downed the hot liquor in one smooth gulp.

"I wish I were that glass of Vodka," the server cooed in his ear.

"Stick around," David said, turning back to the table, "You just might be."

Getting three-of-a-kind in hand on the flop, he could taste a full house in the making. Sliding a hundred grand worth of chips forward, David exhaled. "Luck be a lady tonight."

Standing at his side, the waitress watched the game unfold.

As the dealer flipped the turn card, David could feel his heart racing. He glanced at the pile of chips growing in the middle of the table as the bet was raised to one hundred and fifty thousand. With a single bet he could recover all of the money he'd lost today plus some pocket change.

"Your bet, Sir," the dealer said, looking at David.

"I'll raise," David said, tossing another hundred and fifty grand into the pile.

The two players in front of him folded on the spot. Tasting his pot of gold, David cut his eyes at the old man sitting across from him.

His face void of the slightest emotion, the remaining competitor, lowered his eyes to his cards. A hint of a smile formed on his lips. "I call," he said smoothly.

Sweat glistening on his reddened forehead, David took another long look at his cards. With three Kings and a Jack on the turn, this was the best hand he'd been dealt all day. Down to his last fifty thousand in chips, David knew he needed to turn things around quick. He was putting his faith in the cards he was holding, and that matching jack-on-the-river to do just that.

David steadied his breathing as the dealer tapped the table lightly before drawing the final card. He stared down at the seven of clubs, and happily called along with his competitor. Confidently, David lowered his three Kings onto the table. His heart quickly sank when he saw the straight draw of clubs in his competitors' hand. The old man high-fived his buddy as he collected the chips.

Luck was proving to be anything but a lady tonight.

"Let me get another one of these," David said, raising his empty glass to the waitress, still standing there.

"You got it," she said with an empathetic smile.

Rising from his chair, David shook the hands of a few players, buttoned his blazer, then made his way through the crowd surrounding the table. Approaching the gold bars behind which the cashier's cool smile beckoned, David pulled out the only credit card he hadn't pressed past the limit.

"Cash or casino chips, Mr. Michaels?"

"Chips," David replied, anxious to get back to the poker table before his seat was taken.

"Hey you!"

Turning, David did a double-take when he saw her standing there looking more than ready for action.

"Long time no see, Handsome," the woman said, hugging him in a way that made it clear they were more than friends. "I've missed you."

"It has been a while," David said, taking a step back in order to admire the fine sista. Oh how he did love black women. Just thinking about the special time he and the woman had spent together in one of the casino's hotel room's three weeks ago, made him hard as granite rock.

"I see you're still at it," she said, glancing over at the teller.

"What can I say," David said with an ironic chuckle, "I'm an addict."

"Not all addictions are so bad," she said, smiling as her eyes wandered to the bulge in his Armani slacks.

David's lips formed into a cocky grin. "Good point."

"You're all set, Mr. Michaels," the cashier said, handing him the tray holding his fifty thousand dollars in chips.

Breaking his gaze with the woman he'd already planned to bed tonight, David nodded to the cashier. "Thank you very much," he said, sliding a hundred dollar chip back to her.

"Thank you Mr. Michaels," the brunette said, beaming.

David tucked the tray under his arm, turning back to the bronzed beauty standing beside him.

"So what brings you back to the Sands?" David asked, trying to find out if she was here entertaining another man.

She pressed her body into his side and cooed, "I was hoping to run into you again."

"Really," David said, feeling his manhood straining against his thigh. "And why would you want to see a little old white boy like me again?"

"You're white," the woman said, her hands easing toward David's midsection, "but we both know you're anything but little."

A spark of energy shot up David's spine. After a rough afternoon at the tables, he was in desperate need of the release the freak, discreetly squeezing the tip of his Johnson, could provide.

"I'm feeling especially cagey tonight," she said, running her tongue slowly across her full lips. "If I remember correctly you're rather *energetic* in bed."

It took everything David had not to do her doggie-style right there in the casino as she brushed her lips across his earlobe.

"But, let's play a little first," the woman said, liberating five hundred dollars in chips from David's tray.

Tongue wagging, David followed the juicy piece of ass back into the gaming room.

"You're back," the waitress said, when she saw them approach.

David smiled as the two women exchanged cool looks. Settling into the chair he'd vacated not ten minutes earlier, he felt once again like a man at the top of his game.

"Bring out a bottle of Cristal for the little lady here," David said, wrapping his hand around the backside of his date.

"I guess your luck isn't so bad after all," the waitress said, coolly.

"Think she might want to play with us?" the woman asked, eyeing the server as she walked away.

David almost jumped out of his skin, but kept his poker face in tact. He had forgotten that the girl had shared with him that she was bisexual, and wouldn't be opposed to a ménage a trios...if the price was right, of course.

"Would you like that?' David asked.

"Very much," the woman said, taking another five hundred dollars worth of chips from the tray.

"Then consider it done—"

"I wouldn't be so confident if I were you," the waitress said, returning to the table with the champagne.

David grinned. "You heard?"

"I heard enough." The waitress lowered the glasses onto the table. "What makes you think I'd be interested in playing with the two of you?" she asked playfully.

"Because you're too smart...and too sexually charged to pass up a golden opportunity to have some great fun...and make a week's salary doing it," David said, his hand resting on the small of her back. "That's how."

David removed a handful of chips from the tray, placing them in the waitress' hand. "But you have to be willing to be and do anything I ask," he said carefully. "Can you do that for me?"

The waitress pondered for a moment, before, turning on her heels, "I'll be right back."

"Place your bets!" the dealer called out.

David snatched up a fistful of chips from his tray, handing them to the woman. "Why don't you go get us a room?" Swatting her across the rear, he returned his attention to the table.

"Welcome back Davey Boy," one of the other players said with a sly grin as he watched David's skimpily-clad companion slither away.

Once again focused on recouping some of his earlier losses, David gave the man a distracted nod. As the dealer dolled out two cards, he checked his watch. It was now half-past four. Montana probably wouldn't be returning from the spa for a while yet, giving him ample time to get in a few more hands, and get *inside* the two ladies.

His ten thousand in chips added to the pile, David picked up his two cards. Confident he could build on the pair of aces, he placed another ten thousand in the pot.

David took a careful breath as the next card was dealt. It wasn't his ace, but he was pretty sure the unsuited non-face cards on the table didn't help anyone else either.

"We're ready," two voices rang out simultaneously in each of his ears.

Looking first at the ladies, then down at cards, David weighed his options. As much as he loved what the looks on both of the women's faces promised there was no way he was getting up from the table with a hand like the one he was holding.

"Go ahead and get started without me," David said, taking a long sip of the champagne. "Daddy'll be up in a few."

"But we want you now," the woman said with a lusty pout.

"We could always do him right here," the waitress chimed in.

Impressed and terribly aroused by the server's newly acquired aggressiveness, David sat his cards down, turning to face them. "Just let me play out this hand...then I'm all yours."

Satisfied, both women nodded in agreement.

"Four of clubs," the dealer said, dealing out the last card.

"Check," the man next to David said, tapping his hand on the table.

David tapped the table to return the checked pot. He was sure his pair of aces would be enough.

"Damn it," David smarted as his competitor proudly placed his full house on the table.

"Tonight just isn't your night, Davey Boy."

"Not at the tables anyway," David said with a sigh.

"We'll make it all better," the woman said, urging him up from the table, but not before liberating the remaining few chips from his tray.

Standing, David tilted his none existent hat to the other players, then followed his two girls to the elevator. Going at it like mad banshees the entire four flights up, the threesome made their way to the suite at the end of the corridor.

Just as he stepped into the room, David felt the vibration of his cell against his waist. "Shh," he said, to the giggling women as he flipped it open. "Hey you."

"David," Montana said with a hint of stress in her voice. "How's work going?"

"It's work," David said, biting his bottom lip as the woman lowered to her knees before him. "Are...umm...you...you enjoying your retreat with the girls?" he asked, trying not to lose it as his stiff penis was released from his slacks.

"Ooh, shit," David moaned, as the woman took him into her mouth polishing his pole like the consummate pro. The waitress licked her lips as she stood there watching.

"What's wrong?" Montana asked.

David winced. "Nothing baby," he said, straining. "I just hit my leg against the desk...umm listen, I...I gotta get to a meeting...see you at home."

Before Montana could respond, David flipped the phone closed, tossing it on the dresser. Motioning for the waitress to join in, he struggled out of his wrinkled blazer, dropping it haphazardly to the floor.

Pulling the woman to her feet, David slid down the straps of her rhinestone cocktail dress. "Let me play with those big-puppies," he said, groping her breast as if they belonged to him. Snatching the waitress by the hair, he pulled her to her feet.

"Get on the bed," David instructed them both.

The women did as they were told.

"Don't just sit there," David said roughly. "Kiss each other."

While the women got to know each other better, David made his way over to the bar, pouring himself a glass of Grey Goose. Heading back over to the bed, he pulled up a chair and watched the now naked twosome as they rolled around on the king size bed.

Resurfacing from deep between the waitress' quaking legs, the woman looked over at David, stroking himself as he sipped on his drink. "Don't be stingy," she said, licking her tongue as she eyed his penis. "We want to play with it too."

Rising from the chair, David unbuttoned his dress shirt, laying the diamond-studded cufflinks Montana had given him for his birthday on the table. He slipped out of his slacks and underwear, then headed over to the bed.

Stopping short, David snapped his fingers. "Condoms," he said, doubling back over to the pile of clothes on the floor.

Retrieving the Trojan from his pocket, he made his way back to the bed. "Ready or not here I come!"

Chapter Three

"*S*peed up you ass-wipe!" Montana yelled out the window as she zipped past the compact car. Pressing her foot down on the accelerator, she increased her speed, desperate to make up some lost time in the bumper-to-bumper traffic. Weaving in and out of lanes, she glanced at the clock rolling her eyes in complete irritation. If she didn't hurry, the bank was going to close before she could get answers.

Cutting across four lanes, Montana exited from the freeway. At this time of day, her best shot of getting anywhere fast was by taking the surface roads. Driving like a bat out of hell, she raced down the intersection, barely avoiding drivers not smart enough to simply give her the road.

Her pulse racing, she held onto the steering wheel with one hand, retrieving the cell from her purse with the other.

"Somebody's going to tell me what the hell is up, I know that much," Montana said, fuming as she speed dialed David's office.

Blowing a frustrated breath through her lips, she pressed the END button, then speed dialed her MIA fiancé's cell.

"Where the fuck are you, David Michaels?" Montana glared at nothing in particular. "Answer the phone....hey yourself," she said, relieved when he finally picked up. "Listen, something weird happened at the spa...David...David...are you okay?" She asked when she heard the sound of his moan. "What did you do?"

While the guttural sound he made sounded more pleasure than pain, Montana accepted David's explanation that he'd hit his leg against the table. "I'm sorry about that," she said hastily. "As I was saying, I went..."

Hesitating, Montana's brow lifted in suspicion. "What are you doing, David? Fine...bye," she said, tossing the cell onto the passenger seat.

Taking her eyes off the road for only a moment, she squealed when she glanced up to see the black blur flying in her direction.

"Son of a bitch!" Montana shouted at what looked to be a tire continued barreling toward her head-on.

Panicked, she hit the horn with her hand as if doing so would cause the giant piece of rubber to change course. When it didn't, Montana gripped the steering wheel tightly, swerving the Range

Rover off the highway, shutting her eyes as the truck came to a stop only inches shy of the railing that separated her and the mountainside.

Slowly Montana reopened her eyes. "Sweet Jesus," she said, clutching her chest. "That was close."

Bringing his beat up pick-up to a screeching halt, the overall-clad man jumped out, running toward Montana's SUV.

"What the fuck is wrong with you?" she asked, glaring at him through the opened window. "You almost killed me?"

The man took a step back as Montana opened the door and got out. "I'm very sorry about that," he said, apologetically. "Are you all right?"

"No thanks to you," she said, snappishly. Making her way around to the front of the Range Rover, she checked for damage. Thankfully, there was none.

"Ma'am I'm really sorry," the man said, retrieving his tire. "The tailgate lock must have—"

"Spare me," Montana said, cutting him off.

"I'm really sorry about this," he said, studying her intently.

Montana folded her arms across her chest defensively. "Yes?"

"Anybody ever tell you how much you look like that supermodel?" the man asked, resting the tire up against his leg.

Her eyes rolling back in her head, Montana snarled, "Look Mister—"

"The name's Richard," he said, flashing a set of the whitest teeth Montana had seen in her entire life. "But my friends call me Red."

"Look Mister Richard," Montana said uninterested in making a friend. "I strongly suggest you learn how to keep your tire in your truck...where it belongs."

"I plan to do just that," Red said with a sly grin. "Until I find a better place to store it, that is."

Montana smirked as she watched him toss the rubber onto the back of his pickup. Even in oil-stained overalls, the fair-skinned brotha wasn't anything near hard on the eyes. While she had no doubt that many a woman would happily drop her drawers for the attention of his curly headed, bedroom-eyed, hands the size of boulders self, Montana was immune to Red's blue-collar charm. Okay, that wasn't entirely true. But it didn't matter. She was engaged to another, *wealthier* man.

Red double-checked the lock on the tailgate, then turned around to face Montana. "Why do you keep looking at me like that?" she asked annoyed.

"Because you're an exquisitely beautiful woman."

Blushing despite herself, Montana guffawed. "Whatever."

"You really do remind me a little of that supermodel. What's her name," Red said snapping his fingers. "Naomi—"

The smile on Montana's face morphed into a frown. "Campbell?" she asked, looking at him like he'd just called her out of her name. "I'm not nearly as dark as she is."

Red gave her a curious look, but kept his thoughts to himself.

"It's been real," Montana said, turning on her heels, "But, I have someplace I need to be."

Opening the door for her, Red smiled. "Drive safe."

Montana couldn't help but smile back. "And you try not to kill anyone," she said, starting the engine.

"Goodbye, Mrs.?"

"It's Montana," she said, then sped off.

Five minutes later she pulled into the Bank One parking lot. Once inside, Montana quickly pushed her way to the very front of one of the long lines.

"Excuse me," she said, elbowing the man standing at the teller's window, "but I need to speak with someone about my account."

The man gave her a *so what* look.

"It's important," Montana said, planting herself in front of him.

Cutting her eyes, the teller said, "Ma'am, I'm sorry but you'll have to wait--"

"I need to speak with someone immediately about my account," Montana said interrupting.

"As does everyone else standing behind you," the teller said, motioning toward the crowd of people waiting their turn for service. "And like them, you're going to have to get in line."

Montana didn't move.

"Ma'am I'm sorry but you have to get in line," the teller repeated.

Her hand rising to her hip, Montana glared at the bank employee. "Obviously, you don't know who I am."

"No, I don't," the teller said. "But you still have to wait in line. It's only fair to the other customers who are being courteous enough to do the same."

"Get your manager out here...*now*." Montana said, done dealing with the little people. The moment felt strangely reminiscent of her earlier encounter with the snooty clerk at the spa.

Leisurely, the teller picked up the phone. Moments later a uniformed officer approached Montana.

"What seems to be the problem, Miss?"

Montana turned to the guard. "Are you here to escort me out for causing a fuss?"

"I'm just here to make sure that everything is okay."

"How 'bout you make yourself useful then," Montana said, giving him a fake smile, "and go fetch me a manager."

"I'm sorry but I can't do that," the guard said, his jaw tensing. "If you need to speak with someone, then you can just wait in line for the next available teller."

Just then, an older woman approached. "Hello, I'm Mrs. Reynolds."

"Are you the manager?" Montana asked.

"Yes, I am," the woman said, motioning for Montana to follow her. "If you'll come with me, I'll see what I can do to assist you today."

"Gladly," Montana said, giving the teller an arrogant smile.

Once in her office, Mrs. Reynolds took a seat behind the desk. "What can I help you with?"

Montana sat down in the empty chair, crossing her legs. "I need you to look up the account of a Mr. David Michaels please," she said, trying to sound above it all. "There seems to be some kind of error that the bank has made with our credit cards, and I need it resolved immediately."

"The account isn't in your name?" Mrs. Reynolds asked with a curious eye.

"David Michaels is my fiancé," Montana said, placing her credit card and driver's license on the desk. "I assure you he won't mind your giving me information about *our* account."

"Well I'm sorry Miss...?"

"James."

"Ms. James, we need the authorization from the primary account holder before we can release any information."

"I'm sure I am listed on the account," Montana said, holding up the plastic. "Otherwise I wouldn't have this card. Now please tell me what's going on with the account."

"We'll need authorization from the primary account holder before we can release any information," Mrs. Reynolds' repeated.

Montana rolled her eyes at the unhelpful manager. "Do you realize how much money my fiancé and I have sitting in this bank?" she asked snappishly.

"I'm sorry Ms. James," Mrs. Reynolds said, towing the company line. "But there are strict rules in place for the protection of our customers that prevent me from giving you any information about Mr. Michaels' account."

"So you're telling me that I can't find out what's going on with my own account?" Montana asked, infuriated.

"If you were, in fact the primary account holder, then it would be my pleasure to afford you access."

Reaching into her desk the manager pulled out some forms. "If Mr. Michaels would like to give you full access to *his* account," she said handing the papers to Montana, "he can fill—"

"My name isn't listed anywhere on the account?" Montana asked, not accepting the forms.

Mrs. Reynolds turned to her computer. "It appears your name is listed..."

An arrogant smile began to spread across Montana's face.

"As a secondary card holder."

"Meaning?" Montana asked with a raised brow.

"Meaning you don't hold any rights to the account itself, or the funds therein," Mrs. Reynolds said. "Your access to Mr. Michaels' account begins and ends with the use of the credit card you're holding in your hand."

Montana fell back in her seat, mortified, and pissed beyond words.

"I'm sorry but there is really nothing more I can do without Mr. Michaels present," Mrs. Reynolds said, rising from her chair.

Not getting up, Montana took a slow calming breath. "Mrs. Reynolds I've had a very long day, and I really don't want to be any trouble," she said, eyeing the manager intently, "but if you refuse to be more helpful, I will insist to my fiancé that we move *our* account elsewhere."

Carefully considering her options, Mrs. Reynolds sat back down at her desk. "Is there any way we can contact Mr. Michaels?"

Montana reached into her purse. "The top number is David's direct line," she said, handing the woman the business card.

Mrs. Reynolds dialed the number, lifting the receiver to her ear.

Her heart threatening to pound right out of her chest, Montana clutched the edges of the chair praying the fault belonged to the bank, and not David.

"He's not answering at this number," Mrs. Reynolds said, lowering the phone. She studied Montana carefully, rightly sensing she was at her wits end. "I'll tell you what you can do."

"And what can *I* possibly do that *you* can't?" Montana wanted to ask. "What's that?" she asked instead.

"Place that credit card into our ATM and enter your personal pin number," Mrs. Reynolds instructed. "You'll only get an account balance, but it's better than nothing." Mouthing a weak thank you to the manager, Montana exited the office, racing toward the ATM at the front entrance of the bank. While she would have preferred to find out where – or to whom – her money had gone, she'd settle for knowing how much of it actually remained.

When she spied the number that flashed on the screen, Montana almost fainted. How in the hell was it possible that only five hundred dollars remained in the account? From her periodic snooping through David's records, she knew for a fact that the account had housed over five hundred thousand dollars not three weeks ago.

Taking another look at the screen, Montana's eyes formed into angry slits.

"David, what the hell have you done, now?"

Chapter Four

*S*tanding barefoot on the cool wooden deck, Montana stared up at the clear evening sky, then exhaled a weak sigh. It was after eight' o'clock and David still hadn't come home from work, or wherever it was he'd been all afternoon.

Montana thought about just how *not* unusual it was for her to be having dinner alone, then sit for hours wondering what her man was up to while he was away from her. Sooner, than later, something would have to give.

Taking a seat in the reclining lawn chair, Montana lit a cigarette. She picked up the remote from the glass table, pointing it into the house she shared with David. As the sound of smooth jazz floated onto the deck, she reached for the phone sitting beside her. Tonight, she needed a friend.

"Hey girl," Tracy said, the instant she picked up.

"Hey yourself," Montana said, blowing out a white cloud of smoke.

"Are you smoking?" Tracy asked.

"Umm hmm," Montana said, taking another long drag of her Newport 100.

"I know what that means," Tracy said.

Montana rolled her eyes. "I'm getting tired of his shit Tracy. At first I liked the time to myself that David's little disappearances afforded me, but now..." Her voice trailed off.

"Did you find out what was going on with your bank?"

"Other than the fact that there's only five-hundred dollars in the account," Montana said bitterly. "No, and that asshole David has yet to show his face, so I can't get any answers out of him."

Tracy grunted. "He'll...umm...show up."

"Please tell me you are not taking a shit while you're on the phone with me?" Montana asked, turning up her nose.

"I don't know what it is," Tracy said with an embarrassed giggle. "But sometimes talking to you makes me have to use the no-no."

Montana laughed. "The no-no?"

"Don't make fun," Tracy said laughing as well. "What are you going to say to David?"

Montana exhaled. "I'm going to ask him where the hell my...*our* money is."

"That's as good a place as any to start," Tracy said.

"There is one other thing I learned today," Montana said, rising from the chair.

"What's that?" Tracy said.

"David didn't have my name added to the account like he'd promised to do six months ago," Montana said with a hard roll of the eyes, "which means I don't have access to shit."

"Wow," Tracy said, then waited a beat. "So how did you find out the money was gone?"

"After I cursed out everybody in the bank, I finally went to the ATM to check the balance," Montana said. "I damn near fainted."

"I'm sure David will have a rational explanation," Tracy said, trying to reassure.

"If he ever finds his way home," Montana said, darkly. "Something ain't right Tracy...I can feel it in my gut. I bet you that pale motherfucka is back to gambling again--"

"Tana, don't jump to conclusions about David just yet," Tracy said. "He's innocent until proven guilty."

"David is anything, but innocent."

"Do you think he's cheating?"

Montana did a double-take at the phone. This wasn't the first time Tracy had asked that question. "David knows he's got the best thing going right here," she said smugly. "If he's stupid enough to go sniffing elsewhere he can be my guest."

"You don't care if he is seeing someone else?" Tracy asked skeptically.

"Right now I'm far more concerned about David's shrinking finances than his fucking some other chick," Montana said, flicking the cigarette butt over the railing. "Listen, I need to go. I'll check in with you tomorrow."

"Okay," Tracy said. "Everything's going to be—"

Montana hit the END call button before Tracy had finished talking.

Heading back inside, she snatched up her keys from the counter, and marched to the front door. She needed to get away from this house. A nice long drive might help to clear her head.

Hopping into her black Mercedes SL500, Montana let down the top, then sped off into the Las Vegas night. Sinking into the dark leather seat, she turned up the volume on the stereo. She was about to get onto the freeway, but the blinking yellow light on her dash board, suggested she get some gas first.

Pulling into the first service station she saw, Montana snatched up her purse and stepped out of the car. Moving briskly, she entered the building, making her way over to the counter.

"Twenty please," Montana said, handing the male cashier a fifty dollar bill. "And correct change."

"On what pump?" the man asked, ignoring the suggestion that he was shady.

"The one where you see a car," Montana said condescendingly.

"The Mercedes?"

Montana didn't bother answering.

"Nice car," he said with a smile. "My brother has one just like that."

"I'm sure he does," Montana said, staring out at her vehicle to make sure it was still there. Noticing the truck pulling up to the pump next to hers, she turned back to the clerk.

"He's cool," he said, reading the concern on her face. "Red is—"

"Whatever," Montana said, snatching the thirty dollars out of the clerk's hand.

"You enjoy the rest of your evening," he called out to her back as she strutted out.

Approaching her car, Montana tightened her grip around the pepper spray in her purse. Careful not to make eye contact with the man, she reached for the nozzle.

"Good evening to you, Ma'am," he said with a respectful nod.

Ready to tell the bothersome stranger to kiss her ass, Montana snapped her head in his direction, stopping short when she saw the familiar wide smile.

"Hey, Pretty Lady," the man said, recognizing her. "Long time no see."

"I'm sure we don't know each other," Montana said, continuing to pump her own gas.

"I must be losing my touch," the man said with a chuckle that assured he didn't believe his own words. "You've forgotten me in less than four hours."

Montana turned her head back in his direction, giving him a visual once-over. Making a mental note of how good his hair-dusted chest looked peeking out from the wife beater, she said in a bored monotone, "Tire boy."

"The name's Red," he said with a smile.

Recalling that the clerk had just called him by the same name, Montana now wished she'd listened to the back story.

"But you can call me anything you'd like," Red said, retrieving a card from his pocket. Writing his cell number on the back, he handed it to Montana. "Just so long as you call."

Montana fought against the urge to smile. She had to give him credit for being smooth. "I'm engaged."

"Good for you," Red said.

"Take your card please," Montana said, extending it toward him.

Red settled his sexy sleepy eyes on hers. "Why don't you hang on to that...just in case."

"Just in case, what?" Montana asked smoothly, "Hell freezes over?"

"Stranger things have happened."

"Fine," Montana said, dropping the card haphazardly into her purse. Starting to enjoy the give and take with Red more than any engaged woman should, she returned to the pump, and headed around to the driver's side door.

"I look forward to talking more with you," Red said, his easy confidence both annoying, and wildly attractive.

"Don't hold your breath," Montana said, shutting the door. Eyeing Red in the rear-view mirror as she left him in the dust, she chuckled to herself. "That man's gonna give some woman the flux."

Chapter Five

*M*ontana was still smiling from her second encounter with Red as she pulled into the valet parking structure of the Sands Casino. Coming to a stop, she removed the key from the ignition, her smile morphing into a frown as she reached for her purse on the passenger seat. Thanks to David, she only had thirty dollars to her name. Hopefully a few rounds with the one armed bandit inside would not only improve her mood, but her financial bottom line as well.

After smoothing out her bone-straight weave – that fell to the center of her back -- Montana got out of the car. Unclenching her jaw, she walked toward the elevator, determined not to let her David completely ruin her Friday night. The thought of him returning home to find her gone pleased her greatly. Rattling around in that big place all by his lonesome might help him appreciate how she felt on the many occasions she'd sat alone, staring at the front door, waiting and wondering.

Stepping into one of the gaming rooms, Montana squinted as her eyes adjusted to the lights. The place was packed with people, and the nearly naked waitresses were busting their ample asses to ensure that each of them got nice and drunk. Carefully maneuvering her way through the crowds, she headed for the cashier station to exchange what little cash she had for casino chips. For the next few hours anyway, Montana was going to live as if she didn't have a care in the world.

"Montana?" a female voice yelled out.

Turning slowly, Montana tried not to grimace when she saw the woman approaching. "Hello Sharon, you back-stabbing, two-faced, man stealing, stank bitch," she wanted to say. "Hey girl," she said instead.

Acting as if she wasn't the woman who'd slept with Montana's football star boyfriend their junior year of college, Sharon gave Montana an enthusiastic -- and two-seconds longer than it needed to be -- hug. "You lookin' good."

"Thanks," Montana said, maintaining her plastic smile. Of all the nights to walk out of her house wearing something as unflattering as a crewneck t-shirt and black driving shoes, she had to pick the one when she'd run into her old college rival. Fortunately, Sharon looked like shit warmed over as well. "You...you look good too."

"Well, thank you," Sharon said, buying the lie. "I do what I can."

Montana studied her old *friend* barely able to maintain her balance in the six-inch come- fuck-me stiletto heeled pumps she was wearing. With her porn-star ass, and clearly store-bought D-cups, spilling over the low-cut, too-sizes-too-tight red rhinestone dress, Sharon looked like a call girl, two years past her prime.

"What brings you out to this damned-to-hell place tonight?"

Certainly not the same thing that brings you here, Montana thought. While still an attractive woman, years of hard living, and way too much sexing had taken its toll on Sharon.   "Was bored, so I decided to come on down here and waste a little cash, is all."

"I hear that, Girl," Sharon said, invading Montana's personal space big-time. "I've already lost a few thousand myself."

"A few thousand?" Montana cringed. "That's gotta hurt."

"Well, when it's somebody else's money," Sharon said, offering a sly grin. "It takes some of the sting out of it."

"Somehow I don't think you're referring to your husband," Montana said sardonically.

"Husband!" Sharon said, missing the insult. "Girl please, I am far from married...you wouldn't happen to have a cigarette would you?"

"Uh, yeah," Montana said, reaching into her purse, retrieving her last cigarette. "Here you go."

"I've been jonesing for one of these bad boys since I finished..." Sharon said, catching herself. Chuckling, she lit the cigarette and took a long drag. "Got me this little white boy, I spend time with every now and again," she said as if proud. "He's not hard on the eyes, and he ain't stingy with the money."

Montana listened, stunned and a bit amused as she realized that Sharon was whoring. The skanky heffa who had caused her many a sleepless night back at UNLV was now an honest to goodness whore. And, not some high-class call girl either. Sharon was a bottom of the line, fishnet stocking wearing hoe.

"He's still around here somewhere," Sharon said, brightening as the idea formed in her clouded little head. "Let me go find him and see what he's got left. He's a big trick girlfriend."

"A trick?" Montana said, ignorant to whore lingo.

Sharon rubbed her thumb over her fingers to signal his large bankroll.

"No, that's okay," Montana said, trying not to show her disgust. "I'm not really in the mood to spend time with some old geezer on the off chance he might toss me a few dollars."

"He's far from an old geezer," Sharon said, proudly. "And trust me, with this guy you can get more than a few bucks. He loves dark-skinned black girls like you most."

Montana had heard about as much as she needed to hear about Sharon's chosen vocation. It was time to say goodbye, and good riddance.

"Thank you for the compliment," Montana said dryly. Lifting her left hand to ensure Sharon got a good look, she smiled smugly. "I'm engaged."

"What?" Sharon squealed in surprise. "Who's the lucky fuck?"

Montana demurred. "I doubt if you know him--"

"Wait," Sharon interrupted. "Don't tell me you and old Donald Haines from college got back together after all these years."

"No we never got back together," Montana said tightly. "I couldn't bring myself to forgive him for fucking another *bitch* behind my back."

Sharon gave Montana a guilty grin. "You know he was just something to do, Girl."

"Of course he was," Montana said.

"I was so pissed when I saw that that Negro wasn't packin' like I'd heard he was," Sharon said, rolling her eyes. "He was a total waste of all my time..."

Montana smirked. She could have told Sharon that and saved her the trouble.

"But this guy I've hooked tonight," Sharon said, returning to the business at hand. "This dude's got a monster in his pants...and I'm not talking about his wallet."

"How wonderful," Montana said, desperate to get away from this woman. "I need to get going. It was nice seeing you again."

"Wait," Sharon said, reaching for her arm. "Aren't you gonna tell me who you're marrying?"

"So you can fuck him too?" Montana asked rhetorically. "Not a chance."

"To tell the truth," Sharon said, leaning closer. "I'd rather fuck you."

Montana's jaw fell to the carpet.

Sharon licked her lips. "But you're probably still too square to have any fun."

"I beg your pardon?" Montana asked aghast. "I'm far from square, Sweetheart. I'm just strictly dickly."

"Of course you are," Sharon said, with a disbelieving grin. "Well, it was wonderful seeing you again, Beautiful."

"Likewise," Montana said, but didn't mean it.

Sharon reached into her purse. "Here's my number..."

Oh snap! Montana thought as Sharon handed her the card. *Hoe's have business cards!*

"Give me a ring so that we can make up for lost times..." Sharon said, stopping short, when she saw her john. "Oh there he is!" she squealed, waving at the man staggering toward them. "Davey Boy, come here. I want you to meet my girl."

"I really need to get going--" Montana said.

"No wait," Sharon said, thwarting her getaway. "It'll only take a second."

Exhaling a bored sigh, Montana turned to face the high-roller Sharon was so desperate for her to meet. Her heart dropped.

"This is Dave," Sharon said, introducing the two.

David's mouth fell open when he saw Montana. His hands visibly shaking, he took a nervous sip of his drink, discreetly dropping his other hand from where it rested on Sharon's lower back.

Not uttering a word, Montana dressed him down with her burning eyes. David looked a damned mess. His tie was gone, the top three buttons on his wrinkled shirt were undone underneath his open blazer, and his pants hung low on his waist. His eyes bloodshot and glazed, it was clear that he'd been drinking like a fish.

Looking like a boy caught with his hand in the cookie jar, David placed more distance between himself and Sharon.

Sharon watched the two curiously. "Did I miss something?"

"Not at all," Montana said, finally taking her eyes off David. She turned to Sharon. "You said his name was Dave?"

"Yes it is," Sharon said, reaching for his hand.

David snatched away from her.

"Is something the matter, Baby?" Sharon asked.

David didn't say a word.

"It's very nice to meet you," Montana said, extending her hand to him. "I've heard so much about you."

Looking as if he was about to collapse, David wiped his forehead with the sleeve of his designer shirt.

"Davey Boy, what's wrong--?"

"Don't call me that!" David barked at his whore.

Sharon drew back. She looked over at Montana, who was glaring at David. "What's going on here?" she asked, becoming irritated. "Do you two know each other?"

"No we don't know each other at all," Montana said, shaking her head. "I have to get going Sharon." It took everything she had to keep her anger in check. "You two enjoy the rest of the night."

"Good to see you again!" Sharon called out as Montana marched away from them.

Montana had barely made it to her car before the tears started to fall from her eyes. She couldn't believe what she'd just witnessed. In an instant, things had gone from bad to worse.

The bright lights of the casino in the distance, she drove as fast as she could to no place in particular. She wanted to crawl into bed and cry, but didn't dare go home. Alone and utterly brokenhearted, Montana searched her mind for an answer.

Wiping her eyes, she reached into her purse, removing the card Red had given her. Studying it carefully, a pale smile formed on her face. In addition to being too charming for his own good, Red was also the proprietor of the gas station she'd visited earlier tonight.

"Red's Gas and Collision," Montana said, flipping the card over. "Well, all right for you."

As impressed as she was to learn Red was more than a worker-bee, did she dare turn to him, a complete stranger for comfort? She needed someone. Lisa and Tracy would take her call, but neither would be able to offer Montana the non-judgmental shoulder on which she so desperately needed to cry.

Montana tossed the card onto the passenger seat.

I can't call a man I don't even know. He might be crazy.

From the corner of her eyes, Montana spied the card.

But what do I really know about anybody? Hell, the man I'm sleeping with is buying the services of prostitutes.

Scooping up the card, Montana dialed the cell phone number Red had written on the back. Taking a deep breath, she waited for the call to connect. After the fourth ring, she was ready to give up.

Just as she lifted her finger to tap the END button, he answered.

"This is Red."

Montana swallowed nervously. "Hi."

Chapter Six

*M*ontana was nervous, but it was too late to turn back now. Smoothing out her curve-hugging red dress, she took a deep breath, then walked inside the small, dimly-lit hole in the wall. The place was nothing like the swank environments she was used to. Still, it was more than she'd expected. There was a bar in the center of the room with several small tables and a few private booths surrounding it. The large plasma screen televisions in each corner were the only quasi luxury items to be found in the joint.

Maneuvering carefully around the cigarette butts and unidentifiable substances on the floor, Montana took a seat at the far end of the room, just as Red walked in. A broad smile spreading across his face, he almost tripped over himself making his way to the table.

"I'm so sorry I'm late," he said, wiping his hand on his jeans before extending it toward Montana. "I couldn't find anything to wear."

"You look just fine," Montana said, trying not to stare at Red as he settled into the chair. He looked so much different than the man she'd remembered seeing only yesterday. His dark gray jacket covered a surprisingly clean and neatly pressed dress shirt. The curly locks really did compliment his caramel-complected face. And from what she could make out of it, Red was in excellent physical shape. While she wouldn't have chosen them, the well-worn jeans were working on him as well.

Taking Montana's hand, Red kissed it softly. "You look stunning," he said, his eyes smiling into hers.

Montana blushed. "Thank you."

"You really are a beautiful woman..." Red said, pausing as if he was trying to pull the perfect words from the depths of his soul. "Almost ethereal."

Usually Montana didn't allow such dribble to set her pulse racing, but coming from Red's sexy-assed lips, she bought it.

Lowering her eyes to the menu, Montana prayed that the heat this man was inspiring in her wasn't visibly evident.

"You're not hungry so I don't know why you're looking at that menu so intently," Red said, reading Montana's dirty thoughts.

I should not be finding this brotha so damn sexy, Montana thought as she sat there squirming in her seat. "A couple of hours talking to me on the phone, and already you think you know me," she said, trying to play it cool.

"It was four hours actually," Red said. "And you'd be surprised how much one can learn about someone by simply listening."

Montana sighed. "I'll give you that."

Red chuckled. "How nice of you."

"Whatever," Montana said, blushing once again. "So tell me more about you."

"Let's see," Red said, settling back in the chair. "I told you about my tour of duty during the Gulf War, right?"

Montana nodded.

"And, how when my mom got sick I returned home to help out instead of reenlisting," Red said, staring off into the middle distance. "I'm glad I did..."

Thoroughly mesmerized, Montana listened intently as he spoke.

"Six months later she was gone..." Red said, struggling not to get choked up.

Reaching across the table, Montana placed her hand on top of his, a spark of electricity shooting through her body as she did.

"It's important to live life while you can," Red said, forcing a weak smile. "There are no guarantees."

Sitting there with him, Montana was struck by how genuinely caring Richard "Red" Howard was. Despite the sly grin, and smooth confidence, there was a depth of character about him that she found more attractive than she'd ever thought possible. With most of the men she'd known prior, spiritual and emotional wealth always took a back seat to financial wealth.

"So tell me more about you?"

"No," Montana said, shaking her head. "I bent your ear enough last night."

"I don't mind," Red said, and sounded like he meant it.

Bracing as another spark shot up her spine, Montana asked, "Were you serious when you said you'd like to open up a chain of full-service gas stations throughout the state?"

"Oh absolutely," Red said, that delicious confidence returning. "I'm working on securing a small business loan now. But first I've gotta finish putting together a business plan."

"I can help you with that," Montana said.

Red eyed her incredulously.

"Don't look at me like that," Montana said with a smirk. "I do have a degree in business in case you've forgotten."

"Oh right," Red said, remembering their conversation from the night prior. "You graduated from UNLV, right?"

"With honors," Montana said proudly.

"Of course," Red said, a sly grin forming on his freshly shaven face. "Perhaps you'd want to consider being my business partner. I get the feeling the two of us would make a great team."

"I'm not looking for a partner," Montana said. "But I will help you with your business plan."

"I appreciate that," Red said, locking her in his gaze. "I'm glad you came tonight."

Montana smiled softly. "Me too."

"Big Red," the waitress said, appearing out of nowhere. "How you doing tonight, Handsome?"

"I'm blessed Becky," he answered. "How you doing?"

"Great, now that you're here."

Montana cleared her throat. Red wasn't her man, nor did she want him to be. Still, she'd be damned if this top-heavy woman was about to disrespect her.

"Oh hi there," the server said as if just noticing that Montana was there.

"Could you bring me a glass of water," Montana said, uninterested in pleasantries. "With a thin slice of lemon...fresh lemon."

Giving Montana a look, the waitress turned to Red. "Your usual, Sweetie?"

"Sounds good to me," Red said.

"Be right back."

Don't rush, Montana thought to herself as she watched the server walk away. "I take it you're a regular here," she said, glancing around the bar.

"Cheap liquor and good food," Red said with a light chuckle. "Can't beat that with a stick."

"I bet," Montana said, quickly shifting gears. "Were you surprised that I called you last night?"

"Not really," Red answered. "Pleased...but not surprised."

"You're so arrogant."

"But an otherwise good guy," Red said. "Do you regret calling?"

"Not yet," Montana said.

"And, when do you think you might start regretting your decision to be with *him*?"

Montana exhaled slowly. She was hoping that Red wouldn't bring up David. She hadn't planned to tell him about catching her fiancé with another woman, but it just slipped out. The part about Sharon being a whore, however, she'd managed to keep to herself.

"I don't think that's any of your business," Montana said, tensing. "I barely know you."

"That didn't stop you from calling me last night to bear witness to your pain and hurt," Red said, not backing off, "did it?"

Montana gritted her teeth. She liked him a lot more last night when he was doing more listening than talking.

"Does he know you're here?"

"I haven't seen him since I talked to you last night," Montana said.

"Why do you stay with someone who obviously doesn't respect you enough--?"

"Don't," Montana said, raising her hand to stop him. "David isn't perfect, but he takes very good care of me."

"So he can be a complete jackass, so long as he can he can keep you fitted in designer clothes, and driving fancy cars?"

"Yes...no," Montana stammered. She collected herself before continuing. "Material things may not buy happiness, but it gets you damn close."

"You're spoiled rotten," Red said as a matter of fact.

Montana drew back. "I beg your pardon!"

"I meant that in the best way possible."

"Umm hmm," Montana said, rolling her eyes.

"I can see that a regular Joe like me doesn't have a chance in sweaty hell with a sista like you."

"You see correctly."

Ignoring the sour look on her face, Red grabbed Montana by the hand. "Let's dance."

"I don't dance," she said, not budging from her chair.

"You do tonight," Red said, pulling her to her feet.

"Red...what are...don't you dare!" Montana squealed with delight as he lifted her into his arms and carried her toward the floor.

Red smiled. "I dare."

Montana turned on the hallway light, making her way toward the foyer.

From the darkened living room, David said, "You look nice tonight."

Without responding to him, Montana continued up the spiraling staircase and into the master bedroom.

David walked into the room as she undressed. "Did you have a good time?"

Montana stood with her back to him as he moved toward her. He had some nerve trying to act as if nothing was wrong. The man really was an asshole of epic proportions.

"I'm sorry," David said, placing the trinket around her neck.

Inhaling wearily, Montana went over to the mirror, spying the large diamond and ruby tear-drop necklace, sparkling like wet ice cubes on her dark skin.

David turned her around, cupping her face. "I'm so sorry."

The foul smell of stale liquor and cigarettes on his breath caused Montana to cringe. After spending the night fucking some other woman, the least David could have done was taken a shower and brushed his damn teeth.

"I never meant to hurt you, Tana," he said, staring into her cold eyes. "I love you too much to hurt you."

And yet you hurt me just the same, Montana thought as she turned back to the mirror, carefully studying David's latest in a long line of make up gifts. She ran her fingers lightly across the jewels, barely listening to her fiancé continue to plead his case.

"I love you. I need you in my life," David said imploringly. "I made a stupid mistake. I fucked up, Tana."

Montana remained silent.

"I know what I did was wrong and stupid," David said, talking to her back. "I'll do whatever it takes to make this up to you. I promise you."

Spinning her around, David's glazed eyes twinkled with excitement. "Let's get married, right now...tonight," he said, lowering to one knee. "Marry me Tana."

Placing the song playing inside her head on pause, Montana looked down at David as if he were a complete stranger. In so many ways he was. Besides knowing he came from a family of old money and that he was a real estate developer with a fondness for black women, Montana knew very little about the man she'd agreed to marry. Perhaps she didn't want to know for fear David would ultimately prove unworthy of her time and affection.

"Excuse me?" Montana said, pushing past David.

"What do you say, Tana?" he asked, rising from the floor.

Montana looked at David like he was dog crap on the bottom of her designer shoe. "You expect me to still marry you?" she asked, unable to believe his audacity.

"Tana, you're the only woman for me," David said with such sincerity in his voice, Montana almost believed him. "I want to spend the rest of my life with you and only you...forever."

"Where's the money David?" Montana asked. "Did you spend all of it on your little whore?"

David lowered his head.

Removing the necklace, Montana dropped it into her swelling jewelry box. "I'm just asking because at least one of the accounts was completely emptied out," she said, turning to face him. "But I'm guessing you know that already."

Angered by her condescending tone, David marched over to Montana grabbing her by the arm.

"Is that all you give a fuck about is money?" he asked in a shout. "Is the money I give you all I'm fucking good for?"

"It would appear that way," Montana said without emotion.

David tightened his grip on her arm. "You don't mean that."

Montana jerked away from him.

"Do you love me, Tana?"

"I'm starting to feel a lot like Tina Turner when it comes to that question," Montana said, walking away from him.

David snatched her back. "Answer me."

"Let go of me," Montana said.

Pulling away from him, she marched into the walk-in closet, slamming the door shut behind her.

"Don't make a mistake you can't afford to make!" David yelled from the bedroom.

"You've made more than enough mistakes for the both of us!" Montana yelled back.

"You're willing to give up everything we have...everything I give you because I let some tramp suck my dick?"

David's words made Montana's blood run cold. She'd always felt there was more than a small possibility that he was cheating on her, but hearing him admit it was too much.

With her pale pink dress and matching sling backs in hand, Montana reemerged from the closet.

Glaring, at her as she strutted across the room, David took off his jacket, tossing it onto the bed.

"Where the fuck do you think you're going?"

Laying out her chosen ensemble, Montana didn't respond to David's question. Infuriated, he rushed toward her, pushing her down on the bed.

"Who the fuck do you think you are?" David asked, climbing on top of her. "I own you damn it. Don't you ever fucking forget that!"

"David!" Montana squealed as he pinned her arms back. "Get off of me!"

"You belong to me," David said, kissing her roughly on the mouth.

Panic rising inside her like a building tide, Montana struggled to break free. "Get the fuck off of me!" she shouted.

Ignoring her, David forced Montana's legs apart with one hand, while freeing himself from his wrinkled trousers with the other.

"David...no!" Montana's voice insisted as he began forcing himself inside her. "Please don't do—!"

"Shut up," David demanded, forcing Montana's dress over her head.

With all the force he could muster, he pumped into his fiancée's uninviting body.

"I own you damn it," David said in a crude growl. "I own you."

As if staring down from the ceiling, Montana watched haplessly as David violated her in ways no human should ever violate another.

Clutching her hair as he buried his face in her neck, David's thrusts increased in power and frequency.

When the pain became more than she could bear, Montana cried out. "No. Stop it, David!"

"Shut up!" he shouted, not letting up on his physical abuse.

Now fearing for her life, Montana freed her hand, wedged behind her back, smacking David hard across the face. It didn't faze him.

"You're hurting—"

"I told you to shut up...*bitch*," David growled.

Tightening his hands around Montana's throat, he rammed himself deeper inside her.

Tears streaming down her face, she fought not to lose consciousness.

"Please stop," Montana's frail voice begged. "Please, David... please..."

"You're mine and you always will be," David grunted into her ear. "We belong together."

Closing her eyes, Montana prayed for God to save her from David...and herself.

Chapter Seven

The smell of bacon and eggs filled her nostrils as Montana struggled to open her eyes. Squinting to avoid the blinding sunlight streaming in through the blinds, she leaned over to check the clock, almost knocking over the tray resting beside her.

Smiling, she spied her breakfast. Beside the plate were two long-stemmed red roses, sticking out from a mayonnaise jar. Next to it was a mug emblazoned with a Red's Gas and Collision logo, filled with coffee. Lifting herself carefully up against the headboard, Montana removed the fork from inside the neatly wrapped paper towel. So focused on the food, she didn't notice at first, the sleepy eyes staring at her from the chair placed in the corner of the room. Her knight in shining armor smiled broadly as their gazes finally met, but he didn't say a word.

Montana smirked playfully. "Whatever," she said, stuffing the scrambled cheese eggs into her mouth.

Shaking his head, Red chuckled as he watched his overnight guest woof down the breakfast. "Had I known you were that hungry, I'd have made you four eggs instead of two."

Montana slathered the strawberry preserve onto her toast. "Leave me alone man," she said between bites.

"Don't be mad at me 'cause you eat like a wild Amazon," Red said, laughing.

"Forget you," Montana said, trying to catch the food dribbling from her mouth.

"Nobody's gonna take the plate from you," Red said. "You can take your time."

Laughing, Montana continued eating. "You make me sick," she said. *But, you look too damn cute in that T-shirt and those shorts,* she thought.

"I bet," Red said, rising from the chair.

Montana smiled to herself as he made his way into the bathroom. The thought of Red in the kitchen cooking for her, especially after she'd kept him up all night balling into his chest, touched her.

Having regained consciousness last night, Montana had crawled out of bed. Leaving David snoring in the chair, she'd snuck out of the house. Her body and heart aching, she drove into the night not sure where she'd wind up. Knowing that her husband Robert was in LA shooting an underwear commercial, she'd considered going to Lisa's, but Montana didn't have the courage to face her friend. After calling him on her cell in tears, Red met her at the gas station and drove her back to his place.

"So you wanna move in?" Red asked, stepping back into the bedroom.

"You crazy," Montana said with an uneasy laugh. "I've got too many problems for you."

Sitting down on the edge of the bed, Red looked at her with serious eyes. "The only thing you've got that I don't want is David," he said. "Everything else I can handle."

"That's what you think," Montana said.

"What he did to you was absolutely unacceptable," Red said, spying her bruised cheek.

Montana took a pensive breath, grateful she hadn't told him the grotesque details of all she'd endured at David's hands. Besides the slap to her face, all Red knew was that her fiancé had admitted to cheating on her.

"I'm serious about the offer to stay here," Red said. "At least until you can find a place of your own."

"I already have a place," Montana said.

"You're joking right?" Red asked, not waiting for an answer. "That punk-ass man doesn't deserve you—"

"Red, please...don't."

"And assuming this is the first time he's hit you," Red said, giving her a look to suggest he believed otherwise. "You can rest assured that it won't be the last."

Angrily, Red shook his head. "A brotha who would even dare raise his hands to a sist—"

"David's not a brotha," Montana said. "He's white."

Red almost fell off the bed. "He's white?" he asked, shaking his head. "Ain't that 'bout a bitch."

Montana noticed the immediate change in Red's demeanor. Black men had a real problem with black women leaving their trifling behinds in the dust for white men.

"That explains a lot," Red said with a cryptic chuckle.

"And exactly what is that supposed to mean?"

Red stood up from the bed, desperate to put some distance between them. "The comment you made about Naomi Campbell being too dark...the long weave," he said, staring at her head, "It would make sense that you'd only date white—"

"Hold up!" Montana shouted. "I never said I *only* dated white men. And who the fuck are you to comment on my damn weave?"

"Let me ask you a question," Red said staring at her intently. "If David was black would you stick around after he'd hit you?"

"That's a hypothetical—"

"Answer it anyway," Red pressed.

"I don't have to answer anything." Montana jumped up from the bed. "How dare you stand there and try to psychoanalyze me," she said, glaring at Red. "You don't know a damn thing about me."

"I know enough—"

"No," Montana snapped, "you don't know jack about me!"

"I know you are so in love with the all mighty dollar that you're willing to prostitute yourself — "

"Prostitute!" Montana shouted, pointing her finger at Red. "How dare you call me that!"

Taking a step back as she approached, Red clarified. "I didn't call you a prostitute, Montana."

"You might as well have," she said, snatching up her sneakers from beside the chair. The veracity of Red's words cut her to the core. As much as she might have denied it, he wasn't telling her anything that she hadn't told herself on more than one occasion. On some level Montana knew that a man as spoiled and shallow as David could never offer her the love and affection she so desperately craved. The one thing that he could give her – wealth – he had done expertly, but at great cost to her self-respect. For years Montana had purposely sought out men like David. They paid her rent, and bought her clothes. In truth, the only difference between her and a whore was that the whore had no illusions about what or who she really was.

"Thank you for your hospitality," Montana said, marching toward the front door.

"Montana wait," Red said, following her down the hall. Grabbing her carefully by the shoulder he stopped her. "I'm sorry."

"It's okay," Montana said, damning the tears burning her eyes.

"Come on," Red said, wiping her moist cheeks, "don't cry."

"You're right about me," Montana said, continuing to sob. "I'm a vapid gold-digging bitch--"

"*Shhh*," Red said, drawing her into his waiting arms. He rocked her slowly as she cried. "Whenever you're ready, you can choose to be someone different."

Chapter Eight

Montana waved goodbye to Red as he pulled out of the gas station. Reaching for the cell sitting on the passenger seat where she'd left it last night, she sighed when she saw Tracy's name appear on the screen. She was in no mood to talk to anyone, but she knew her friend would call out the National Guard, if Montana didn't check in soon.

"Scorn the Devil!" Tracy exclaimed the instant Montana picked up the line. "Where in the world have you been?"

"Busy," Montana said, hoping the answer would suffice.

"Busy my ass!" Lisa snapped.

"Don't say that nasty word!" Tracy said aghast. "It's Sunday."

Montana sighed. "Great, it's the infamous three-way curse out call."

"Don't try to be cute little girl," Lisa said. "And, Tracy?"

"Yeah?"

"Kiss my ass...tomorrow."

"You're going to hell in a hand basket," Tracy retorted.

"And what will *you* be arriving in?" Lisa shot back. "Now to the issue at hand," she said sucking on her teeth. "Montana where have you been all weekend?"

Montana could feel the hairs tickling the back of her neck. There was no way she could tell them about David. "Did you ladies forget I have a wedding to plan for?"

"*We* have a wedding to plan for," Tracy corrected. "You know you're not allowed to make any decisions without Lisa's and my input."

"All right now Tracy," Lisa said, impressed. "That's the bitch I like to see."

Tracy giggled. "I try."

"I'm sorry you two feel left out," Montana said, popping in the headset, "but I've got enough to deal with without you two hussies giving me more gray hairs."

"I got your hussy," Lisa said playing along.

When she heard the sound of the call waiting, Montana glanced down at the cell, flinching when she saw David's name. The thought of him was enough to make her stomach ball up in knots.

"Is somebody ringing?" Tracy asked.

"It's Montana....but I know she better not hang up on us to answer it," Lisa said as a warning. "Your husband-to-be can wait."

"I'm not going to hang up on you broads," Montana said, only too happy to let David's call go to voice mail.

"Tracy and I have taken the liberty of selecting a caterer for your wedding."

Montana flipped down the visor. "Can we not talk about the wedding, right now?" she asked, her hand rising to her bruised cheek as she stared into the mirror.

There was a moment of loud silence on the shared line. Finally Lisa asked, "Did something happen between you and David?"

Montana swallowed carefully. "David and I are fine," she lied. "I'm just not up to dealing with planning right now."

"What are you not telling us?" Lisa asked, not buying it.

Exhaling a dejected sigh, Montana returned the visor to its original position. "I'm not ready to discuss—"

"Don't tell me there's another woman in the picture," Lisa said, cutting her off.

"If you're referring to the bitch David was fucking all day while I was searching for spare change in our bank account," Montana said, spilling the beans, "then yes, there is another woman in the picture."

"Oh sweet mother of Jesus," Tracy said in a stunned whisper.

"Montana, I'm so sorry," Lisa said.

Beep.

Montana rolled her eyes as she spied the call screen.

"I'm guessing that's David on your other line," Lisa said.

"Yep," Montana said.

"Tana, maybe you should talk to him," Tracy suggested. "See what he has to say for himself."

"And why should she talk to that son of a lyin' motherfucka?" Lisa asked bitterly. "He's the one who fucked up the best thing he had. I say let him stew in his own shit for a while."

"You don't give up on the love of your life just because he makes a mistake," Tracy said.

Montana cut her eyes at the phone. She cared for David, but the man was nowhere in the vicinity of being the love of her life.

"Don't be stupid, Tracy!" Lisa barked. "A mistake is getting a dress in the wrong color. What David did is unfucking acceptable," she said emphatically. "Montana shouldn't put up with that weak bullshit just because that white bitch put some flimsy ring on her finger."

Flimsy, Montana thought to herself as she spied the shimmering rock. *This ring is anything but flimsy.*

When the phone beeped again, Montana snarled, "Son of a bitch." She knew that David would keep calling until she at least answered, and hung up on him a few times.

"Hold on, ladies," Montana said, quickly clicking over before Lisa could argue. "What is it, David?"

"I'm sorry," he said, his voice ragged and strained. "I'm sorry for everything."

"We're beyond the sorry stage," Montana said.

"I love you Tana," David said, pleading. "I need you--"

"What do you need from me?" Montana asked, interrupting. "Besides being one of your fuck toys, what do you really need from me David?"

Wisely, he didn't respond.

"Does Sharon like it rough?" Montana asked. "Does she like you to take it from her the way you took it from me last night? Hmm, does she David?"

"Sharon means nothing to me," David said. "I'm sorry for cheating on you, Tana. I promise you on my life that it won't happen again. I'll do whatever I have--"

"Save the bullshit lines for another one of your skank bitches," Montana said, shutting him down, "'cause *this* bitch is done with your tired ass."

"Don't do this to me...us," David implored. "You gotta believe me when I say I'll do whatever I have to do to win you back."

"The only thing you can do for me David is cut your cock off," Montana said smoothly.

"I know I need help," David said, sounding desperate.

"You didn't seem to need help sticking your dick in another woman," Montana said, not letting up. "And you sure as hell didn't need help forcing it into me last night."

"What are you talking about?" David asked, sounding genuinely baffled. "We haven't had sex in I don't know how long."

"You son-of-a-bitch!" Montana shouted. That this man would try to ignore his deplorable actions was the height of disrespect. "We definitely didn't have sex. You raped me," she said, spitting out the words. "Hopefully you got your rocks off nice and proper last night because it'll be the last time you fuck me...you heartless sonofabitch!"

Slamming the cell shut, Montana punched her fist into the steering wheel, boiling in anger for both David and herself. They were a match made in heaven. He believed money could buy him whatever he wanted, and she proved it by allowing herself to be bought.

Snatching up the ringing cell, Montana barked, "What David?"

"Open the door!"

Montana almost jumped out of her skin when she saw him standing outside her driver's side door.

"Open the door, Montana!"

"Fuck you!" She said, quickly, starting the car. "Leave me alone, or I'll have a restraining order filed against your ass!"

"I love you Tana!" David yelled, barely dodging the side mirror as she hurriedly backed out of the gas station.

Montana slammed on the brakes, barely avoiding a collision with a car pulling up to one of the pumps.

"Go away David!" she shouted through the half opened window.

"I'm getting help for my problems," he said. "I'm seeing a therapist first thing tomorrow."

That got Montana's attention. "I don't believe you," she said.

David held up the piece of wrinkled paper. "You can call and check," he said, moving carefully toward the Mercedes. "I know I can be the man you want me to be, Tana. But I need your help."

"I can't David," Montana said in a weak voice. "I can't."

"Please don't leave me," David begged. "I love you so much. First thing tomorrow I plan to put all the money back into the account," he promised. "*Our* account..."

Wrecked with indecision, Montana closed her eyes.

"Tana, please say you'll stay and see me through this," David said, imploring. "After all I've given you...you owe me that much."

Despite the pain he'd caused her, Montana felt a strange sense of obligation to the man who'd given her the world. Life with David wasn't always perfect, but it was the life she'd chosen, and the one she deserved.

Slowly, she opened her eyes. "I'll stay."

Chapter Nine

"You like?" Lisa asked, holding up the rhinestone-encrusted stiletto pump.

"It's a wedding, not a Saturday night party," Tracy said, holding up a more conservative alternative. "These say *I do*...not *take me now*."

Lisa rolled her eyes as she dropped her suggestion back into the box. "Were you born with a tight ass, or did you have to grow into it?"

"I'm simply trying to make sure you don't ruin things with your sometimes questionable tastes."

"Questionable?"

"Yes," Tracy said, not stuttering. "You know how you can get."

"And how is that?" Lisa asked, daring her to answer.

Sitting quietly in the corner, Montana exhaled a bored sigh as her friends went about their usual routine. Turning her head toward the store's front window, she stared out at the puddles, hoping to find in them some answers. She'd been back with David for a month now, and she was already second-guessing her decision to return. Although he was seeing a therapist for his *issues*, Montana remained unsure whether he truly had the capacity, or desire to change. The fact that she couldn't get Red out of her head didn't help matters one bit.

"Don't you agree, Montana?" Lisa asked, holding up the pair of lavender Stuart Weitzman's. "Montana?"

"Huh?"

Giving Tracy a bemused look, Lisa waved her hand. "Never mind."

Rising from the crushed velvet lounger, Montana asked, "Are you guys ready yet?" It was the second time she'd posed the question in the past hour.

Tracy glanced over at Montana as she continued examining the myriad options the sales woman had presented. "Your bubbly excitement is just spilling over," she said drolly. "What's on your mind, Girl?"

Montana walked over to the window. "Just thinking," she said, staring out at nothing in particular.

"You've been 'just thinking' all daggon day," Lisa said, snatching the pink Blahnik's out of Tracy's hand. "Not right for the dress," she said tossing them into the building pile of rejected items. "So, do you finally want to talk about what happened?" she asked, cutting her eyes to Montana. "Or, shall we keep shopping for a wedding that was *sooo* not gonna happen only a few weeks ago?"

"Can't you just be happy that Tana and David are back together?" Tracy asked, annoyed, "And working out their problems?"

"They may be back together," Lisa said, studying Montana as she stood there looking like a lost puppy. "But, the bride-to-be is anything but happy."

"We've already covered this Lisa," Montana said, trying not to show her irritation. "David is getting help...we're over-the-fucking-moon happy. End of story."

"Is that your head or your heart talking?" Tracy asked, realizing that Montana might not be as ready to move forward with David as she'd claimed. "Tana, if you don't think this is the right thing—"

"Right is relative," Montana said, interrupting. "The smart woman knows that she doesn't burn down bridges if she can't walk on water."

Lisa cocked her head to the side. "What the hell does that mean?"

"Nothing," Montana said, not interested in sharing how her deep-seeded fear of being broke and destitute, may have propelled her back into a man's arms she knew she didn't truly love. "Let's just get those in an eight," she said, pointing at the lavender open-toes in Lisa's hand, "and get the hell out of here."

Placing the shoes in the box, Lisa rolled her eyes. "These weren't for you," she said under her breath as she followed Montana and Tracy to the register.

The instant the cashier handed her the receipt, Montana snatched the bag and walked out of the store. Marching through the parking lot, she stopped dead in her tracks when she saw him. "Shit..."

"What?" Lisa asked, almost mowing her down.

Montana wanted to make a run for Lisa's yellow Hummer, but couldn't bring her quaking legs to move. Of all the people she didn't want to see right now, *he* was at the very top of the list.

"Girl, what is wrong with you?" Lisa asked, staring at Montana. "Why are you standing there frozen?"

Before Montana could respond, Red turned around, his face brightening when he spotted her. Finally willing her limbs to cooperate, she rushed toward the truck without returning his wave.

Jumping into the back seat, Montana demanded, "Lisa will you get in already!"

"Uh...you're screaming at me," Lisa said, taking her sweet time climbing inside. Turning back to face her bitchy passenger, she asked, "Are you losing your mind?"

"*Dayum,*" Tracy said, licking her lips as Red approached. "Who is he?"

"Can we just go please," Montana said, sweating bullets.

Taken aback by her friend's agitated behavior, Lisa hesitated for a moment. "Montana what is going—?"

"Will you just..." Montana said, stopping short when she heard the taps against the window.

Tracy cracked her window. "Yes?" she asked carefully.

"I'm sorry to trouble you," Red said, "but, I thought I saw my friend Montana get into the backseat..."

Tracy and Lisa looked at each other, then turned to Montana.

"I was hoping to have a word with her."

Ignoring Lisa's questioning eyes, Montana opened the door and got out.

"You weren't trying to hide from me, were you?" Red asked, smiling that familiar, easy smile.

"Actually I was," Montana said, wiping the moisture from her brow.

"I thought we were better pals than that," Red said, trying for levity.

Montana didn't respond.

"So how've you been?"

"Fine," Montana said, averting her eyes from his.

"I've called you a few times," Red said. "Did you get any of my messages?"

"Yep," Montana said. "I've been really busy, is all."

"Busy with what?" Red asked, not taking his eyes off of her.

Vacillating, Montana finally said, "Planning for the wedding."

The smile on Red's face faded. "I see."

"David and I..." Montana said, struggling to sell to Red a vision she barely bought herself. "We've worked out our issues and—"

"No need to explain," Red said, taking a step back. He tried to remain upbeat, but it was well apparent that the news had unsettled him. "So when's the big day?"

"Why?" Montana asked, suspiciously. "You plan on coming?"

Red let out a weak laugh as he ran his fingers through his mop of hair. "No, I wouldn't consider being someplace I wasn't wanted."

"Listen, Red," Montana said, feeling the need to defend her actions. "David isn't perfect, but he's trying to do better. I can't just turn my back on him. Not now."

"Fair enough." Red sighed. "I just hope you know what you're doing."

"I know exactly what I'm doing," Montana insisted. "David's getting help," she said, careful not to speak so loud as to be overheard by Tracy and Lisa, staring at her and Red from the truck. "He's seeing a psychiatrist..."

Red studied Montana carefully as she rattled off her reasons for returning to the man who just four weeks ago had sent her racing into his arms.

"And he's promised never to force himself on me again..." Montana said, stopping short when she realized what she'd just said.

"Wait a minute," Red said, twisting his head as if shaking off a sucker punch to his jaw. "What did you just say?"

"I didn't mean to say that," Montana said, backing up toward the truck.

"But you did," Red said, taking a step toward her.

"Look I gotta go," Montana said, gripping the door handle.

Red reached for her arm. "Talk to me, Montana."

"Goodbye Red," she said, hopping back inside the SUV.

Lisa twisted in her seat to face Montana. "What was that all about?"

"Nothing," Montana said, staring straight ahead. "Let's go."

Chapter Ten

"May I take your plate, Mrs. Michaels?"

"Yes, Gretchen," Montana said, leaning back in her chair.

Seated at the opposite end of the table, David smiled lovingly at his wife. Montana returned his tender gaze, absentmindedly strumming the diamond tennis bracelet around her wrist with her fingers.

"That's gorgeous," Tracy said, eyeing the expensive trinket.

"Thanks," Montana said. "David got it for me during his recent business trip to Los Angeles."

Lisa eyed Gretchen intently as the server continued clearing the table. She leaned over to Montana, sitting beside her. "What happened to Sasha," she asked, referring to the Michaels' former maid.

Montana's eyes twitched, but she remained composed. "She didn't work out."

"Really?" Lisa asked incredulously. She took another look at Gretchen.

"Dinner was absolutely amazing, Mrs. Michaels," Robert said, raising his glass to salute her.

"Why thank you Mr. Foxworth," Montana said with a gracious nod.

"Don't act like I don't feed you at home man," Lisa said, feigning irritation with her husband.

The three married couples laughed.

From the corner of her eye Montana watched David watch Gretchen as she leaned over to pick up the fork that had dropped from the tray.

"Gretchen could you bring in desert and coffee," Montana said, a bit more sharply than she'd intended.

Her eyes moving from Montana to David's, to the pretty young maid, Lisa sighed wearily.

"Will you all excuse me for a moment?" David asked, rising from his chair.

"Where are you going, Darling?" Montana asked.

"The restroom," David said, not appreciating being questioned. "Unless you have a problem with that."

Sitting on either side of Montana, Lisa and Tracy observed the tense exchange with peaked interest.

"Of course not," Montana said, smiling for the benefit of her guests. "Just don't take too long."

"Is everything okay between you two?" Lisa asked the instant David stepped out of the room.

"Everything is fine," Montana said, rising from the table. "Will you all excuse me please?"

Stepping out of the dining room, Montana made her way toward the kitchen, taking great pains to remain as quiet as a church mouse as she did. Her heart pounding in her chest, she slowly pushed open the swinging door.

"*Oooh,* shit," David groaned as he stood with his slacks hanging around his ankles. "That's it...swallow it all," he instructed.

Tears welling in her eyes, Montana watched in stunned silence as her maid blew her husband.

Sensing he was being observed, David glanced back over his shoulder.

"It isn't what it looks like," he said, not bothering to remove his penis from Gretchen's mouth.

Backing up slowly, Montana turned to leave.

Stuffing himself back into his pants, David followed her down the hall. "Montana, wait."

"I really don't want to hear it David," Montana said calmly as she checked her drag in the mirror.

"She means nothing," David assured.

"I know," Montana said, plumping her hair. "She was just sucking your dick, is all." With that she turned on her heels and walked away.

"Tana, are you okay?" David asked, pursuing her. "Are you okay...?"

"Tana, are you okay?"

The squeeze of David's hand to her forearm snapped Montana out of her daydream. "I'm sorry," she said, struggling to regain her bearings.

"I asked if you were okay," David said concerned. "You look a little flushed."

"I'm fine," Montana said, turning back to the priest. "Let's keep going."

Clearing his throat, Father Charles resumed. "Montana Abigail James, do you take David Preston Michaels to be your lawfully wedded husband?"

Montana could feel the word *yes* on the tip of her tongue, but couldn't push it through her lips.

Giving her a strange look, the priest repeated the question.

Feeling the stares of the family and friends gathered for her wedding, Montana took a deep breath, then opened her mouth to speak.

The "yes" still refused to come out.

"Tana," David said in an irritated whisper. "What's the problem?"

Studying him carefully, Montana finally found her words.

"I can't do this," she said, exhaling as the reality hit her. "I deserve better than you...than *us*."

David drew back. "What?"

Montana shook her head resolutely. "I don't want to be married to you," she said, finally seeing things clearly.

"We need to take a few minutes," David said, turning to the slack-jawed priest.

"No we don't," Montana said.

"Baby," David said, trying to remain calm. "Don't say or do something you'll regret for the rest of your life."

"Good-bye David," Montanna said, stepping back. "Good luck."

The guests let out a collective gasp as she hiked up her gown, and raced down the stairs from the pulpit. Instantly, Lisa and Tracy jumped out of the line of bridesmaids and chased after her. By the time they finally caught up to her, Montana was hopping inside the waiting limo.

"What the hell are you doing?" Lisa asked, jumping in behind her.

Tracy joined them. "I can't believe you just did that Montana," she said, placing her hand against the runaway bride's forehead. "Are you sick?"

"I can't marry him," Montana said, breathlessly. "I don't love him."

"Well, it took you long enough to figure it out," Lisa said, relieved.

Tracy's eyes bugged. "Montana you can't be serious?"

When she saw David rushing out of the church, Montana shouted at the stunned driver. "Hit it!"

Doing as told, the man burned rubber. "Where are we going?" he asked, speeding away from the crowd of people shrinking in the distance.

"Red's Gas and Collision...East Desert Inn at Cambridge."

"Interesting choice," Lisa said.

Montana snatched off her veil. "Could you step on it please?"

Happy to oblige, the driver drove down the highway like a bat out of hell.

"Are you trying to get us killed?" Lisa asked, clutching the seat as the limo made the turn onto Cambridge.

"This feels like a scene from *Charlie's Angels*," Tracy said, loving it.

"More like a bad episode of *Cagney and Lacey*," Lisa smirked.

When the limo came to a stop, Montana swung the door open, racing inside the station. "Where's Red?" she asked the clerk.

"Umm...he's in his office," the teen said, looking at Montana like she'd just stepped off of a space ship. "Do you want me to call—"

Not letting him finish, Montana raced toward the back of the station, Lisa and Tracy fast on her heels.

"Absolutely John..." Red said, hesitating when Montana and company burst into his office. "Ah....John, hang on a sec," he said, covering the phone. "Montana, what are you doing here?" he asked utterly confused.

"I need to talk to you," she said impatiently.

Red uncovered the phone. "Umm...John...let me...let me call you right back," he said, not taking his eyes off Montana. "Sure. Bye."

Lisa cut her eyes at Tracy. "Tell me she is not about to do what I think she is?"

"It's like Romeo and Juliet," Tracy beamed.

"Montana," Red asked, rising from the desk. "What are you doing here?"

"I need to ask you a question?"

Tracy cooed as she watched. "This is *sooo* good."

Lisa smirked. "This is *sooo* crazy."

"What question is that?"

Montana took a deep breath. "Are you still interested in having me as a partner?"

Red made his way around the desk. "What's going on?" he asked.

"I'm making the choice to be different than I was yesterday," Montana said, moving toward him. "But I need your help."

"Who am I fooling," Lisa said, clutching her chest. "This shit *is* good."

"Does your offer still stand?" Montana asked desperately.

"Absolutely," Red said, wiping the tear from her cheek. "My offer still stands."

ENOUGH

Darrious D. Hilmon

Prologue

My eyes eased open as I felt the body slip into bed beside me. Resisting the urge to turn toward the masculine energy nuzzling up against my backside, I re-closed my eyes and pretended to be asleep. This wasn't the first time Mark had made his way into my room in the middle of the night. During each visit we'd kiss for a while, then spoon, allowing our hands to *accidentally* caress each other's sweet spots. After about an hour of pseudo sex, we'd finally fall off to sleep, our hearts and bodies in *no-words-needed* synch. I wanted more from him, but had come to grudgingly accept that I'd probably never get it.

Mark Theodore Cannon was an absolutely incredible man. I know, people say that kinda stuff about their 'special guy' all the time. But, in Mark's case it was the God's honest truth. The man was breathtaking. He was kind and gentle – though deliciously rough when the occasion called for it. Without a second thought, he would give you the shirt off his back…literally. Mark was also an infuriatingly insecure man-child, with deep emotional scars caused by the almost unbearable weight of his father's inflexible judgment and insistence that his only son be a *man*. The man he wanted him to be, anyway.

Taking a discreet breath, I tried not to quiver as Mark's massive hands swallowed up my own, his grip tender, but oh so very sure. From the moment I first laid eyes on him outside the student union three weeks into our freshmen year, I knew Mark would be the first and quite possibly *only* man I'd ever love. In his eyes I could see my future. His laugh – a throaty, full-bodied chortle was contagious and quickly came to represent the sound of my own joy. The late night walks we used to take together around campus were heaven for me. It was as if Mark had stepped out of my dreams. Nothing was ever the same after he'd come into my world.

But, none of that sweet crap mattered at the moment. Right about now, Mark was at the very top of my shit-list. I was amazed he'd even had the balls to slither up next to me tonight. When Rashad arrived earlier to pick me up for our date, Mark had shown his complete ass. It wasn't even a real date. As I was leaving stats class yesterday, Rashad had caught up with me and asked if I'd be his study partner for the upcoming mid-term. I agreed. So what if he was a cutie. After we went to the movies, then had dinner with maybe a beer or two, we were going to go right back to his place and get in some *study* time. If his pants happened to fall down around his ankles, then so be it.

As soon as he saw Rashad standing in the living room of our apartment, the shit-eating grin on Mark's face morphed into a sinister snarl. What should have been a simple "what's up" was instead a passive-aggressive, testosterone-driven pissing match between the two. Before long they were exchanging snide comments and thinly-veiled insults. I'm telling you, men can really be some territorial so-n-so's when they thought another guy was trying to piss around their tree – more precisely their roommate/fuck-buddy.

Mark nudged me with what I could only assume was the fully erect, nine-inch anaconda between his thick legs. It certainly wasn't a flashlight. For as many times as that brotha had come creepin' late in the midnight hour, he could find his way to my bed in the dark.

"You sleep?"

"Duh," I said annoyed. After his deplorable behavior earlier, I was in no mood to talk to Mark. Being next to Rashad had made me horny as a billy goat though, so a little bump-n-grind would be okay. But, words? I had no use for Mark's words, unless they were the ones forming his apology for being such a jackass.

Mark exhaled a heavy sigh, before going silent. His hard-on however continued screaming into my lower back. I take it back. I wasn't even in the mood for a little PG-rated roll in the sack, and believe me, with Mark they were always PG. What I really wanted was for him to climb his 6'4" muscular, hairy-chested, size thirteen wearing, bubble-butted self out of my bed so I could try to go back to sleep and forget how good it felt having him this close to me.

Nudging me again, he whispered, "I'm sorry."

I hated him for being so forgivable, and for having the uncanny ability to read my thoughts. Mark made it next to impossible not to genuinely like him, even when he was being an utter jerk which – tonight not withstanding – he wasn't often.

Attempting to remain sour I said, "You were completely out of line tonight."

"I know, Mark said in a slow, sexy drawl.

I wish I didn't like him as much as I did. Don't get me wrong. Mark was crazy cool, and being his friend was all good. The two of us could talk for hours about something as trivial as the Pistons' chances of winning back-to-back championships, then shift effortlessly into a debate about the country's chances of survival with Bush in office another four years. Mark was kind-hearted with one wickedly funny sense of humor. He laughed at my jokes even when they weren't funny. In so many ways we were a match made in heaven. When it came to maneuvering this gray area that was him in my bed looking for anything but sleep, things were a little less simpatico.

As much as he might have been attracted to me sexually – who could blame him – the truth was, Mark simply couldn't handle the responsibility that came with being my lover.

Squirming a bit, Mark exhaled again. "It's just...it's hard to see you..." he said, his voice trailing off.

Something about him was different tonight. I could sense it in the way he held me, the heaviness of his breathing...not to mention the fact that he was currently easing his finger between my butt cheeks. Oh my God, this man was easing his finger between my butt cheeks!

A moan escaped my lips as he entered me. This was certainly not the same sexually timid Mark I knew. The guy wrapping his leg around me was more assertive, surer of what he wanted. Tonight, Mark had arrived with an agenda. I just wasn't sure if either of us were ready to go where we seemed to be headed.

"I don't like seeing you with other guys," Mark said, the bass in his voice turning me on like you wouldn't believe. "Especially not guys like *Rashad.*"

"Because he's a punk-ass nigga'?" I asked, repeating the hateful words Mark had let slip through his lips as Rashad and I were leaving the apartment. Now I was pissed all over again.

"You know I didn't mean to say that," Mark said. "I was just... jealous."

"But you did say it," I said, determined not to process that last comment. Six-months ago hearing Mark tell me he was jealous would have sent me to the moon. Now, the admission seemed like little more than an empty gesture on his part, offered up to keep me from pulling completely away.

"You have no reason...or right to be jealous of anyone I choose to spend time with."

"You're so sexy when you're mad at me," Mark said, pulling me closer.

With everything in me I resisted the urge to respond physically as his hot breath brushed across the nape of my neck. "Push up off me," I said snatching away.

Drawing me back into his strong hold, Mark allowed his full soft lips to graze against my ear. This is exactly why I should have never, ever told him that that was one of my g-spots.

"I'm sorry," he said, returning his hand to my butt.

"Yeah, you are," I said, forcing down the hope – and sexual energy -- building inside me. I needed to stay mindful of the cold hard reality. The chances of my having anything remotely resembling a real relationship with this man -- now positioning his penis between my legs -- were about the same as my winning the lottery. I'd be a damned fool, an utter and complete fool to hand over my body and soul to someone I knew was incapable of returning the favor. Falling in love with this boy would be tantamount to snatching out my own heart and stomping it.

"I thought I could, but I can't," Mark said, his hand caressing my chest. "I can't stand the thought of you with another guy."

How dare he play me like this! Every time I mustered up the courage to try and put this – whatever this was he and I had – into perspective, he'd man-up just enough to lure me back into his web. Well, not this time buddy boy. This time I was going to stand my ground, call a spade a spade. Let him know that I wasn't as stupid as he'd been playing me.

Spinning around to face him, I glared at Mark. "Let's see if I understand you correctly. You don't want me, but you don't want anybody else to have me either."

"That's not what I'm saying," he said, having the nerve to sound angry, "and you know it."

"All I know is what your actions tell me," I said, matching his salty tone.

Mark's eyes almost bugged out of his head. "You gotta be kidding me! "

Sitting up in the bed, I reached over to turn on the lamp. "Let's look at the facts, shall we?"

"Here we go," Mark growled under his breath. Placing his hands underneath his head, he stared toward the ceiling, bracing for my tirade.

"You and I have been *friends* for what, two years now?" I asked, rhetorically. "I've been your roommate almost a year of that…"

Trying not to hear me, Mark lay there, purposely not covering himself with the blanket. His large biceps, hairy legs, and six-pack abs -- rising and lowering with every agitated breath -- dared me to stay mad at him. Ooh, that boy makes me sick! Well, if he thought the sight of his naked body was going to throw me off, Home Slice had another thing coming.

"In that time we've messed around maybe six, seven times," I said, looking past him. "When you get horny enough you'll toss me a bone...a kiss here...a little dry-humping there..."

The truth of my words making him squirm, Mark finally pulled the blanket up to his chest...thank God.

"You can't keep having it both ways, Mark," I said, getting out of the bed. "I'm done with the mixed signals, and half-stepping." With every word, my level of anger over the position in which I'd put myself increased. "You are my boy, my ace...my partner in-crime..." Hesitating, I mustered up the courage to say the words, "but, I think I need to find another place to live."

Mark gasped. He pulled himself up against the headboard, the look in his eyes -- a combination of fear and shock -- causing my breath to stick in my throat.

"Chris, please don't say that—"

"It's for the best Mark, and you know it," I said, cutting him off before he could say, or do something to break me. With everything in me I knew I had to put some distance between us. It hurt too much to be this close.

"Come here."

Standing with my back to him, my heart quickened as I sensed his approach. "Go to bed, Mark," I croaked. "You don't want me so stop—"

"I want you so bad it hurts." Grabbing me by the waist, Mark pulled me close enough that I could feel his heart beating a mile a minute beneath his chest. "You have to know that."

"Come on Mark," I said, my eyes welling up with tears. "Don't do this to me. You don't...you can't mean it so don't—"

Before I could finish the sentence, he'd turned me around, lifted me into his arms, and lowered me onto the bed. In no time, I was lying on my back with Mark on top of me. There was nothing more exciting – or scary – than feeling his energy, smelling his scent. Part of me wanted to push his hand away as he reached for my t-shirt, lifting it over my head. But a greater part of me didn't want him to stop.

"Don't leave me," he pleaded, between kisses to my lips, and neck, and shoulders. "Don't ever leave me."

"You know how much I care about you, Boy," I said, trying to catch my breath as he lifted my butt off the bed in order to remove my underwear. "But you don't want to be g—"

"*Shhh.*" Mark's finger rose to my trembling lips to silence me. "We can deal with the reality tomorrow," he said, his eyes locking on mine. "Tonight you belong to me...and I belong to you."

Every inch of my body on fire, I gripped the sheets as Mark's oral exploration shifted from my earlobe, to my lips, to my heaving chest on down to the visibly excited area between my now quivering thighs.

"Damn you," I moaned, the sensation of his tongue against my pulsating skin sending me to the edge. "What you doin' to me?"

"You like that?" he asked, continuing to work it out.

"Hell yeah...ooh shit," I stammered. "Mark....ooh..."

For a virgin – that five minute fiasco with his high-school prom date didn't really count – Brotha Man had mad skills.

Just when he had me on the brink, Mark came up for air. Looking me dead in the eye he said, "Stop seeing him...*please?*"

Shaking my head like a mad-banshee, all I could manage to push through my dry lips was a weak-assed, "OK."

The shit-eating grin returning to his face, Mark went back to work between my legs. For a good five minutes he worked me over something awful. I tried to focus my eyes on him in order to take a mental snapshot of him making me feel so damned good, but I couldn't lift my head from the pillow. It took every ounce of energy I had not to explode as I lie there on my back, gasping and growling, squealing and howling. For so long I'd fantasized about what this would be like. Never in my wildest dreams could I have imagined one man, one mouth being able to set me off like this.

Not wanting to appear greedy, and afraid I was a nano-second away from erupting like Mount St. Helens, I pulled Mark up.

"Something wrong?"

"No," I said, planting a tender kiss on his lips. "Sit on the edge of the bed."

Mark gave me a nervous grin. "What you 'bout to do?"

"Now did I ask you that?" I said smiling as I stood in front of him. "What, you don't trust me?"

Mark's expression grew serious. "With my life," he said, and meant it.

How could I not love this man?

"Ease your legs over the side of the bed."

Tentatively but surely, Mark did as told.

Lowering to my knees before him, I ran my hands up and down his thick legs. He squirmed a bit, but withstood my touch.

"Damn," he whispered, closing his eyes as I placed wet kisses on each of his inner thighs. Though I wanted him in the worst way, I was determined not to rush this. Who knew if it was ever going to happen again.

The deepest, sexiest, most guttural moan escaped his lips as I took his pipe hard member into my mouth, teasing the throbbing head with my tongue.

Mark cried out softly as his hips pumped upward. "You are blowing my mind, Baby."

Not wanting him to reach the Promised Land too quickly, I pulled away. Like a man possessed, he snatched me down onto the bed, flipping me over onto my stomach.

I inhaled slowly as he slipped two fingers inside me. Initial pain quickly gave over to blissful ecstasy.

"You got any condoms?"

His question stopped me cold. Swallowing the scream lodged in my throat, I struggled to regain my bearings. Did he just ask me if I had any condoms? Was this really about to happen?

Turning onto my back, I stared at the massive mound of hardened flesh jutting upward from his midsection. "Mark," I asked pensively, "you sure?"

He nodded. "Yes."

Before either of us could change our mind, I reached into the nightstand drawer and pulled out the pack of under-used Trojans along with the tube of Wet lubricant. My hands shaking, I handed the items to Mark. Easing the pillow underneath me, he leaned over, kissing me long and hard on the lips. The taste of his tongue intermingled with my own made me high. I couldn't believe this was finally about to happen. On so many occasions, I'd laid in this very bed daydreaming about him being inside me. The thought alone had been enough to bring me to orgasm. And now it was really about to happen.

The room spinning around me, I watched in silent awe and eager anticipation as Mark ripped open the package, struggling to fit the large condom around his extra large penis. His eyes burning with desire, he lifted my legs, bringing them to rest on his broad shoulders.

As he slathered his latex covered penis with lubricant I closed my eyes and took a deep breath. "Careful."

"Okay."

Digging my nails into the sheet, I struggled to relax as he eased himself inside my body. "Oh...Ma...Mark...slow," I stammered. I'd been this intimate with only one other guy and he was no Mark, if you catch my drift.

Cringing, I pressed my hands against his chest.

"Am I hurting you?" he asked, concern coloring his flushed face.

"A little," I winced, carefully repositioning myself on the pillow.

"Want me to stop?"

"Hell no!" My head screamed. Wrapping my hands around his waist, I drew him into me. "Just go slow."

In no time any residue of discomfort was washed away with the mind-blowing pleasure of his thrusts into the core of my very being. Soon our lovemaking took the form of a well-orchestrated dance. Our bodies moved as one, giving and taking of their own accord.

"Mark!" I cried, tightening the vice grip my legs had formed around his neck. "Fuck me Man...harder...don't stop. Please don't stop!"

The sound of my strained, sex-craved voice got Mark even more excited. Balancing his weight against his outstretched hands, he plunged himself deeper into my now fully accepting body.

"You like that?"

"Ye...ye...yes," I stuttered.

Locking his hands around my butt, Mark pulled me closer, his thrusts – determined, forceful and utterly sure – pushing me closer to orgasm.

Before I could scream for him not to stop, he shouted, "Oh fuck! I'm...Chr...Chris, I'm com..."

Both approaching our shared apex, I grabbed onto Mark's furry backside, forcing him to give all that he had to me. The muscles in his legs twitching, he bit down on his bottom lip to stifle the sound of his cries as the power of his explosive orgasm overtook every inch of his being.

When the aftershocks finally subsided some minutes later, Mark slowly pulled out of me. Lowering his head onto my sweat-drenched chest, he sighed softly before falling off to sleep. Barely able to keep my eyes open, I stared at the man lying beside me, a bittersweet smile forming on my face. For better or worse, Mark had me...mind, body and soul.

Chapter One

Nine years later...

Watching Pastor Cannon grin from ear to ear as he went on about the union of his emotionally mute son to the cloyingly perfect Asia Stallings, I couldn't help thinking that I should have been the one standing up there next to Mark. But, he wasn't marrying me, unfortunately. He was marrying *her*.

"Asia," the Pastor said, turning to his soon-to-be daughter in law. "What father wouldn't want his son to marry such a beautiful, loyal...?"

She was loyal all right, like an attention-starved lap dog. Bitch.

Draining my glass of wine, I motioned for the waiter to bring me another. This shit was too thick to be endured sober. I really thought I could do this, but now I realized that I should have said no to Mark when he asked me to be a part of this farce. It was all rather pathetic, actually. That man – my supposed best friend -- had about as much business marrying that plastic Barbie doll as I did. None. So what if Asia was sweet, kindhearted, *apparently* intelligent with one killer rack? The fact remained: She wasn't right for Mark. I was.

"She could have chosen to be anything that she wanted," Pastor Cannon said, eyeing Asia. "But this God-fearing woman chose to educate young minds."

Oh *puhlease*! If my parents owned the most successful chain of funeral homes in Detroit, I could *choose* to be a fuckin' goodie two shoes as well. Oh how I hated that pretty, rich, man-stealing bitch!

Tabitha's head snapped in my direction. Oh good God, how I hoped I hadn't just said something evil out loud. Swallowing the venom surely reeking from every pore of my lock-jawed face, I flashed my old friend a bright smile. She returned a look that made it clear she wasn't buying my cheeriness. At that moment, however, I really didn't give a damn what Tabitha, or anybody else in the restaurant thought. I was being forced to bear witness to this train wreck of a marriage in the making, and it was killing me.

You know what? If Mark wanted to ruin his life, that was his business. Why should I care? He had made it perfectly clear when he moved out of our apartment seven months ago that anything we may have had was over. I was out and Miss Asia was in. And that was just fine by me. Good riddance to him. Good luck to her. Fuck them both.

I bet you Mrs. Cannon would have something to say about her son getting married if she were still alive. She wasn't giddy with joy over the prospect of Mark and me being together, but at least she was able to put her personal views aside for the sake of her son's happiness. Despite that bright smile on his chiseled, dark-chocolate, deeply dimpled face, I could tell that Mark wasn't as joyous about his impending nuptials as he put on.

Not six weeks after his mother passed, Mark's cock-blocking father went into overdrive, trying to put a wedge between me and his son, hell-bent on getting me out of Mark's life once and for all. If this cozy little celebration dinner for one-hundred and fifty was any indication, he'd won.

"I trust my boy will waste no time giving me some grandbabies," Pastor Cannon said with a not-so-playful wink at his son.

Asia squeezed Mark's hand as they stood there basking in the glory of this breathtakingly manufactured moment, while Pastor Cannon said some nonsense about their union being God's will. I don't know why he was trying to blame this on God.

And, why in the hell did anybody need to invite three-hundred people to their wedding? Ego and shallow boastful pride, that's why. Asia's rich, but class-free daddy, with an assist from his surgically enhanced, fifteen years his junior second wife, had invited every damned body under the sun to attend what would surely be a gaudy, emotionless wedding.

"I have known Marva and Douglass Stallings for well over twenty years now..."

It took everything I had not to chug up my four-course meal as Mark's old man fawned over his future in-laws. I hated all of them, but I *reeealy* hated that Asia chick. I hated every inch of her five foot seven, size eight wearing ass. Hated her long flowing honey blond hair and snow white teeth. And, I really, really hated the way she kept glancing over every fucking two minutes at Mark, flashing him that *I love me some you* smile. Hated it!

Turning to his son, Pastor Cannon choked back emotion. "In a few days my boy is getting married," he said, the relief in his voice almost palpable. He looked at Mark intently. "You be the man I raised you to be and commit yourself, mind, body and soul to this lovely woman..."

I glared at Mark, nodding obediently to his father/oppressor. I take back my hate for Asia. She's not my enemy. That poor girl was as much the victim in all this as I was. Mark was the one I hated. Okay, that wasn't true either. Despite everything -- the wishy-washiness, and inability to commit emotionally, the not standing up to his pious holy roller father, the moodiness, and guilt-filled silence every time we made love -- I still loved that bastard's dirty drawers.

I'll tell you what I really hated. I hated the fact that the man I gave my heart to was about to give his heart – legally anyway -- to another. I don't care what Mark said, there was no way he could possibly love Asia the way I knew he loved me. Every time he touched me, drawing me into his forty-six and a half inch chest, there was no doubt in my mind that he loved me. Every kiss told me so. It was in his eyes, even when it was absent from his words. I was…I *am* his soul mate, not Asia.

"Please raise your glasses," Pastor Cannon instructed the crowd, "and help me toast the happy couple."

Happy my ass! I shook my head resolved. No matter how badly the good reverend may have wanted it, this wedding was not going to happen. Nope, this travesty was not going to take place because I wasn't going to let it. Mark didn't belong with Asia and I wouldn't be his best friend if I allowed him to destroy three lives – hers, his and mine – by going through with this desperate attempt to be the man his father insisted he be.

"Chris?"

Later tonight I would march right over to Mark's apartment, sit him down and talk some sense into him. Sure, the last time I tried to do that he'd refused to hear me. I'd just have to try harder this time.

"Chris?"

He doesn't love her. He can't possibly—

"Christian!"

The sound of Tabitha's borderline shout jolting me out of my reverie, my hand jerked, causing the half full glass of white wine I was holding to spill onto the cream table cloth, and my navy suit.

"Why are you screaming at me?" I asked, snatching up a napkin. "Look what you made me do."

Unfazed that every eye in the restaurant had turned toward our table, Tabitha, or Tabby as Mark and I had taken to calling her, replied, "If you had answered me the first three times I called out your name I wouldn't have been forced to raise my voice."

Dabbing at the stain on my new silk tie, I rolled my eyes. "Whatever."

"Are you okay?"

"I'm fine," I lied.

"Really," Tabby said, dunking her napkin into the water before moving in to help me clean up my handy work. "You looked like you were lost in another world for most of Pastor Cannon's toast."

"I wish." The words were out of my mouth before I could stop them.

Tabby drew back. Eyeing me incredulously, she asked, "Have you told Mark how you feel?"

"How I feel about what?" I asked, failing miserably in my effort not to sound defensive. Tabby had never been big about beating around the bush. I was amazed she'd resisted asking me point blank whether or not Mark and I were lovers.

"You need to tell..." Tabby began, then trailed off. Her head snapped in the direction of her twin daughter and son seated on the other side of her. "Suzanne Elizabeth, do not put your finger in your brother's mouth again. "

She turned back to me. "Where are you going?"

Rising to my feet, I smirked. "To clean up the mess you made," I said, holding up my tie.

"I'll come with—"

"No, that's okay," I said, waving her off. "Besides, Miss Suzanne is about a nano-second from losing a finger."

Tabby's head twisted back toward her offspring. "Suzanne Elizabeth," she said through a tight smile, "don't make Mommy have to act unladylike up in this piece."

While mother and daughter handled their business, I made my way toward the bathroom to handle mine. Stopping at the door, I turned around, studying Mark as he leaned in to kiss his fiancée on her blushed cheek.

"It ain't over till the fat lady sings," I said in a determined whisper "Or Asia -- so sugary sweet she makes my teeth hurt -- says I do."

Chapter Two

"**W**hat?" I asked, noting the look on Chris' face. "You don't like it?"

"It's fine," he answered, continuing to study the ring. "It's absolutely fine."

"You think I should have gotten her something else, don't you?" I asked, now unsure of my selection. Between the two of us, Chris had the better sense of style by a mile. Most of the clothes in my closet, as well as the furniture in my apartment had been selected and/or blessed by him. That was exactly why I was a little upset when he kept making excuses for not going to select Asia's wedding band with me. With the wedding date fast approaching, I had to go pick out something on my own. Now, if his chilly response was any indication, I'd made the wrong choice.

"Why do you care what I think?"

"'Cause you my boy," I said, ignoring the coldness coming from across the table.

"Right," Chris said with a disbelieving chortle. "I'm your boy." He took a final look at the ring, then closed the box. "I'm sure your *girl* will love it."

"Man, I sure hope so," I said, relieved.

Chris looked away as he wiped at his eye.

"You all right, man?" I asked, concerned that maybe something was going on that he hadn't let me in on. Usually Chris and I shared everything – like best friends do. But between the big case he'd been working on at the ACLU – he was a lawyer there -- and all the planning for my wedding, we hadn't been able to find much time for each other these past few weeks. That was too bad. I really missed spending time with Chris. Didn't matter whether we were shooting hoops or shooting the breeze, everything just felt better when he was around. In a lot of ways, I thought of him as the brother I never had. Well, not exactly a brother, but just as close.

"I'm fine," Chris said, tossing the ring at me. "Take your ring."

Overlooking the fact that he damn near popped me in the eye with the box, I slid it back across the table. "No, you keep it."

Chris glowered at me like I'd spat on him. "Why?" he asked, his voice dripping with hostility. "It's not for me."

What the hell was wrong with him? I'm telling you, I loved Chris, but sometimes the brotha could be as moody as a woman. As far back as college, he tended to be a bit on the over-emotional side. Having ten years of experience dealing with him, I'd learned to ride out the wave until he finally emerged from his funk. That wasn't always so easy when we lived together. Despite his flaws, I've got nothing but mad love for the guy. Very few people understood me as Chris did. At least he used to.

Taking a calming breath, I explained, "It's tradition for the best man to keep the ring until the wedding day."

"Fine," Chris said, placing the box next to his cell phone. "I'll hold your woman's ring."

"Thank you," I said, a bit more sardonically than I'd intended.

There was a good two minutes of silence between us before I made another attempt at having a civil conversation with him.

"Hey, what happened to you last night?"

Not bothering to break his stare out the window of Union Street, Chris said, "I don't have a clue what you're talking about."

Like a fool I pressed forward. "Tabby said you'd gone to the bathroom, but when I came looking, you were nowhere to be found."

"Umm hmm," Chris said, barely paying attention. "I had a more pressing engagement."

More pressing than his best friend's pre-wedding dinner? Oh, see, now this Negro was starting to piss me off.

"Dude, what is your beef?"

"What's my beef?" Chris asked, looking at me like I was supposed to know the answer already. "Mark Cannon, you are such a selfish asshole."

"Me!" I said almost shouting. "I'm not the one sitting here pouting like a little bitch."

"I got ya' bitch," Chris smarted.

Slowly inhaling, I reminded myself that I sincerely liked the man sitting across from me. "Did I do something to you?" I asked, baffled by his apparent anger with me. "If I did, let's talk about it, so we can quash all this hostility."

Chris chuckled bitterly as he raised the glass of water to his lips. "Were it only that simple."

Leaning into the table, I reached for Chris' hand, stopping short when I remembered we were in a public place. I wasn't big on PDA's, not even with Asia. She'd actually commented on it a few times. I'd had to explain to her that it was just the way I was. She knew how I felt about her, just as Chris knew how I felt about him. There was no need to bring the rest of the world into the mix. Color me private, but I subscribed to my father's view: Some things are best left behind closed doors.

"Is it something at work...your mom...sister?" I asked, trying to identify the problem so I could help my friend find a solution.

"Spare me the feigned concern for my well-being," Chris said, dryly.

"Fuck it then," I said, irritated. "With all I got on my plate right now, I don't have time for this passive-aggressive crap."

Chris lowered his glass. "My bad," he said with mock sincerity. "Forgive me for not being singularly focused on your comfort. Lord knows its gotta be hard on you seeing how you're a day away from making the biggest mistake of your—"

My hand shot into the air to silence him. "Don't even start with that shit, Chris." I shook my head in disbelief. "I can't believe you."

"You can't believe--" Chris said in an angry whisper, stopping short when he saw Tabitha approaching our table.

"Hey Frick and Frack," she said giving us both pecks on the cheek.

Cutting my eyes at Chris, I said, "What's up Tabby Cat."

"Sorry, I'm late," she said, taking a seat next to the guy well on his way to becoming my ex-best friend. "What you doing in a suit," Tabby asked Chris, brushing her hand across the lapel of his jacket.

"Duh...work," he said. "The ACLU may not be as prestigiously saditty as the blue-chip law firms you two work for," Chris said, eyeing me and Tabby, "but they still expect us to look like professionals."

"That's not what I meant, smart-ass," Tabby said, popping him in the arm. "I thought you had taken the day off," she explained, glancing over at me. "What with the bachelor party tonight and the wedding tomorrow, I just knew you two wouldn't have time for work."

"I did take the day off," I said, tugging at my Michigan Law School t-shirt.

"You're the one getting married," Chris said, sharply. "I on the other hand, gotta get ready for the case we're bringing against the state."

"Umm hmm," Tabby said, correctly sensing that Chris wasn't being completely on the up-in-up. "So what time does the *boyswillbeboyspalloza* start?"

"You're picking me up at eight, right?" I asked, turning to Chris.

"About that," he said, unable to look me in the eye. "Looks like I'm going to be at the office later than I thought." Chris fiddled with his cell phone. "It might be best if we just...umm...meet at the club."

"What?" I asked stunned. "Dude, you my road dawg...we're supposed to ride together."

"Shit happens," was Chris' smug response.

"It's all good," I said, trying to shake it off. "I'll just follow you back to your place—"

"Why don't we play it by ear?" Chris suggested. "I might have other plans later."

I fell back in the chair floored by his pissy attitude. For the life of me I couldn't understand why Chris was acting this way. Okay, that wasn't completely true. Considering our *interesting* history together it only stood to reason that this might be a little difficult for him. But damn, this guy was acting like I was divorcing him to marry Asia.

Sensing the tense energy between Chris and me, Tabby sighed. "Somebody wanna tell me what I've missed?"

"Absolutely nothing," Chris said, tapping his cell phone on the table.

Tabby's eyes widened when she noticed the box sitting in front of him. "Is that the ring," she said, snatching it up. "Nice." She smiled as she spied the platinum band. "Asia's a lucky girl."

"She'd be a lucky girl even without a seven thousand dollar ring," I said, trying for levity. "She got me."

If you weren't watching too closely, you might not have noticed the smirk on Chris' face. I noticed.

Tabby looked over at him. "Did you help pick this out?"

"Nope," he said simply.

"Chris doesn't like it," I said, half-joking.

"I didn't say that," he said super-seriously. "And since I'm not the one marrying your confused..." Chris added, before catching himself. He waved his hand in surrender. Even he knew he was crossing the line. "Not my business."

"Whatever Chris," I said, irritated. His reservations about my marrying Asia, the ones he'd shared with me every chance he got, were inconsequential at this point. Tomorrow I was getting married and that was that. Chris needed to stop being such a wet pussy, grow up, and get over it. Were the tables reversed, I'd support his ass whether he was right, wrong or somewhere in the middle.

The sound of my ringing cell phone snapped me out of my angry haze. Reaching for my waist, I spied the caller-ID, my heart jumping when I saw the name. "Hey, Babe."

While I was on the phone with Asia, Tabby turned to Chris. "What's wrong with you?" I heard her whisper.

"Uh...yeah..." I said, barely listening to my fiancée. "That sounds good."

"Nothing," Chris whispered back to Tabby. "I'm just tired of the bullshit."

Sitting there half-listening as Asia outlined a list of wedding plans I cared little about, I wondered exactly what bullshit Chris was talking about. When we got back to his place after the bachelor party tonight I was going to get to the bottom of whatever it was that was eating him. I know I said I didn't care, but when it came to Chris, it was impossible not to care.

"Me too," I said into the phone, praying Asia wouldn't press me to say the words.

Chris' head snapped in my direction, the look on his face sending a chill up my back. I should have gotten up from the table to take the call.

Tabby continued probing. "And exactly what bull—?"

His hand rising to stop her, Chris' eyes remained fixed on me, daring me to say it.

"I love you too."

The words were barely out of my mouth before Chris was on his feet. "I need to go."

Tabby cocked her head to the side. "We haven't even ordered lunch yet," she said curiously.

"Lost my appetite."

"Chris wait," I said, covering the phone. "No, not you...Asia hang on."

Reaching for his arm I tried to stop him from leaving. "Dude—"

"Let go of me," he said, snatching away.

Stunned, I stood from the table. "What the fuck is your problem!"

"What the fuck is my problem?" Chris shouted back.

Tabby jumped into the small space between us. "Fellas, let's use our indoor voices please," she said carefully.

Still on the phone, Asia asked what was going on.

Taking a breath I answered, "Nothing important."

"You got that right," Chris said, turning on his heels.

"Chris wait!" Tabby called out after him.

"Let him go," I said, stopping her before she could follow him. "Asia, I need to call you back...I won't forget...bye."

Slapping the phone closed, I retook my seat.

Tabby fell back into her chair. "What was that all about?" she asked, eyeing me like it was my fault Chris was acting a fool.

"Your guess is as good as mine."

The expression on Tabby's face made me squirm. For a split second I wondered if Chris had told her something he shouldn't have. But I knew he'd never do that to me.

"May I get you something to drink Ma'am?" the waiter asked.

"Umm...let me get a glass of iced-tea," Tabby said. "You know what...bring me a glass of merlot instead."

Nodding, the waiter turned to me. "Would you like another beer sir?"

"Yes...no," I said changing my mind. "Make it a gin and tonic instead." Why wait until my bachelor party? I saw no reason to delay the start of my celebration.

"Will the other gentleman be rejoining you?" the waiter asked, acting as if he'd not just witnessed Chris' diva-like march out the door.

"He had to get back to work," Tabby said.

"Very well, then. I'll be right back with your drinks," the waiter said, then dashed off.

"I can't believe him," I said, still smarting over Chris' outburst. "Of all the times for him to show his ass he chooses now... *unfuckingbelievable.*"

"Cut him some slack," Tabby said. "Surely you of all people can understand how difficult this must be for Chris."

"Difficult for Chris!" I guffawed. "What about how difficult this is for me. I'm the one getting married."

"And you don't think seeing the man he lov—" Tammy stopped talking abruptly. Reaching for Chris' glass of water she took a long sip. "Not my business."

"No, finish what you were about to say," I said, my heart beating a mile a minute. What did she know? I wondered.

Tammy pondered for a moment. "How long have I known you and Chris?"

"Seven, maybe eight years."

"In all those years, I can't call to mind a time when you two guys were apart from each other more than 48 hours," Tabby said, not taking her eyes off me. "It's always been Mark *and* Chris....Frick and Frack."

I chuckled, recalling the first time Tabby had dubbed us that. In so many ways it seemed like yesterday that she'd moved into the apartment next to ours. Chris and I were in our first year of law school, Tabby was in her second. I could still remember the day she'd asked me how long Chris and I had been lovers, to which I *aggressively* assured her that we were not. My father was a minister for goodness sake! Gay was the last thing I'd be. A bemused look on her face, Tabby apologized, adding that she'd only assumed we were since we were so close to one another...just like Frick and Frack.

"Losing you can't be easy on him."

"I'm getting married, Tabby, I'm not moving to Antarctica," I said flippantly. "Chris and I will still be best friends."

"What you and Chris have is more than *just* a friendship, Mark," Tabby said, nodding to the waiter as he sat the drink before her. She waited until he left the table before continuing. "How would you feel if he got married to some guy?"

Swallowing my discomfort, I tried to make a joke. "Surprised since it's illegal."

Tabby rolled her eyes, not appreciating my failed attempt at humor. "You know what I mean."

Blowing air nervously through my lips, I said, "I've never judged Chris for being gay. If that's what floats his boat—"

"Stop it," Tabby said, cutting me off.

"Stop what?" I asked, shifting my weight in the chair, thoroughly afraid to continue this conversation. "It's not my fault that Chris is acting like a five year old."

"Chris isn't acting like a five year old," Tabby said, taking off the gloves. "He's acting like a man with a broken heart. And I'd think you of all people would appreciate that."

Before I could get in a word edgewise, Tabby continued. "You can call what the two of you have had all these years whatever you'd like Mark, but don't sit there and insult both of our intelligence by acting like you're utterly clueless as to why Chris is falling apart."

"Look, I don't know what Chris has told you, Tabby," I said, shame and guilt flushing my cheeks. "But I'm not like that."

"I lived next door to you guys for two years," Tabby said sharply. "So before you sit there and tell me what you aren't, keep in mind that the walls between our apartments were paper thin...and my hearing pitch-perfect."

The lump in my throat the size of a boulder, I reached for the gin and tonic. With an unsteady hand, I raised the glass to my lips, taking a long gulp of the liquor. Sitting there I could feel the room and my world closing in around me. Tabby had just exposed my deepest secret and darkest shame. Slumping in my chair, I felt like everyone in the restaurant was looking at me, their eyes filled with judgment, hating me as much as I hated myself.

"Are you in love with her?"

"Yes," I croaked. "I love my fiancée."

"I didn't ask you if you loved her," Tabby clarified. "I asked if you were *in* love with her."

"I'm marrying her aren't I?" I asked rhetorically.

Tabby was my girl, but she was completely out of line here. She had no right to call me on the carpet like this. I'd been to hell and back in the past year. The one person in the world who I could always count on to support and protect me was gone. My whole world shifted off balance when Mamma passed. Had it not been for Asia's friendship, and unique insights to what I was dealing with, I don't think I could have survived. Having lost her own mom when she was just fifteen, she knew what I was feeling without me having to say a word. Asia held my hand, and witnessed with me through the darkness. I owed my life to that girl, I really did.

Tabby reached across the table, covering my trembling hand with her own. Before I could stop it, the tear was making its decent down my cheek. Damn it! I was a man. Men didn't cry. They got married to women and they built families together. That was what the Bible said, and what my father demanded. I had no choice in the matter.

Pulling my hand away, I rose from the table. "Listen, I gotta get going," I said, reaching into my wallet.

"Talk to him, Mark."

I placed the bills on the table, then leaned over to kiss Tabby goodbye. "I'll see you at breakfast tomorrow."

Racing toward my truck, I jumped inside. Lowering my head onto the steering wheel, I exhaled a pained sighed.

"Chris. I am so sorry."

Closing my tear-filled eyes, I prayed to God for the strength to do what I knew I had to do.

Chapter Three

Waiting for my father in his office, I pulled out my cell phone and pressed the number three to speed dial my home phone. I wasn't in the habit of checking there for messages during day, figuring that anyone who I really needed to talk to knew my cell number. Something in my gut, however, suggested that today I make an exception.

I inhaled slowly when the message began to play. After ten years the sound of his voice still had the power to make me lose my breath.

"Umm...hey it's me," Chris said tentatively. "Look man, I'm not trying to make things harder..." There was a moment of hesitation before he continued. "I just...I...I think it would be best if I didn't come to the bachelor party tonight..."

Rubbing my forehead, I blew through my lips. His decision not to come tonight bothered me, but I could live with it. Chris just needed a little time to deal with everything.

"...or be your best man tomorrow..."

"What!" I leapt up from the chair. "Son of a bitch!" I shouted, then glanced up to the ceiling, hoping the Lord wasn't listening.

Not bothering to let the message finish, I hit the END call button, quickly punching the number one. Anxiously, I paced around the office as I waited for the call to connect.

"Hi this is Chris Weaver—"

"Shit...shoot," I said, again remembering where I was.

Canceling the call, I hit the number two. If Chris wasn't answering his cell, maybe I could catch him at home.

This was madness. If his point was to unsettle me, he'd succeeded. I got it. Chris was pissed with me. Maybe I hadn't handled all of this in the best possible way, but that was no reason for him to pull some shit like this.

"Chris if you're there pick up," I demanded into the phone. "Pick up!"

Realizing he either wasn't home, or was screening his calls, I swallowed my pride and began pleading my case. "Chris, man I'm sorry. You my...you my boy. How could you even consider not being my best man?"

Falling into the chair, I lowered my face into my hand. "I realize how hard this must be for you." Heaven knows it was utter hell for me. "But please, Man…please don't turn your back on me. Not now."

I waited a beat, hoping he'd pick up the phone. He didn't.

"Come on Chris, talk to me," I said, now full-out begging. The thought that I'd finally pushed him too far was more than I could bear. We'd had our ups and downs like friends do, but I couldn't imagine my life without Chris in it. As unfair as it might have been, I couldn't let him go. I wouldn't let him go.

Struggling to keep it together, I cleared my throat. "Please come tonight. Okay, if you don't feel up to the party, I understand. But promise me you'll be standing at my side tomorrow," I said, the level of desperation I was feeling in that moment threatening to swallow me whole.

"I love you Christian." The instant I uttered the words, the magnitude of my feelings for him rushed to the surface. My voice cracking, I begged some more. "Dude, you gotta try to look at this from my position—"

Sensing someone standing behind me in the office, I discreetly snatched back the tears readying to fall from my eyes.

"Just call me alright," I said, then quickly closed the phone, praying that my father hadn't heard anything too damning.

Making his way into the office, Dad took a seat behind his large cherry wood desk, his face expressionless. As if stating the temperature he said, "It's for the best."

"I'm sorry," I said distractedly. "What's for the best?"

"Chris not being part of yours and Asia's wedding." Still, calm as a cucumber, Dad loosened his tie as he reclined in the chair. "Divine order if you ask me."

Though his words had pissed me off in the worse way, I had the presence of mind not to let the words, "But I didn't ask you," slip from my lips. My father wasn't an abusive man, but he wouldn't hesitate to knock me into next week if I ever disrespected him.

"Chris is my best friend," I said, careful to keep the bass in my voice at an acceptable level. "And he's my best man."

"You're no longer in grade school, Mark," Dad said, searching for his glasses, hidden somewhere beneath the mountain of files on his messy desk. "And the only person you *need* standing beside you at your wedding is your wife…and the Lord."

He'd never said it point-blank, but my father had made it clear that he wasn't particularly fond of Chris from the moment he first met him. He was even less of a fan after what happened senior year. Chris was staying at my house over Spring Break. My mom, who adored him, had made up one of the spare rooms for him to sleep in. Most nights after shooting the shit until the wee hours, however, Chris would wind up climbing into my bed with me. Nothing even remotely sexual ever happened. We both had far too much respect for my parents to do anything in their home. Other than a few glances here, or a prolonged touch there, we were careful to keep everything above board.

Well, one morning my old man walked into my bedroom – that'll teach him for not knocking first -- and found us asleep in my bed. I almost pissed my boxers when I awakened to find him standing over Chris and me, looking as if he was witnessing a train wreck. To his credit he didn't make a scene, he simply backed out of the room, closing the door behind him. Later that day, Dad suggested to me that perhaps it would be best if my *friend* spent the remaining days of the break with his own family. Guilty – for what I wasn't sure – I simply said, "Okay."

Chris hadn't stepped foot back into my parents' home since.

"Your mother and I worked hard to give you every privilege in life," my father said, pushing the wire-rimmed glasses up his nose. He looked over at me, his eyes saying what his words wouldn't. "Unto whom much is given much is required."

I swallowed nervously as he eased forward in the chair. "The time for youthful experimentation is over," Dad said, locking me in his gaze. "It's time for you to be the man I raised you to be…and do the right thing."

"I'm not so sure what that is anymore," I said in a whisper.

Dad exhaled. "The right thing…the only responsible thing for you to do is to carry on our family name," he said, fighting to keep his temper in check. "Asia is a good woman, Son. She'll make a good wife and mother."

"But, Pops I'm not sure that I love her enough to—"

"Cold feet," he said, cutting me off. "That's all it is."

It wasn't as simple as that and we both knew it. My father took great care to speak in generalities so as not to deal with the shame, guilt and fear that came with directly addressing the big gay elephant standing in the room – Chris.

"Think about your future," he said, rightly sensing that I was wavering on my decision to marry Asia. "You are a junior partner with a blue-chip law firm. If you want to move up, there are certain expectations..."

Pinching the bridge of his nose, Dad considered his words carefully. "Son, you need to have a *woman* like Asia at your side. Whatever you think you feel for..." he caught himself before saying Chris' name aloud. His hands tightening into a fist, my father took another breath. "It's God's will for men and women to marry and procreate. The Bible is very clear about this."

"What if I'm not in love with her?" I asked, fighting back the tears my father told me men didn't shed.

Standing to his feet, Dad made his way around the desk. As he stood behind me, I braced myself, certain he was about to knock me in the back of my head, barking out something like, "Now you listen to me you little fudge packer. No son of mine is going to be a Nelly boy. You are going to marry that girl and never talk to that faggot Chris again...period, end of discussion!" Instead he squeezed my shoulders and sighed. "The day your mother told me she was pregnant with you was the happiest day of my life."

He sat down beside me. "After three first-trimester miscarriages, the good Lord had blessed us with a child."

There were many things about my father I questioned; his love for me wasn't one of them. He wasn't the most demonstrative man in the world, but in his own way he made sure I always knew how important I was to him. His rather severe religious beliefs made him unbearably inflexible sometimes, but I loved and respected my pops more than words could say. The last thing I'd ever want to do was hurt him. Never again would I put myself in a position to see the look of pain I saw in his eyes the morning he'd found Chris and me in my bedroom.

"It wasn't easy for me and your mom," Dad said. "But we stuck it out, committed to our union. That's why God gave us the miracle."

His words, while uplifting, weren't exactly accurate. Two years ago, my mom had shared with me how their inability to create a child had almost resulted in the end of her and my father's marriage. After catching Dad and the church secretary in a less than Christian-like embrace, Mom had walked out on him. Even while she showed up to church every Sunday, continuing to play the role of loving wife and first lady, she and Dad lived under different roofs. Separated for six months, he'd only asked to come home after finding out his wife was four months pregnant with his son.

"Were you in love with Momma when you married her?" I asked, not wanting to offend my father, but needing desperately to know the answer.

He hesitated for a moment before finally answering, "No."

Sitting straight up, I blinked. Did he just say what I think he said?

"I cared deeply for your mother," Dad explained. "But it wasn't some mad passionate love affair."

Rising from the chair, my father walked over to the window. "Peggy was a good woman from a fine upstanding family. I was a young, newly ordained minister. We were a good fit."

Listening to him made me shudder. To think that two people got married simply because they were 'a good fit' didn't sit well with me. Wasn't life supposed to be lived with passion, preferably with someone you felt some passion for?

"In time I grew to love Peggy deeply," Dad said, staring out the window into the courtyard garden where my Mom had planted roses, tender lilies, and sunflowers every spring. "Life isn't always as simple as it appears on the movie screen, Son," he said, turning around to face me. "We don't always get what it is we think we want. But God always gives us what we *need*."

What I needed was a sign from the Father that I wasn't about to make the biggest mistake of my life.

"This is for you," my dad said handing me a box. "I meant to give it to you sooner." My heart leapt into my throat as I stared inside. "This is Mom's wedding ring," I said, in a stunned whisper.

"She would have wanted you to have it."

"I don't know," I said, shaking my head.

"It's up to you to carry on the Cannon name," Dad said, more a plea than a statement of truth. "Now that your mom is..." he said, choking back emotion, "you're all I got."

And with that, my decision had been made. In less than twenty-four hours I was going to commit my life to Asia Stallings. It wasn't a love supreme, but Asia was a good woman who I adored. The sex wasn't the greatest, but with time – and a lot of practice -- it would get better. As man and wife, we'd create the family I'd always wanted, giving them the traditional, stable upbringing my Mom and Dad had afforded me. Tomorrow I was getting married.

So it is said, so it is done.

Turning to face my father, I said, "I won't let you down."
A prideful smile formed on his face. "That's my boy."

Chapter Four

*F*rom the curb I stared up at the house in which I'd grown up. The tattered basketball hoop, minus net, still hung from the garage. Mark and I had played countless games out there during his visits over the past ten years. The porch swing we'd sat in while we talked for hours about the life we'd live together, was still there as well. Whenever things got rough, I always found my way back home, a place where the good memories far exceeded the bad.

With the key my moms insisted I keep when I moved out, I opened the front door. "No matter where you are, or what you're going through, you can always come home," was what she'd told me.

The instant I walked inside, my spirits brightened. My stomach growling, I inhaled the heavenly scent of whatever Delia Weaver was cooking. That woman knew she could work it out in the kitchen.

I smiled as I gazed around the living room. Everything remained in meticulous order. The framed print of Bearden's *She-Ba* held its usual place of prominence over the black sofa with overstuffed cream pillows. On the opposite side of the large box-shaped room, stood the same black lacquer entertainment center Mom had bought almost twelve years ago with the first check she'd received after returning to teaching. My father had made her stop working shortly after Stacey was born. Since the divorce, Mom had been diligent in living her life the way she chose, imploring my baby sister and me to do the same.

From the Fisher stereo and compact disc system – a gift from Stacey – the sound of George Benson's sweet guitar wrapped the house in melodious sound. As usual, the 36-inch television I'd bought Mom a few years back was turned off. It was rarely ever turned on. "I can get my news from a newspaper and my entertainment from a good book," Mom would say whenever Stacey or I pressed her about her aversion to the big black box. The three exceptions Delia Weaver made to her *television is a waste of perfectly good brain cells* rule, however were to watch *The West Wing, Desperate Housewives,* and *Alias.*

Lucky, our family's seven-year old black lab, poked his fat head through the banister spokes. The moment he saw me, he came barreling down the stairs, barking at the top of his lungs.

"Come here boy," I said, trying to catch him before he could run back into the kitchen to tell his mother that her *other* son was home. "How ya' doin' fella," I said as the high-strung animal lapped up my face. There really was no place like home. And right now I needed the unique comfort found here something awful.

Stacey appeared at the top of the stairs, frowning. "Lucky if you don't cut out all that..." she said, stopping short when she saw me.

"Oh my--!"

My finger zipping toward my lips, I shushed my sister before she could build up to a full scream.

Hurrying down the stairs, Stacey wrapped her arms around my neck, planting a kiss on my cheek. "I thought you'd fallen off the face of the earth," she said in an excited whisper. "Did Momma know you were coming over?"

"No I was just out driving and wound up here."

"I see," Stacey said knowingly. She stepped back, giving me a visual once-over. "Ooo la la," she cooed, squeezing my bicep. "Somebody's been working out."

"Stop that," I said, blushing as I pushed her hand away.

"*Sooo,*" Stacey said, grinning coyly. "Paul told me that he invited you to the opening of the Harris Sifuentes exhibition at the Taggert Gallery."

"Yep," I said, hoping that would be the end of my sister's latest attempt at matchmaking. Just because she'd fallen head over heels for a Washington man, didn't mean lightning would strike twice.

I'd never seen a woman happier than Stacey was the day she married Patrick two years ago. The aforementioned, Paul was his younger brother's best man. I gave my Stacey away – grudgingly. Spying Mark as he sat with Tabby, in the row directly behind my mom, I wished it was he and I getting married that day. But alas, this was America, and well, Mark was Mark.

"Why didn't you go?"

"Why didn't I go where?" I asked, playing dumb.

"Don't even try it," Stacey said with a smirk. "Paul really likes you Chris."

"And I like him."

"So, why won't you give any play?"

With a weary sigh, I looked at my sister. "Can we not have this conversation today?" I couldn't count the number of times Stacey had tried to push her brother-in-law into my arms. A senior design engineer with General Motors, Paul was a nice guy and -- like his brother Patrick -- was the very definition of tall, dark, and handsome. Most men and a few desperate women would have jumped at the chance to date him. I wasn't one of them.

"It's time to face the reality," Stacey said. "Mark is getting married tomorrow--"

"I know that," I said cutting her off. "Believe me, I know that."

"Sorry," Stacey said, stroking my forearm. "I just want you to be happy, Chris."

Unclenching my jaw, I said, "I know."

"So you gonna call him?"

"You're getting fat," I said as if noticing her extra girth for the first time.

Stacey's mouth fell open. "That's because I'm seven months pregnant you butt wipe!" She squealed, punching me in the arm.

"Ouch," I said, stepping out of her reach. "Are you having twins?"

"You are such an ass," Stacey said, laughing.

"I'm joking," I said, kissing her cheek. "You look beautiful."

"Thank you," she said, then sighed. "But man am I horny as hell."

"Too much information lady," I said, covering my ears. "Too much damned information."

"God bless my husband," Stacey said, empathetically. "I know I'm working that poor man out."

Standing there, I flinched as the thought popped into my head. What if Stacey's husband had been some homosexual/bi/curious-confused brotha carrying on a ten year affair with another man? Worse yet, what if he'd continued seeing the man after marrying and knocking up my sister, claiming the two were just *boys*? Would there be any logical justification he could offer Stacey for fucking her life up so royally? I'd be the second one in line -- Mom being the first -- demanding that Stacey toss Patrick's trifling *confused-not* ass to the curb with the rest of the rotting trash. I didn't know Asia all that well, but from what I could tell she was good people. She'd always been nice to me. Lord knows I didn't always return the favor. As much as it pained me to say it, I knew in my gut that she loved Mark, almost as much as I did. And while I may have felt like one, Asia was the true victim in this little love triangle from hell. At least I was in on the lie. I'd made the choice to take part in the madness. Asia remained clueless.

"You okay, Bro?" Stacey asked, noting the far away look in my eyes.

"I'm good," I said, shaking off the dark thoughts. "A little tired is all."

"Well you need to get more rest," she said, then added, "or find someone worth losing sleep over."

"Don't start."

"Nobody's starting anything," Stacey said, following me down the hall. "But let me just say this one last thing."

Turning to face her, I sighed. "Say it."

"If genetics hold true, Paul has a lot to offer," she said with a wink. "If you know what I mean."

"Ugh," I said, cringing. "You are such a freak."

"I'm just saying," Stacey said, laughing.

I couldn't help but laugh too. "Oh, I think you've said enough."

Bounding past us into the kitchen, Lucky planted himself under the table. Rising onto her tip-toes, Stacey watched from over my shoulders as I stood in the doorway watching Mom go about the business of living her life.

Delia hummed to herself as she alternated between checking on the cornbread warming in the oven, and the collards simmering on the stove top. I could never get enough of seeing Mom when she was like this; happy even when the world wasn't looking. In that moment, all of the pain and confusion...and anger I was experiencing over Mark marrying Asia melted away. I was home, and for the time being anyway, I was happy.

"Hey, Ma."

Stilling herself for a moment, Mom made sure her ears weren't failing her. Turning toward me, her face lit up. "My Baby's home?"

"How you doin' Beautiful?" I said, going over to embrace her.

Delia held me tightly before finally taking a step back. "Are you eating okay?" she said, her voice brimming with maternal concern.

"Mother, will you stop it," Stacey said. "Chris looks fine."

"Yes he does," Delia said proudly.

"*Maaaaa!*" I protested as she pinched my reddening cheeks.

"Is the Baby embarrassed?" Stacey teased.

"You be quiet, pregnant lady," I said, swatting her on the butt as she passed.

"Well, I don't care if I embarrass you," Mom said, running her fingers through the mess of curls on my head. "You are my Baby," she gushed. "Always will be."

Stacey made her way over to the stove. "He knows he likes it," she said.

"Come sit down," Mom said, pulling out a chair for me. "I'll make you a plate."

Stacey cut her eyes at our mother. "I asked you to make me a plate not ten minutes ago and you told me to go to hell," she said, feigning irritation.

"Get out of that pot girl," Mom said, pushing Stacey aside so she could fix my plate.

Make no mistake, my mother loved both of her children dearly, but it was obvious to everyone, including Stacey, that I was the favored one. I was Delia's first, and for five years, only child. As a little girl, Stacey had been resentful of the special bond between Mom and me, until she realized that she hadn't suffered because of it. Delia Weaver had more than enough love to go around.

"If I'd known you were coming by I would have had more than leftovers waiting for you," Mom said as I finished wolfing down my second helping of the ham, macaroni and cheese, collards, and cornbread.

"I love your leftovers Ma," I said, stuffing the last fork full of greens into my mouth.

"How 'bout some pie?"

Shaking my head no, I pushed myself away from the table. "I don't think I can eat another bite," I said, rubbing my full stomach. My appetite had been one of the casualties – along with my self-respect -- of the stress I'd been under lately. Being back in Momma's house however brought it right back to life. Let's hope my self-respect would soon follow suit.

Pleased that her son had eaten every bite, Mom picked up the empty plate and carried it over to the sink. "How's Mark doing?" she asked casually.

"Who cares," I said tight lipped. "I've decided not to be his best man tomorrow."

"You wanna tell me what happened, or should I try to guess?" Mom asked smoothly.

"Well that's my cue," Stacey said, rising from the table. "It's good to see you big brother," she said, giving me a light smack across the back of my head.

"You too," I said a bit distracted.

Stacey kissed Mom goodbye. "I'll call you tomorrow."

"Okay, Hun," Mom said. "Drive carefully...and under the speed limit."

"I will."

Once my sister had waddled out of the room, Mom turned from the basin. "What's going on, Christian?"

Exhaling in frustration, I rubbed my wrinkled forehead. Part of me wanted to just lie and say everything was okay. Assert that I was at total peace with the fact that the man I loved – the same man I'd wasted a decade of my freakin' life pining for -- was getting married tomorrow. Past experience, however had taught me that it was wasted effort trying to convince Mom I was okay if I wasn't. The woman was like a heat-seeking missile when it came to her children. She knew when something wasn't right with one of us -- sometimes before we did.

"This is tougher than I thought it would be," I said, my voice quivering. "I feel like such a fool."

Mom sighed softly as she wiped her hands across her apron. Making her way across the kitchen, she took a seat in the chair beside me. "You are not a fool," she said with gentle certainty. "You, my dear son, are loving and kind-hearted..."

Tears clouding my vision, I listened as my mom worked to rebuild my sense of self-worth.

"Mark is the one missing out here," Mom said, shaking her head adamantly. "He doesn't deserve a man as wonderful as you."

As much as I appreciated what she was trying to do, there was nothing my mother could say that was going to make me want Mark any less than I did.

"Maybe I should just find some girl to marry," I suggested, more as a wishful thought than anything.

"Why would you want to do something so foolish?" Mom asked, taking me seriously.

"It would make it easier."

"For whom?"

"Come on Mom," I said, wearily. "Don't you wish I were straight?"

"Sure," Mom answered. "I also wish I were twenty pounds lighter...and independently wealthy. But the fact is I'm neither of those things, just as you're not straight."

"Can I ask you something? And please tell me the God's honest truth."

Mom straightened in the chair. "*Okaaay.*"

"Are you ashamed—?"

"Don't finish that question," she said quickly. "I am proud of, and amazed by you Christian Teshawn Weaver. I'm also terribly worried and concerned..."

Hesitating, Mom placed her hand on mine. "Hear me when I say this," she said, fixing her eyes on mine. "I have never ever been ashamed of you. *Ever.*"

Lowering my head, I wiped away the tears streaming down my cheek. My mother may not be, but I was very much ashamed of myself. For the past ten years I'd been hoping for a dream that, on some level, I had to have known would never come true. But like a fool, I'd chased and hoped, ignoring brutal reality each and every time it bitch-slapped me across the face.

"If I could I'd wave a magic wand, enabling you to see that you deserve so much more than what Mark can give you," Mom said. "But I can't."

Drawing me into her full bosom, my momma rocked me gently as I sobbed like a baby. "Only you can save you," she said, softly. "The decision to no longer dishonor you by accepting anything less than Mark's complete, utter and exclusive love has to be yours," Mom explained. "Whether you say it today, tomorrow, or a year from now, you have to be the one to say it."

Sniffing I asked, "Say what?"

"Enough," Mom said simply. "Enough."

Chapter Five

*L*eaving my mother's house shortly before nine o'clock, I drove back to my apartment, shedding my business suit the moment I walked through the door. Wearing only a pair of gray boxer briefs, I crawled into bed, tired and heartbroken, yet oddly hopeful. The wedding hadn't happened yet, which meant anything was still possible, including a miracle.

Lying there, I stared at the ceiling, my mom's words and Mark's calls keeping me from sorely needed slumber. Finally dozing off shortly after midnight, I was jolted into full consciousness a few minutes later.

"Shit!" the all-too familiar voice cried out.

Annoyed, but unconcerned, I rose from the bed and headed down the hall without bothering to demand, "Who's in my living room bumping into my shit?"

There was only one man arrogant, and stupid enough to come calling at such an ungodly hour – uninvited, no less. Had every one of the twelve calls he'd placed to both my cell and home phone over the past four hours went unanswered, a *sensible* man would have gotten the freakin' hint. But, not Mark Cannon's spoiled ass. Besides being too weak to admit he was gay, he was too accustomed to getting whatever he wanted, whenever he wanted it. My needs had always taken a back seat to his. We were a couple *only* when Mark decided we were a couple. If he wanted sex, then we had sex. But, let me ask for something I wanted – his heart, a real commitment – and Mark's punk-ass went running for the emotional hills just as fast as his size big feet would allow.

Making my way into the living room, I turned on the light.

"What are you doing here?" I asked, both pissed and happy to see him standing there. Even disheveled from a night of too much partying, Mark looked incredible. Leave it to me to do something as dangerous as falling for a guy who could pass for Taye Diggs' twin. Forget Stella's groove, right now it was hard not to go in search of my own.

"We need to talk," Mark said, struggling to dislodge the black, silk muscle tee tucked inside his jeans.

"Not at damned near one in the morning we don't," I said, determined not to let my physical attraction for the man-child staggering toward me weaken my growing resolve.

Violating my personal space big time, Mark asked, "Why you acting like this, man?"

"I'm not acting like anything," I said, taking a step back. "And you're drunk."

"I am not drunk." Mark smirked. "I'm relaxed."

"Go home," I said, keeping him at arms length. "Wouldn't want you puffy-eyed on your big day."

"Not until you agree to be my best man," Mark said, one sheet away from being three to the wind.

"Then I suggest you settle in and get some sleep," I said, turning on my bare heels, "in the guest room."

"Chris!" Mark called out after me.

"Good night playa," I said, disappearing into my bedroom.

Climbing back into bed, I slid under the covers and closed my eyes. With everything in me I hoped, prayed that Mark would still be in my apartment when I opened my eyes later that morning. How pathetic was that? How in the world could I justify to my mom or myself the fact that I still held out hope that this man might still choose me over...his father?

A few minutes later, Mark crept across the threshold of my moonlit bedroom. Lying on my side with my back to the door, I remained completely still. His gait was that of a five-year old with an inner-ear infection. Mark made his way over to my bed. Balancing himself against the wall, he attempted to take off his shoes, only to trip over his own big feet.

"Get off me," I snarled.

"My bad," Mark said, giggling as if anything about this was even remotely funny.

Somehow managing to return to the upright position, he asked in a slur, "Were you sleep?"

"I was until you stumbled in."

"I'm sorry."

"Yes you are."

"Maybe this wasn't such a good idea," Mark said, backing away from the bed.

I turned to face him. "Maybe what wasn't such a good idea?" I asked, bitterly. "Coming to my house at damned near one in the morning...or marrying someone you're not in love with?"

Mark made a face. "Why you gotta go there?"

"Why I gotta…?" Sitting up in the bed, I glared at him. "You're fucking kidding me right?" I asked, not bothering to wait for an answer. Waving him off, I lied back down, yanking the covers over my head. "Go home, Mark."

"Not until you agree to be my best man."

"Not gonna happen dude," my muffled voice retorted.

Mark sat down on the edge of the bed, vacillating for a few moments before whispering, "I need you Chris."

The touch of his hand on my shoulder made my heart ache. As much as I wanted to be stronger, demand that Mark get out of my apartment, insist that he respect me enough *not* to pressure me into doing something that would dishonor me, I was simply too weak.

"Please, Chris," he said, his voice laced with desperation. "You gotta do this for me."

Swallowing the "Okay, fine I'll do it," about to pass through my tight lips, I closed my eyes and sighed. It was pretty much guaranteed that I would ultimately break down and give Mark what he wanted, if only because it afforded me a little more time with him. Can you say masochistic, boys and girls?

Frustrated, Mark rose from the bed. "Damn Chris, I've always had your back," he said, growing angry. "No matter what, you're supposed to be there for me."

Eyes still closed, I remained silent. I'd let him grovel a few more minutes before finally relenting.

"What do I have to do to get you to agree?"

My eyes popped open.

"I'm desperate man," Mark said, sounding like it. "I need you to help me get through this. Don't make me do it alone, Chris."

Alone, was exactly what I was going to be once Mark -- the man I loved, and had sacrificed my happiness for -- walked down that aisle tomorrow. Who was going to be there for me? Who had my back? Who the hell was going to help me get through this nightmare?

"Tell me what you want me to do?" Mark asked, pleading.

A sadistic grin spread across my lips as the thought formed in my head.

"You want me to wash your car for a month? Clean you house… kiss your feet? I'll do anything you want man," Mark said. "Name it?"

And we have a winner!

"Anything?" I asked, sitting up in bed.

"Within reason," Mark said, correctly sensing I was up to something.

Rolling my eyes, I reached for the blanket resting at my waist. "Good bye—"

"All right!" Mark blurted out. "Anything."

The glimmer in my eye returned as I leaned back against the headboard, preparing for the start of the show. "Take off your shirt."

Mark stood there smiling, his awakened manhood stretching the fabric of his jeans. If sex was the *anything* to which I was referring, he was more than game. He'd soon change his tune.

"Dance for me," I instructed.

Mark played along. Pulling the T-Shirt over his head, he swung it in time to his gyrating hips, before tossing it toward me.

Inhaling his scent on the discarded clothing, my own manhood sprung to life beneath the sheets.

As he sang some wordless tune off key, Mark unfastened the buckle of his belt, pulling it through the latches nice and teasingly slow.

"You like that, don't you?" he asked, giving me a confident wink.

"It's *aiight.*"

Completely undressed, Mark began moving toward the bed.

"Stay there."

Mark eyed me incredulously.

Licking my lips, I spied the impressive member hanging majestically between his thick thighs. "Play with it."

A soft moan escaped Mark's lips as he stroked himself to full excitement. My own sex rising, I got up from the bed, motioning for him to come to me.

"Lie down," I said.

Sure he was about to get the blow job of his life, Mark plopped onto his back, hands behind his head, penis pointed skyward.

"Turn onto your stomach."

Mark's eyes widened. "What?" he asked, now stone sober. "You know I don't play that—"

"Do what I ask...or go home."

Nervous as a high school virgin about to have her cherry popped, Mark traced over his full lips with his tongue, then turned over.

Enjoying my role as the *top*, I forced his tightly shut legs apart.

"That's better," I said, taking in the sight of his hairy cheeks quivering at my touch.

"Chris...don't," Mark said, weakly. "You know I'm not into that shit."

Ignoring him, I continued kneading his tender flesh. Tonight I was going to be the one calling the shots.

"Oooh, shit!" Mark gasped. "Man, I'm not into...you...you know I don't...ooh, damn *boyeee*."

My confidence building, I eased a second finger inside him.

"Umm...oh, shit," Mark moaned as my tongue joined my fingers. "What you doin' to me Chris?"

Whatever I damned well pleased.

The taste of him had my penis throbbing like crazy. I needed to have him in the worst way.

Reaching into the night stand, I pulled out a condom and jar of lube.

When he noticed what I was doing, Mark flipped over. "No Chris," he said, about to rise from the bed.

Climbing on top of him I pinned him down. "I don't wanna hear that shit," I said, glowering. "You invited yourself up in here."

"But you know I'm—"

"What?" My eyes burned with anger. "You're too much of a man to give me what I've been giving you for the past ten years? Huh? Is that what you're saying?" I asked daring him to answer in the affirmative.

It was hard to explain the conflicting emotions swirling inside me as I locked my knees on either side of Mark to keep him still. On the one hand, I was as turned on by, and attracted to him as I'd ever been. On the other hand, I hated the man, wanting badly to inflict upon him the pain and shame he had inflicted on me each time he'd told me – by way of his actions – that I was good enough to fuck, but not good enough to love.

"Tell me that's what you're saying and I'll stop."

Mark didn't say a word.

Shifting my weight, I handed him the pillow. In stunned silence he placed it under his back, his cock brick hard. Like hell he wasn't into this.

"Go slow...okay?" Mark's voice was a frail whisper.

I bent down and kissed him on the lips without giving a response. I didn't think it fair to make him any promises I was certain I wouldn't keep. Tonight might very well be my last chance to touch Mark, taste him; feel the power of his heady passion as he exploded in ecstasy onto my chest. I was going to fuck him so good, and so hard that he'd either leave Asia at the altar, or be haunted by the vision of me inside him every time he was inside her.

"Oh fuck!" Mark cried out as I spread him open, inserting as much of my seven and a half inches as his body would allow.

"Oh…ooh…shit!"

"That's it, take that dick," I said in a testosterone-drench growl. "Take it."

"Chris…ah…ooh...shit man…" The sound of Mark's strained voice almost caused me to prematurely reach my peak. But, I was determined not to give in to the white hot passion raging inside me. I'd been waiting a decade for this night. I'd be damned if it was going to be over in five minutes.

Pushing Mark's knees back into his chest, I pressed my midsection into his. Like a man possessed, I drove into him, each thrust more powerful and determined than the last. This was fucking blowing my mind, man! I felt like I was having an out of body experience, watching in amazement from the sidelines as Mark and I went at it with wild, animalistic abandon. Never in my wildest dreams could I have imagined just how good the sensation of being inside him would be. The muscularity of his body, the way it wrapped around my manhood like a custom-made glove. I felt like an exposed live wire, every inch of my being crackling with electricity.

Squeezing my taut backside with his large, strong hands, Mark demanded me deeper inside him.

"You like that?"

"Ye…yeah…ooh," Mark said, struggling to get out the words.

"That's it," I said, roughly. "Take all that dick, baby."

Pumping wildly, I braced my legs against the edge of the bed in order to keep them from buckling beneath me. This felt so damned good.

Mark shut his eyes tightly. "Oh fuck!" he wailed, locking his legs around my neck. He wrapped his fingers around his engorged penis.

"I'm 'bout to com…come."

"Not yet, baby," I pleaded, reaching for his hand. "Please…not…not yet."

"I can't wait." Mark winced. "I gotta come!"

The sight of his warm sex shooting up against my chest like an erupting volcano propelled me to orgasm.

"Son of a bitch!" I shouted as I exploded inside him.

Ten minutes passed before the aftershocks of our lovemaking had subsided enough for me to attempt words.

"You okay?"

"Uh huh," Mark answered in a hoarse whisper.

"Open your eyes."

Mark focused his tender gaze on me. "What's up?"

Forcing the lump back down my throat, I stared into his sleepy eyes, wondering how I could ever bring myself to let this man go. He wasn't perfect by a long-shot, but he was beautiful, and funny... and good.

"I love you."

His smile bittersweet, Mark replied, "I love you back."

Chapter Six

*T*he sound of the telephone rocked me out of a deep sleep. Disoriented, I reached over Mark, lifting the receiver.

"Hello?"

"Where is he?" the irritated voice demanded.

"Hmm--?"

"Chris, wake up!" Tabby said exacerbated. "And tell the asshole lying beside you to do the same."

Freeing myself from Mark's hold, I sat up in the bed. "What's wrong?" I asked, flinching when I realized what day it was. "Oh shit, the breakfast."

"That's right Sherlock," Tabby said acerbically. "Pastor Cannon is about to blow his stack."

"Mark, wake up," I said, prodding the sleeping giant sprawled out beside me.

"Let me...yeah," he spoke in gibberish as he turned over to his side.

"Mark!" I said, hitting him harder, "Get up!"

Slapping at the air, he opened his eyes. "What the hell you punching me for?"

"Your father is looking for you," I said, knowing that would snap him out of his sleepy fog.

Jolting up in bed, Mark looked at me. "What...where...why?"

"The wedding breakfast."

His head twisting toward the clock, Mark gasped. "Son of a bitch!" He jumped up from the bed, so quickly he lost his balance falling to the floor. Struggling to get to his feet, he looked at me, his face awash with panic. "Where my drawers?"

Instinctively, I covered the phone so Tabby wouldn't hear him say something that could be misconstrued, or in this case, *properly* construed.

"Chris, where are my shoes?" Mark asked, barreling around the bedroom like a madman on crack. "Did I take my shirt off in here...?"

"You can't wear those again," I said, pointing at the wrinkled jeans he was forcing up his leg.

Glancing back over at the clock, he frowned. "Shit, I don't have time to go home."

"Check the closet in the guest room," I said, trying not to laugh as he stood there with the pants hanging around his ankles. "You left a few things—"

"Christian Weaver!"

The sound of Tabby's voice gave me a start. "Will you stop screaming at me?"

"Fine," she said. "I'll just hand the phone to Pastor Cannon and let him do it instead."

Just hearing that man's name gave me chills. "Is he looking for Mark?"

"Duh," Tabby said. "He's the one who had me call."

"Mark's apartment?" I asked hopefully.

"No, yours," Tabby answered.

I flinched.

"The Pastor wanted me to give him your number, but I suggested that I just go ahead and make the call myself. He's standing across the room cutting his eyes at me like I just broke these uppity folk's best china," Tabby said, then paused. "Shall I give him the phone?"

"No!" I said quickly. "Mark's getting dressed now. He'll be at Asia's parents in ten minutes."

"What about you?"

Making a sour face, I smirked. "I ain't coming—"

Just then, Mark stepped out of the bathroom, hurriedly fastening the belt around the gray slacks he'd found in the closet. "Why aren't you getting dressed?" he asked.

I gave him the same funky look I'd just given the phone. "You're on your own G-Monie."

"Like hell," Mark said, pulling back the blanket warming my nude body. "You promised—"

"I promised to be your best man."

"Get dressed," Mark said, yanking the phone out of my hand. When I didn't move he glared at me.

"Mark—"

"You got five minutes," he said, placing the call on speaker. "Tabby...hey, it's me." Lowering the phone onto the dresser, Mark continued getting dressed. "Tell my father you caught me on my cell at the gym."

"All right," Tabby said carefully. "Is Chris coming with you?"

"Yes," Mark said, before I could push the words "Hell no" from my lips. "Go get dressed," he mouthed at me.

Rolling my eyes, I got of bed, making my way across the room like a man headed to his own execution.

"We just stopped over here after we left the gym and—"

"Shhh," Tabby said. "I'm not the one you need to lie to."

Mark and I both stopped dead in our tracks. He was about to say something, but thought better of it. Tabby would play for only so long before she'd let you have it.

"We'll be there in fifteen minutes," Mark said tightly.

"You got ten," Tabby said, then disconnected the phone.

****

Ten minutes later, I pulled up in front of Asia's parents' house, jumping out of my truck the instant it came to a stop. Racing up the winding, pebbled walkway leading to the four-thousand square-foot brick colonial, I formulated the lie in my head. Parked two cars behind me, Chris took his sweet time, the look on his face making it clear that he wished he was anyplace else but here.

As if smelling my scent, Asia appeared at the door.

"Mark Theodore Cannon. Where have you been?" she asked in a tense whisper. "You were supposed to be here for breakfast over thirty minutes ago."

"Sorry, Babe," I said, giving her a peck her on the cheek as I stepped inside. Glancing back at the man who just an hour ago was wrapped snugly in my arms, I added, "Chris and I were playing a game of b-ball at the gym and lost track of time."

I could have sworn I heard Chris mumble "Whatever" as he stomped across the perfectly manicured grass.

"Say you forgive me?" I asked, giving Asia the same puppy-dog eyes I gave Chris on the myriad occasions I'd done something to piss him off.

Unable to resist my charms, Asia softened. "Give me a real kiss and I will," she said, pointing to her mouth.

Leaning in to oblige her, I froze.

"What?" Asia asked, eyeing me curiously.

"I forgot to brush my teeth at the gym," I lied. Truth of the matter was I could still taste Chris on my lips. Damn me for not snatching those breath mints off the dash in the truck.

"Kiss me anyway," Asia said.

Tentatively, I did. Parting my lips, Asia pushed her tongue into my mouth. When she didn't gag or pimp-slap me, my racing heart began to slow. I'd have to be more careful in the future. If my boy and I hung out – which I still hoped we would from time to time – I needed to make sure there were no slip ups. The last thing I needed was Asia finding out something she didn't need to know.

"Excuse me," Chris said, pushing past us.

Asia pulled out of my hold. "Not so fast you," she said calling after Chris.

His eyes twitched, but Chris managed to force a smile. "Sorry about getting him here late."

"Boy's will be boys," Asia said, leading me toward the dining room.

"But men are better," Chris said under his breath as he followed behind us.

When Asia was a step ahead, I turned around cutting my eyes at him. "Cut it out," I mouthed.

"You cut it out," he mouthed back.

"Well it's about time you showed up, Boy," my father said, rising from the table where he was holding court with Asia's father.

"Hey, Dad," I said with a guilty half-grin. "Sorry we're late... umm...Chris and I were at the gym."

"That's what Tabitha told me," my father said disbelievingly. He shifted his focus to Chris. "You boys are men now," he said with an edge. "It's high time you set your priorities straight."

"My priorities are in correct order, Pastor Cannon," Chris said, taking a seat at the table. "But thanks for your concern."

"Well my soon-to-be husband is here now," Asia said. "That's all that matters."

Finally taking his eyes off Chris, Dad smiled at me as I held out Asia's chair for her. "In less than six hours my son is going to be married."

I half expected Chris to twirl his fingers in the air and scowl "Whoop-de-freaking-do." He took a sip of orange juice instead.

Tabby leaned in as I lifted a piece of bacon to my lips. "You need to cut it out."

"What are you talking about?"

"Do you care about Chris at all," Tabby said irritably.

The fake smile on my face fading, I leaned closer to my budinsky friend so Asia, sitting on my other side, couldn't overhear.

"Of course I do."

"Then why don't you start acting like it," Tabby said in a pissed whisper. "You need to pick a side and stop all these games. Your behavior is tired and it's unfair to Chris...and Asia."

"Can we talk about this some other time please?" I asked, massaging the tension building at the base of my neck.

When Asia first suggested inviting Tabby to be one of her bride's maids, my gut instinct was to discourage her from doing so. I wasn't sure why I was against someone I considered a close friend spending more time with my fiancée, until yesterday. Despite a smirk here and a raised eyebrow there, I'd remained fairly confident that Tabby was unaware of the true depth of Chris and my relationship. But, after her "the walls were paper thin" comment at the restaurant, it was painfully clear that she was intimately aware. Armed with that type of knowledge, it was dangerous for Tabby to bond with Asia. Their building a friendship would level the playing field. And all things being equal, women supported each other – especially when it came to dropping the dirt on men.

"You are a sun-warmed mess, Mark," Tabby said, genuinely disappointed. "I don't believe you. The very night before you are to get married you go over to Chris' apartment—"

My head snapped in her direction. "Will you keep your voice down," I said in an angry whisper. "Better yet, drop this entirely."

Tabby lowered her voice, but had no intention of dropping the subject. "I've kept my mouth shut all these years. But Chris is my friend and Asia..." she said, stopping short as the maid approached.

"More pancakes Miss?"

"No, thank you," Tabby said, cutting her eyes in my direction. "I've lost my appetite."

"Is something not to your liking?" The maid's face shaded with concern. "I can have cook--"

"That won't be necessary," Tabby said. "The food isn't my problem."

Ignoring her passive-aggressive bullshit, I looked across the table at Chris, fidgeting uncomfortably as one of the bride's maids put the moves on him. Why couldn't everything be simpler? In a perfect world, I'd be able to be with the one I loved, no matter his race or gender. Unfortunately, my world was anything but perfect.

"Is everything okay, Sweetheart," Asia said, reaching for my hand as it rested on the table.

"I'm fine," I said, trying not to let on that both my head and heart were aching.

"You sure?" Asia asked. "You've barely touched your plate."

"Not really hungry," I said.

Asia chuckled softly as she rubbed my back. "Too much partying last night?"

Tabby's eyes rolled back in her head as she eavesdropped.

"I'll be okay in time for our wedding," I said, kissing Asia softly on the cheek. Turning to Tabby, I discreetly gripped her by the arm. "Your behavior is unacceptable," I snarled into her ear.

"And yours is criminal," Tabby growled back before snatching her arm away. "Either call off the wedding or let him go."

"This is none of your bus—"

"Don't even," Tabby said, cutting me off. "You can't keep doing this to him..."

Feeling like a caged animal as she spoke *at* me, I glanced in Asia's direction to make sure she wasn't witnessing Tabby showing her ass. Thankfully, my fiancée was knee-deep in conversation with her cousin.

When my eyes came to rest on my father, however, my blood chilled. He was watching Chris intently. This was all getting too close for comfort. Me, my lover, my fiancée...and my father were all sitting around a table breaking bread together. I wish my mother were here to help me navigate this treacherous emotional terrain. She never said it, but she'd made it clear that she realized how special Chris was to me. And, while she may have wished the two of us were just friends, my happiness was her principal concern. Whenever Dad got on my case about being too close with Chris, Mom would be the one standing toe-to-toe with him demanding he let me live my own life. Now that she was gone, my life was less and less my own with each passing day.

"You need to grow some cohunes, and decide who you are...and who you want to spend your life with," Tabby said, forcing me to turn my attention back to her. "Either give Chris all of you, or be man enough to let him go so he can find someone who will."

My attention shifted to the other side of the table when I saw Chris pushing back his chair.

"I need to get going," he said, rising to his feet.

"But you just got here," the flirty bride's maid said.

"I've got some things I need to take care of before the wedding."

Leaning back in his chair, Dad folded his arms, giving Chris a disapproving look.

"Mr. and Mrs. Stallings, thank you for the hospitality," Chris said, purposely not making eye contact with me.

The twenty people sitting around the massive dinning room table said goodbye in unison.

"Let him go Mark," Tabby said in a stern whisper.

Not about to listen to her, I stood to my feet.

"Where you going, Hun?" Asia asked.

"Umm...I need to get something out of Chris' trunk," I said, hoping she wouldn't come with me. "I'll be right back."

Tabby was right. What I was doing wasn't fair to Chris or Asia. Still, I couldn't bring myself to choose between them. While my heart belonged to Christian, Asia offered me the life I so desperately wanted. Something in my gut warned that if I didn't make a choice soon one would be made for me.

Chapter Seven

"Chris, wait up!" Mark called out as I walked out the front door.

Ignoring him, I continued to my car. I really wasn't in the mood to deal with him, *her* or their wedding right now. Though it was well worth it, I'd given up sorely needed sleep last night. If I were to pull off my performance in the warped theatre that Mark's wedding would be, I needed to get some shut-eye.

"Dude, will you stop walking?" Mark said, catching up to me.

I turned to face him. "What is it?"

"Are you mad at me?" he asked.

"No," I lied. "Just tired."

I was, in fact, very mad at Mark. I was equally mad at myself. Despite my reasons, I knew very well that what the two of us did last night wasn't right. The man was getting married in less than six hours for Christ's sake.

Mark moved toward me. "You know how much I—"

"Son, your wife is looking for you," Pastor Cannon said, appearing from nowhere.

She's not his fucking wife yet, I thought as I stood there between the two Cannons.

Guilt coloring his face, Mark said, "I'm just gonna walk Chris to his car."

I don't need you to walk me to my car.

"I'm sure Christian can get to his car alone," Pastor Cannon said in a tone that made the hairs on the back of my neck rise.

Now I *wanted* Mark to walk me to my car in the worst possible way.

"I need to get something out of his trunk, Dad," Mark said.

"Fine," Pastor Cannon responded.

Mark breathed a sigh of relief.

"Chris can give whatever it is to me," Mark's father said through a tight smile. "You go tend to your wife."

Cutting my eyes at the Pastor, I wanted to shout, "Enough with the wife crap already! I get it...*aiight*?"

Vacillating, Mark pondered the wisdom of leaving his father and quasi-lover alone.

"Go inside Son," Pastor Cannon said sharply. "Now."

And just as he'd done always, Mark did exactly what his father told him.

Glancing around to ensure that it was just the two of us, Pastor Cannon took a step toward me. I didn't flinch. Unlike Mark, I wasn't about to be told what I could and could not do.

"If you cared about my son, you'd get out of the way and let him get married so he can live the life God intended for him."

"As your son's *fiancée* said not an hour ago," I said, returning the reverend's hard stare. "Mark is a grown man."

"You know what I'm saying, Boy," Pastor Cannon snapped. It was obvious that the man hated my guts. The feeling was mutual.

"I'm not a boy," I said defiantly, "yours or anyone else's."

"I hope your being here doesn't mean you've changed your mind about being Mark's best man," he said, the bead of moisture glistening on his forehead. "You and I both know that you have no business standing up at my son's wedding."

"Mark thinks otherwise," I said, reeking with arrogance. "As of matter of fact, he spent most of last night begging me to stand at his side today."

Usually, I took great pains to respect my elders, but Pastor Cannon was one of those uber-religious, holier than thou types who made my ass hurt. For him there was only one way to do things – his way. There was also only one way to heaven, but a million ways to hell. I held him principally responsible for fucking up an otherwise wonderful man. Pastor Cannon claimed unyielding love for Mark, but if he truly loved his son, he'd want him to be happy above all else. Instead, he exploited Mark's deep love and respect for him in order to control his only child, compelling him to continue living a lie.

"Now, you listen to me," Pastor Cannon said, stalking behind me as I continued toward my car, "you will not be a part of the ceremony today, and that's final."

"With all due deference, Pastor," I said, opening my trunk, "I'm not your son. You can't tell me what to do."

"But I can tell Mark," he said confidently.

After last night, I felt pretty confident that the good Reverend couldn't.

"When Mark tells me he no longer wants me to be his man…I mean *best* man, I'll oblige," I said, retrieving the box of golf balls from the trunk.

"You need Jesus," Pastor Cannon said, pushing up on me.

"No," I said, glaring at his hand. "What I need is for you to get your finger out of my face."

Pastor Cannon didn't move.

"Now," I said, inching forward ever so slightly.

Slowly, he lowered his hand.

"Here are your son's balls," I said, handing him the box. "I'm surprised he remembered he had them."

Mark's father stood speechless as I made my way around to the driver's side door. Starting the engine, I poked my head out the window, flashing him a cool grin. "See you at the wedding, Pastor," I said, then sped off.

Chapter Eight

*R*ising from the chaise lounge, I tried to rein in my scattered thoughts. Nervous and eager, my eyes darted around the living room as I rubbed my sweaty palms against my thighs. This was it. At any moment, the man that I loved was going to step through my front door and choose me.

When Mark called twenty minutes earlier to inform me that we needed to talk, I asked him exactly what there was left to talk about, all the while hoping beyond hope that it wasn't too late for that miracle. Pressing me to allow him to come over, Mark insisted that we had to have this conversation *before* the wedding. My heart nearly jumped out of my chest. Was it possible that he had finally found the courage to step up to the plate; put his love for me above his need to please his father, the church and society?

I had prayed so hard these past weeks to the very God Pastor Cannon claimed would damn me to hell for being gay. "Lord, please deliver to me the man of my dreams," I'd asked on bended knee. "You know my heart. I'm good and kind, Father. Don't I deserve to be loved too?"

"Hey you," Mark said, touching my shoulder.

"Ooh shit," I said, flinching as I turned to face him. "I didn't hear you come in."

"Looked like you were in another world," Mark said, his smile an uneasy one. He was so adorable when he was nervous. How I loved that man, even when he was being everything but lovable.

"I can't stay long," he said, glancing down at his watch, "promised Dad I'd be at the church by three."

Those words sounded like the wedding was still on.

"I'll probably get there by four," I said, trying to hide my disappointment.

Mark shifted his weight from one leg to the other in that way he did whenever he was uncomfortable with a given situation. "About that," he said, averting his eyes. "I think you were right..."

Breathe just breathe, I thought as I wiped the moisture from my brow.

"I should never have forced you into being my best man."

"It's okay," I said surely.

Mark shook his head. "No, it was unfair of me."

He took a seat on the sofa, motioning for me to join him. I remained standing. Something wasn't adding up here.

"I said I'd do it, Mark."

"Chris—"

"I'll do it Mark," I said, finally accepting the bitter reality that the man I loved was going to marry someone else. "I'll be there for you."

"I'd rather you weren't."

Gasping as if the air had been sucker-punched out of me, I fell back against the wall.

"This really is for the best—"

"Best for whom?" I asked, almost shouting. "Why Mark? Why are you doing this?"

Tensing as I approached, Mark bit down on his bottom lip. "Chris don't make this harder—"

"Do you love me?" I asked, tears stinging my eyes

Lowering his head, Mark inhaled. "You know I do."

"Then why are you doing this?" I asked, taking his hand as I sat down beside him. "Why are you marrying her?"

"Asia is a good woman," Mark said, turning away.

Grabbing his chin, I forced him to look at me. If he was going to stab me in the heart, the least he could do was look me in the eye as he did it.

"Do you love her?" I asked, fearing the answer, but desperately needing to hear it.

Pulling out of my grasp, Mark stood to his feet. "Please try to understand the position I'm in. My father..." he said, then hesitated. "Now that my mom is gone, he's all I've got left."

"You have me," I said, going over to him as he stood at the window. "Doesn't that count for anything?"

"Yes," Mark said, his eyes pleading with mine for understanding. "Nothing has to change between you and me. I'm only getting married."

Shaking my head in disbelief, I took a step back.

"We can still hang out and everything," Mark said, moving toward me.

"No," I said, extending my arms to maintain distance between us. "We can't."

"Come on Chris," Mark said, still determined to have his cake and eat it too. "Nothing has to change between us."

"Yes," I said, taking my hand back, "it does."

Standing at the window, I gazed up into the sun-kissed June sky, willing it to fill me with power and regal courage.

"It was one thing to fuck around with a guy who didn't have the balls to commit," I said, each word strengthening my resolve. "It's an entirely different matter when that weak-assed man is married."

"Chris I know you're upset right now..."

Fighting to block out the sound of Mark's pleading voice, I recalled the sage words of my mother...

You deserve so much more than Mark can give you...

Mark drew me into his arms. "I need you to be here for me, Man," he said, pressing his aroused midsection into my lower back.

Closing my eyes, I concentrated on my mom's voice in my head.

Only you can save you...

Turning me to face him, Mark kissed me deeply on the mouth. The taste of his lips, the familiar roughness of his tongue warned that if I didn't let go now, I never would.

It may be today, or tomorrow or next year...

When I tried to pull away from him, Mark grabbed hold of my waist, forcing my body to reconnect with his. "You belong to me."

I moaned softly as he unfastened my belt. "I can't...please..."

You have to be the one to say it...

"We're good together," Mark said, working feverishly to negotiate yet another cease fire between us.

"No," I said in a strained whisper as his hand disappeared inside my boxers. "We can't keep...*umm*...doing this."

"I want you to do to me what you did last night," Mark's heavy voice instructed.

"I can't do this," I said, struggling to separate from him.

"Please Chris," Mark said, stroking my stiffening penis. "Baby, don't say no to me."

You have to be the one to say it...

Realizing I was perilously close to surrender, a feeling of panic overtook me.

"No!" I shouted, pushing him away with more aggression than I'd intended.

Struggling to maintain his balance, Mark eyed me like I'd just lost my ever-loving mind. Quite the contrary. For the first time in more than a decade I was crystal clear-headed where he was concerned; my heart and mind finally of one accord.

"Come on Chris," Mark said, trying to downplay what he sensed was a paradigm shift. "Don't go getting all dramatic on me. Nothing has to..."

You have to be the one to say it...

A silent gasp escaped my lips as the word popped into my head, a word so powerful it changed everything instantly.

"Chris, what we have is—"

"Enough."

Mark did a double-take. "What?"

"Enough," I said, louder and more confidently than before. "We're done."

"Chris, come on," Mark said, following behind me. "We can make this work."

I picked up the velvet box from the coffee table. "Though you can no longer be a part of my life," I said, handing him the wedding ring. "I will always love you, and wish for you the absolute best."

Mark's eyes widened as I walked over to the front door. "Chris, don't do this," he said, sounding desperate. "I need you."

Holding the door open, I turned to him, swallowing the lump forming in my throat. "Goodbye Mark Cannon."

He was about to open his mouth to speak, but I raised my hand to stop him.

"Enough," I said simply. "Enough."

Accepting that the choice had been made, Mark lowered his head, and walked out the door...and out of my life.

Epilogue

Eighteen months later…

Almost tripping over my own feet, I raced out of the lawyer's office. I couldn't get to the parking garage quickly enough. The only thing I could think about was how badly I wanted…*needed* to see him. Speeding down the Lodge freeway faster than the law encouraged, I was in front of Chris' apartment complex in less than twenty minutes.

Now some two hours later, I still couldn't bring myself to get out of the damn truck, walk up to his door, and ring the bell. It wasn't that my desire – desperation actually – to see Chris had waned any; I simply couldn't muster up the courage to face him. Not yet, anyway.

Swallowing the last sip of bottled water, I loosened the tie that felt like a noose around my neck. I sighed as the Jill Scott joint, *Cross My Mind* began to play, promising myself that I'd go ring the bell the very instant the song ended. Then, standing in front of Chris, I would lay it all out for him straight, no chaser.

After less than two years as husband and wife, Asia and I had decided to divorce. As much as I'd tried to, I couldn't make myself the man my father wanted me to be. Each day of my marriage, I'd died a little more inside. In time my desire to be happy; truly, genuinely happy, far outweighed my fear of Dad's reaction to my being gay. There I'd said it. I was gay, and had been ever since I could remember, or at least since my mid-teens when I realized how drawn I was to other men -- their energy and powerful masculinity. The most important thing I'd come to realize in these past eighteen months, besides how much I truly loved Chris, was that my being homosexual didn't make me a punk, a sissy, a jelly-back, or any of the other less than flattering terms my father had used when I came out to him six weeks ago.

I didn't give a damn what he or anyone else thought about me, so long as Chris could find room in his heart to forgive me for hurting him so deeply. Believe it or not, causing that beautiful, passionate, dry-witted, curly-headed man pain was the absolute last thing I'd ever wanted to do. But, in the end, my dishonestly had hurt Chris deeply.

I really did try to be a good husband to my wife, and for the first six months of our marriage I was just that. But soon, it became increasingly more difficult to outrun the lie, the deception on which the foundation of our marriage had been built. When I held Asia in my arms, I saw Chris' face in my head. The night I'd called out his name while she and I were making love was the beginning of the end. My wife pretended not to hear it, but nothing was ever the same after the slip.

Sensing the ever-widening emotional rift between us, Asia had asked me point blank if I was stepping out on her. I said no, of course, though in my dreams and heart I had been cheating on her over and over again – with Chris. No matter how intensely I tried, I couldn't shake that man. Soon, I stopped trying.

At Asia's insistence, we entered into couple's therapy. It was in one of my sessions alone with the doctor that I finally admitted my true feelings, beginning the excruciating, gut-wrenching process of self-discovery and acceptance.

When I saw Chris step outside, I ducked down in my seat. Holding the door open, he spoke to his neighbor about to walk his over-excited chocolate lab. As man and dog made their way down the walkway, I studied the warm smile on Chris' face, a tinge of jealousy rising in my gut. From this distance my view was a little unclear, but I could tell my boy still looked as amazing as ever. It was apparent that he'd been working out too. Damn, how I had missed that man.

Taking a deep breath, I removed the key from the ignition, then stepped out of the truck. My legs felt wobbly as I made my way across the parking lot, but I kept walking, my eyes locked on Chris as he sat down on the stoop outside his building.

"Hey, you."

Chris did a double-take. "Mark?" He rose to his feet, stunned to see me. "What's up?"

"You got it, Bruh," I said, moving in to hug him. He felt so good in my arms. Yes, this was where he belonged.

"Umm...what brings you this way?" Chris asked, pulling away.

"You," I said with a nervous smile.

It wasn't going to be easy, but damn it I wasn't leaving before I had said what I'd come to say.

"You look good, Man."

"Thanks," Chris said, glancing quickly in the direction his neighbor had gone. "You look tired," he said, turning back to me.

"Gee thanks," I said, running my hands over the five o'clock shadow on my face.

"No, you...you still look good," Chris said, with a pensive chuckle. "You just look tired."

"A lots been going on," I said, unable to take my eyes off of him. How could I have let him get away?

"Asia and I got divorced today."

"I'm sorry to hear that," Chris said, his words genuine. "You okay?"

"Working to be," I said, staring into his eyes. "I miss you so much—"

"Mark," Chris said, stopping me.

"No, please," I said, reaching for his hand. "Let me say what I need to say before I lose the nerve."

Shifting uncomfortably, Chris's eyes darted around as if worried someone might overhear us. I didn't care. This time I wasn't going to worry about what the world thought of us.

"There is not a single day that I don't think about you," I said, squeezing his hand. "I know how much I hurt you. I get it...I really get it."

Chris stood slack-jawed as I spoke.

"All you ever wanted from me was my love," I said, choking on the words. "But I was in such denial that I couldn't even accept how very much I adored you, and how much you meant...mean to me."

Chris took back his hand. "Mark, I gotta tell you some—"

"Shhh," I said, placing my finger to his soft lips. "I love you Christian Weaver. I love you so deeply it hurts. You were my world and I let you get away—"

"Chris is everything okay?" the neighbor asked, moving in on the two of us like he was the law or something.

I was about to get in the nosy pin-neck's ass, until I realized who he was.

"Paul, you remember Mark?" Chris asked giving his brother-in-law a careful look.

"Your friend from college," Paul said, unhinging his jaw. "We met at Patrick and Stacey's wedding."

Standing between us, Chris quickly filled in the blanks. "Paul is Patrick's brother."

"Right, right," I said, extending my hand to him. "How you doing?"

"I'm good," Paul said.

"Look at you," Chris said, bending down to play with Paul's dog. "How's my favorite boy?"

Paul cleared his throat. "Your what?"

Chris chuckled. "My other favorite boy," he corrected, continuing to rub the happy dog.

My heart sank as the pieces began falling into place.

"So, how are Stacey and Patrick doing?" I asked, praying I was reading this all wrong. Paul and Chris' only connection was through their siblings. There was nothing more between them. There just couldn't be.

"Husband and wife are doing great," Chris said, rising. "and, the baby—"

"Not such a baby, anymore," Paul chimed in.

"True," Chris said, grinning at Paul. "The Washington men are anything but petite."

"Careful," Paul said, his hand playfully squeezing Chris' shoulder.

"What's he now?" I asked, not interested in Christian's knowledge of any man besides me, "almost two?"

"Sixteen months," Paul said, tightening his grip on the leash as the dog grew anxious. "Those guys are gonna have their hands full once his little sister arrives."

"Stacey's pregnant again?" I asked, trying not to stare at Paul as he spoke. He was no me, but he was a good looking guy, far more attractive than I remembered him being. And if the size of his biceps were any indication, Paul was working out as much as Chris.

"She sure is," Chris said. "Any day now we're gonna have a little niece to spoil rotten."

"As a matter of fact we need to get a move on," Paul said, his eyes dancing as he gazed into Chris'. "We promised to take the little man off their hands for the weekend."

And with that, any chances for the reconciliation I'd hoped for with Chris were gone.

"All right, Paco," Paul said, looking down at the whimpering dog. He turned to Chris. "I better head on up and feed this guy his dinner."

"I'm gonna say goodbye to Mark," Chris said, his eyes asking for Paul's indulgence. "Then, I'll be right up."

"That's cool." Paul said, then turned to me. "Good to see you again, Mark."

"You too," I said, clearing my throat.

Once Paul and the dog were out of sight, I turned to Chris. "You two look happy," I said, trying to take my lumps like a man.

"We are."

"I'm glad."

"Thanks," Chris said. "I hope everything works out for you."

"Me too," I said, my vision blurring. "You know I will always—"

"I know," Chris said, stopping me. "Me too."

Looking away, I wiped away the single tear rolling down my cheek.

"Well, I better get back," Chris said, inching toward the building.

"Okay," I sniffed.

"Take care of yourself Mark."

"You too, Chris," I said to the man I'd loved...and lost. "You too."

Printed in the United States
R1675100003B/R16751PG36351LVSX00001BA/1}